# THERE ARE CREATURES HERE

P.D. WILLIAMS

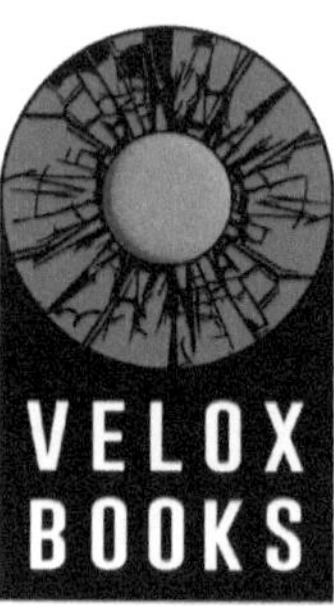

Published by arrangement with the author.

Copyright © 2025 by P.D. Williams.

All rights reserved.

# YOU'RE READING ANOTHER TERRIFYING COLLECTION FROM

**FOLLOW VELOX TO KEEP
THE NIGHTMARES COMING:**

# CONTENTS

# FOREWORD

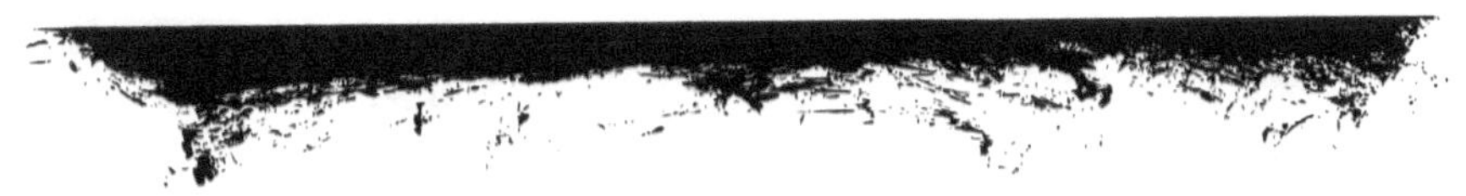

Welcome to the world of cursed objects and demented morticians, a spectral realm where living shadows traverse the darkness of your bedroom at three in the morning—the Witching Hour. We met here once before with my last tome of twisted tales, *Dark House, Many Rooms.* It's nice to see you again. I'm often asked where the stories come from. They don't always come from horrific nightmares. Mine, in fact, come when I'm raking leaves, showering, or sitting on one of North Carolina's magnificent beaches. Many of us, horror heads, are not cackling lunatics; we're dedicated family members, funny co-workers, or friendly neighbors. You wouldn't believe the awkward stares we get right after we've told someone we're horror writers, as if there's inherently something wrong with us. We'd be better off telling them we write pet porn for the Soviet Union. However, for the sake of your reading experience, imagine me as someone you wouldn't want sitting near you in an empty train station late at night. Scared yet? If not, that's okay. These macabre stories will get you there. Enjoy the show!

# THERE ARE CREATURES HERE

A quiet aura permeates this place. You feel it in the cold, damp air, and hear it in the creaking floors, groaning walls, and far-off whispers. Those that trespass in this spectral sanctum awaken the ghostly inhabitants who slumber deep inside its hollow, cobwebbed walls. For a time, the new occupants live unaware of the benign or sometimes ill-intentioned beings that comprise this house like brick and wood, blood and bone. But they will come to know them—fear them.

Curious children engage with the odd visitor, as though they have made a new friend. Laughter, playfulness, and discovery create a fearless bond between the one who lives and the one who lingers. But childhood is not a perpetual state of being. Soon, the distractions and burdens, which the world will imbue within their innocent minds, will replace those once carefree spirits. They will become jaded, too rigid to experience anything that doesn't fit into their pre-packaged existence.

The entities will increase their aggression to ensure they get noticed. The silly friend in old-fashioned clothes will morph into a pungent white mist that pulls life from their lungs. The muted footsteps that sometimes emanate from the upstairs hallway will become an ominous shadow peeking from behind a creaking closet door. A once harmless, disembodied whisper will transform into an icy shroud of dread that exists only in a tight circle of space, chilling their blood, and frosting their breath.

Most of these beings are spiritual remnants of the past: an angry spirit who resents the arrogant interlopers who now call his house their home, or a lost soul who finds neither infernal fire nor eternal light.

Then there are the creatures.

They can appear as a pitch-black spectral shadow that absorbs all light around it or as horrifying figures that fill people with black, inky terror. Rough scales and putrid, slimy oil covers them. Their voices sound like an ancient and otherworldly growl. With an eternity of evil and torment to fuel and guide them, they are patient. Like spindly spiders, they wait with a gnawing hunger that can only be sated when they ensnare a human soul in their web. These tenebrous and insidious miscreations have never felt the sun warm their faces. Never have their cloven hooves touched soft summer grass. Their vile hearts have never experienced love, compassion, or mercy. They exist only to sow fear and despair.

They often begin their work with the most vulnerable. Their whispered words of hopelessness ooze into the ear of a potential suicide victim. They etch their tortured thoughts into the fragmented mind of an armed, unstable person, convincing him that his former co-workers are to blame for his firing. The soulless ghouls haunt their quarry relentlessly until they overwhelm the victim's mind and free will. Only then can they drag their helpless prey deep into the endless pit where demons rule without care or conscience.

These purveyors of pain revel in inflicting violence upon their earthbound toys. With callous cackles and clicking of claws, they gleefully strangle a person while they sleep or give an invalid a powerful push down a flight of stairs. They are agents of misery, destroyers of worlds.

A young mother lives in this house. Her husband spends too much time on the road. The snatching of her children's blankets at three o'clock in the morning awakens them, filling the black house with high, frantic screams. She sees ghosts out of the corner of her eye in the afternoon. It makes her afraid to go down to the laundry room in the basement. She feels glowing, red eyes piercing her soul from the nighttime ceiling. She and her children find themselves caught in the crosshairs of the foulest, most mindless monster from the deepest cage in hell.

Yes, there are creatures here. I know this very well. They watch the bluish tinge of dusk flowing inexorably into the constricting darkness of night. For them, time passes in an infinite circle: a minute feels like an hour and an hour is like a second. And in this house where creatures tread, a dangerous and scream-worthy demon lurks. It now stands beside the bed of a sleeping child, its cracked, yellow claws hooking its blanket. There is only one thing left to frighten them: a mighty tug. I give it and laugh.

# MEMENTO MORI

"That's a good story alright, but I can do you one better. Maybe even two.

I, sir, am a photographer of distinction. You see, unlike my colleagues here in the southwest frontier, I don't take pictures of sunsets, soldiers, or weddings. I take pictures of the dead. I often include live individuals in the photographs along with the departed, but mainly it's the deceased whom I'm there to serve.

In their grief, the bereaved want to have some kind of memento to remind them of happier days when everybody under their roof was alive and well. They don't much care if it's an illusion or not. And here in the age of miracles, when most folks have never seen, much less heard of a camera, that creates a highly marketable demand.

Taking photographs of anyone can be difficult. Just you try getting unruly children, sullen Indians, or the unsophisticated folks who litter the plains to remain motionless for long stretches at a time. Ah, but the dead; they're easy to work with. They're compliant and calm, and they can sit for as long as necessary without complaining.

Oh, don't look at me like that; I'm not a ghoul. I know some folks will find my profession a tad dubious—distasteful even. But death art has been around for quite some time. Statues, pottery, and coins have depicted images associated with death since the sixteenth century. Memento Mori is what it's called. The objects provide equality among the poor, the rich, the proud, and the humble, an immutable reminder that death will come for us all at some point. They've translated the term into many tongues, but essentially, it means, "Remember, you must die."

As for the art of post-mortem photography, the regal Victorians began engaging in this sort of business a while back in merry old England. Some of those blue bloods brought the custom with them when they came to our sandy shores. After a few years, everybody wanted in on it, myself included.

Now I have to admit there's been times when my dark work has overwhelmed me. As I snap photographs of each smiling corpse, I catch myself wondering about the tragic series of events that had led to their demise. Yes sir, every customer has a story. And I've got a couple I'll share with you. But I warn you: They are tragic, dark and gruesome.

I'll start with the one about Ellie Webb.

It was around 1847 when I set aside my work in standard photography to pursue a more lucrative career doing post mortem work. My first job was for a married couple named Edgar and Vera Webb. They'd lost their little girl to disease—a most gruesome and cruel disease, especially for a child. Ellie, who was ten at the time, had died of rabies. Pretty awful stuff. I was told her's was a long and painful demise.

I promptly arrived after her passing. She'd only been dead a day or two, but she was already putrefying. The smell made me gag. And I had to keep reminding the mother that if the whole point of the photograph was to convey one big, happy family, then she'd have to stop bawling.

But in fairness, could you blame her?

For the Webbs, it must have been difficult seeing their deceased child propped in a chair, with her alabaster skin and eyes painted on her closed eyelids to make them appear open. In a situation like that, how in the world do you create the illusion that all is well? Normal? But then again, that's what they hired me to do.

As a child, Ellie had likely thought that she'd live forever. Unfortunately, the raccoon had had something to say about that.

Her parents had warned her many times not to wander too deep into the woods. But the call of her curiosity was too strong, so venture into the woods, she did.

The raccoon had probably looked harmless enough—cute, even. I suppose Ellie couldn't resist holding him. Well, I don't have to tell you what happened next. Even though she'd likely known that something was wrong with the raccoon, she hid the bite mark on her lower arm from her parents and kept the attack to herself. My guess is she didn't want to face the consequences of her disobedience. What child does?

I don't know what kind of parents the Webbs were that their daughter feared their punishment over rabies. I've never had children of my own, so I can't say as I'm fit to judge their parenting. But that's not important to the story.

The girl had kept the incident a secret for a couple of weeks by wearing long-sleeved shirts. But by the third week, the symptoms had become obvious. She experienced a fever and felt disoriented. The sight and sound of water agitated her; she'd bark at it like a dog.

Fearing the worst, the Webbs loaded Ellie in the back of their wagon and took her to the town doctor. Thoreau, I think his name is.

The doc had a difficult time examining Ellie at first. She became aggressive and had to be held down. Once they'd restrained her, the first thing he did was remove her shirt to check for sores or ticks. That's when they saw the bite mark.

By that time, the area around the wound had become red and angry. Puss was oozing from the raised, rotten flesh. The smell must've been awful. By then, the disease had progressed to her brain. The doc said there wasn't anything he could do for Ellie and advised the Webbs to take her home and make her as comfortable as possible until the end. Ah yes, the end—a better place where pain dies and mercy lives. But for those poor parents, watching Ellie suffer on and on must have made them feel closer to the beginning than the end.

As Ellie's condition worsened, she became significantly violent. When she wasn't screaming in agony, she flopped around, whimpering like a sick animal. They said it took that girl almost a month to die. But before that happened, she did some terrible things.

One night, the Webbs noticed a conspicuous silence that had fallen over their house. They looked at one another, wondering if the worst—or in Ellie's case, the best—had happened. Perhaps a compassionate God had allowed her to die at last.

Mr. Webb told the missus to stay put while he went to check on Ellie.

As soon as he entered the girl's bedroom, he was startled to find that she'd broken free of her restraints and climbed out a window. He went to it and hollered Ellie's name repeatedly.

Hearing the ruckus, Mrs. Webb rushed into the room to see what was happening. The stained, empty bed, and the ripped strips of cloth tied to the bedposts told her the story.

The Webbs ran outside, hoping to find her.

They checked the barn first. Empty.

They walked a short distance into the woods at the back of their property, calling for her. Nothing.

They reckoned they needed some help, so Mrs. Webb drove the wagon into town to recruit the Sheriff, Danny O'Herlihy, while her husband fetched a lantern to search the rest of the property.

Mrs. Webb told me she flew into town as fast as she could make the horses go. Once she got there, she burst into the sheriff's office so forcefully, he must've thought that a train had jumped its tracks and made a beeline to his front door. She said after she explained her quandary to Sheriff O'Herlihy; he told her he would need to assemble a search party to scour the deep woods, but that it would take some time to put a group together. They also needed to wait for daybreak, he said, as the woods were too treacherous to navigate at night. That did nothing to ease her mind.

Mrs. Webb returned home and relayed Sheriff O'Herlihy's plan to her husband. Like his wife, he was impatient and frustrated.

Throughout that long night, Mr. Webb paced the porch, cursing the sheriff's lack of urgency and praying for Ellie's safe return.

Mrs. Webb stayed inside, distracting herself with her knitting.

When dawn finally got around to showing up, Sheriff O'Herlihy arrived with a ten-person search party. He instructed everyone not to venture too far away from one another, lest they get lost in the thick woods.

When everyone was ready, Mr. Webb led them to the edge of the woods and the search began in earnest.

After a couple of fruitless hours, a woman's scream penetrated the muted woods. She wasn't difficult to locate—she never stopped screaming.

The mutilated corpse of an unlucky hunter horrified the group. Several deep, jagged bite marks covered his body. His missing face had been ripped off.

Everyone grew quiet. They must've been thinking of the savage animal that had once been a sweet little girl who picked daffodils and sang in the children's choir. Some of the group headed back home. They didn't care to end up being eaten alive by whomever—or whatever—had devoured the hunter. I can't say whether any of them had felt relief or shame as they scurried back to safety. Probably a little of both.

While Sheriff O'Herlihy was directing the remaining volunteers, they heard grunting and shuffling in the distance. O'Herlihy whispered that everyone should remain in place while he went to investigate.

Mr. Webb accompanied him.

Mrs. Webb stayed behind. I guess she didn't want to come across her baby acting like a hungry wolf, gnawing its helpless prey down to its bones.

Mr. Webb said he and the sheriff cautiously followed the sound, like hunters stalking their prey.

When they came across Ellie devouring a rabbit, guts and all, he vomited as quietly as possible; he didn't want to ruin the sheriff's opportunity to take her.

O'Herlihy took off his jacket and stretched it out like a net. He crept as if he were sneaking up on an angry bear.

Mr. Webb heard the man's breathing from where he was standing, said he'd never seen a man so scared.

When O'Herlihy was a few feet away from Ellie, he accidentally stepped on a stick, causing it to snap. To him, it must've sounded like a firecracker going off.

Ellie spun around, catching him red-handed. She dropped the rabbit and lunged at him, knocking him flat on his back.

Now keep in mind that this fellow was a good six-foot and heavy to boot, as Mr. Webb told it. Still, he said, Ellie flew into the lawman's chest like a cannonball, knocking him flat on his back. O'Herlihy thrashed around, holding her off, keeping her from ripping him to pieces. She latched onto the fingers of his right hand with her teeth and shook her head back and forth like a crocodile doing a death roll.

Mr. Webb said it literally scared him stiff as he watched the wild girl chew off some of the sheriff's fingers before going for his face. The man's shrieks were so shrill, Webb couldn't tell if they were coming from O'Herlihy or Ellie.

Finally, Mr. Webb overcame his paralysis and assisted the sheriff. He picked up a large rock near his feet. He said he knew if he didn't do something, O'Herlihy would die an awful death. He hesitated at first—after all, she was his baby girl. But looking at the savage before him and thinking about the slaughtered victim and the other soon to come, he ran to the child and swung the rock at her head. He said that he'd never forget the sound of that rock connecting with her skull, like the sharp crack of a whip.

Mr. Webb said he wasn't sure if he ought to be thankful that she was still alive, or grieved because she hadn't died before becoming a violent beast.

He took off his shirt and used it as a tourniquet for what was left of O'Herlihy's hand. He was relieved when the search party found them.

The posse tied up Ellie with some rope that someone had been wise enough to bring. Then they each took turns carrying the unconscious sheriff out of the woods.

The doctor ended up taking what remained of O'Herlihy's hand. Worse, he couldn't do much about the infection that was coming his way. I wonder if the heroic man ended his life before becoming like the thing who'd mauled him.

As for young Ellie, they took her back home and restrained her securely. Doc Thoreau prescribed Laudanum to ease her pain and to keep her semi-conscious, instructing her parents to administer the powerful drug regularly.

By the end of the ravaging sickness, the child looked like a twisted skeleton. Despite her body's condition, the Webbs desired a final and fitting memento. That's when they heard about death photography. About me. Oh, yes, my best salesman has always been word of mouth.

The mortician they'd hired took great care to make Ellie as presentable as possible: limbering up her joints, fixing her hair, applying rouge to her sunken cheeks. Mrs. Webb provided him with Ellie's favorite Sunday dress; she wanted everything just so.

After they'd delivered the body, Mrs. Webb and her husband arranged the corpse on a lovely, maroon, velvet chair in the drawing room. That's where I first met Miss Ellie. She was sitting up straight and proper, looking for the world like a living soul.

My heart broke for Mr. and Mrs. Webb. But after you've done this work for a time, you treat it like the job that it is. "Make it professional, not personal," I always say. So I did my job, collected my fee, and moved on down the line.

I started with the sad story about the Webb family to prepare you for the more interesting tale—the *Wish You'd Never Told Me* tale. You're probably not going to believe me. You must already think I'm just some old drunk at the end of the bar shooting off his mouth. Well, let me assure you, my good man: Everything I'm about to tell you is as real as this whiskey in our glasses.

One dry summer day, a prospective customer, a Mr. Thomas Teach, telegraphed me about a job offer in a small town nestled in eastern Nevada called Whitford. This would put us about two years ago. Seems a close relative of his had recently lost his wife while she was giving birth, her baby having died inside her.

I replied that I'd take the job and then gave him a rough estimate of what my services and expenses would total.

He promptly responded that money was of little importance and asked that I travel to Whitford at my earliest convenience. I let him know to expect my arrival in a few days.

Mr. Teach met me at the train station. With his tailored suit and meticulously styled coal-black hair, he struck me as a well-to-do and refined intellectual—a bon vivant, courtesy of what my mother used to refer to as "Old money." He was erudite in both appearance and manner. He exuded confidence, a man unwaveringly in control of the things around him. Though these attributes created a measure of intimidation, his face held a visage of kindness and warmth that I found soothing. Turned out he was an amalgam of all of those traits. It was literally a pleasure to meet him.

I presumed that with my luggage and small cases of equipment, I'd been easy to pick out. He came to me, and shaking my hand, introduced himself. I, of course, returned the courtesy. After some brief pleasantries, he guided me to his wagon.

As we were loading my gear and luggage, he filled me in on the particulars.

Some years earlier, his brother, Arthur, had fallen hopelessly and helplessly in love with a pretty, strawberry blonde named Margaret Felton, whom everyone called Meg for short. Whereas the bloom often falls from the rose not long after consummation, Arthur's and Meg's love had formed a beautiful garden. They'd been married for about a year when they decided it was time to have a baby. Unfortunately, it wasn't meant to be.

Meg had been with child for six months when one day something felt wrong in her stomach. She collapsed in pain, dropping into a puddle of her own blood.

The husband had summoned a midwife. By the time she'd arrived, Arthur Teach was a childless widower.

Thomas told me that the corpses were being kept on ice in the basement of the town's only funeral parlor. He said he'd like me to accompany him there to determine if Meg was in good enough condition to be photographed; he never mentioned the child. I wondered about the omission, but decided it would be inappropriate to ask questions. I felt correct in assuming that the infant was likely too underdeveloped to merit a place in the photograph.

After agreeing to the visit, I asked him to take me to the nearest hotel where I'd get checked in and acclimated before heading to the funeral parlor, which he did.

The Harrington Hotel was a tasteful affair. A small brass plaque mounted beside the entrance bragged that the governor of Nevada had once stayed there. I figured if it had been good enough for him, then it should be good enough for me. Besides, outside of a questionable-looking boarding house further up the dusty street, it seemed like the best choice for comfortable accommodations.

Once I'd settled in, we took Mr. Teach's wagon to the funeral parlor.

I hope I'm not being untoward when I say that even in death, young Meg was a beauty to behold. She was a small, delicate thing. And there was something about her face that made me think that she'd been kind and pleasant.

I told Mr. Teach that with some care and artistry from the mortician, she'd turn out fine in the photograph.

The mortician assured us he would properly embalm her, apply makeup, and glue her eyes open.

After finalizing the funeral arrangements, Mr. Teach and I left the man to his craft and took our leave.

He dropped me off at my hotel, then said that he'd talk things over with his brother about the photo session.

I told him to help his brother decide when and where he'd like me to take the picture and to pose the body as they saw fit. He assured me that all would be ready to go before my arrival.

We exchanged a few more pleasantries, shook hands, and parted ways.

I woke early the next morning and went downstairs, where I joined a few other guests in the dining room for one of the most scrumptious breakfasts I've ever partaken of.

I was scraping the last remnants of my scrambled eggs onto my fork when the desk clerk came to me with a note from Mr. Teach concerning his brother's wishes for the session.

The widower had requested that I arrive around noon to set up my equipment in the front parlor. Ahead of my arrival, the undertaker would deliver the body and pose her suitably. Mr. Teach finished by informing me that he would pick me up in front of the hotel just before noon.

The noontime hour worked well for me. I had found Whitford quite charming and wanted to see more of it. The folks there were cordial and reasonably well-educated. With its tree-lined streets, lovely town square, and a bevy of inviting shops, it was reminiscent of a Currier and Ives print. The town was big enough to be interesting, but small enough to traverse in a few hours. I was ever the eager tourist, so I asked the hotel manager about points of interest I could visit that were within walking distance.

He kindly complied.

With my itinerary planned, I thanked the cook for the wonderful meal and set about my way.

I enjoyed my stroll around Whitford, so much so that I lost track of time. Walking at a brisk pace, I made it back to the hotel early enough for a quick lunch before keeping my appointment.

At the agreed upon hour, I was waiting in front of the hotel with my photography equipment.

Just as he'd said, Mr. Teach collected me and we journeyed a short distance away to the widower's house.

The small wooden house was lovely and simple. It was a white, two-story, Victorian-styled home surrounded by a narrow wrap-around porch. A bright trail of flowers lined a short stone walkway that led to the front porch steps. Beside the dark-wooded front door was a large stained glass window depicting Jesus kneeling. He was looking heavenward, as if he were longing for either a touch from God or the splendor of Heaven.

Mr. Teach unlocked the door, then turned to me and said, "I give you warning, sir. My brother is a devout Lutheran and tends to be a tad austere."

I assured him that I would take no offense to his brother's behavior.

He unlocked the heavy door, and we went inside.

Upon entering, I realized how clean the house smelled—like soap and flowers, but not overpowering. Tasteful furniture dotted the small entrance. Expensive rugs and carpets covered tidy oak floors. Pictures and portraits adorned a wall that followed the staircase upwards. I assumed the images were of family and old friends, both living and absent.

Mr. Teach touched my elbow and asked me to follow him into a room directly to our right, a parlor.

The spacious room was awash in a kaleidoscope of colorful afternoon light filtering in through the ornate stain glass window. Something, as a photographer, I was pleased to see.

Seated on the settee to my left was lovely Meg. The mortician had wrapped her strawberry blonde hair in a loose bun. Her cheeks were rosy and her lips straight as a plumb line (you'd think the undertaker would've given her a smile). She wore a formal white dress with matching patent leather shoes. Overall, the undertaker had done his job well enough, I decided.

The other corpse was a different matter.

Nestled in Meg's folded arms, wrapped in a blood-red blanket, was the dead baby. Unlike its mother, nothing looked natural about it. Its eyes were open and peering up at its momma. They were enormous and completely white—no irises or pupils. Its nose looked like a wolf's muzzle. I cannot be certain, but I believe the thing had teeth behind its curled lips. Its misshapen head was the size of a large cantaloupe, perhaps bigger.

I don't mean to offend, but it resembled a monster more than a child. I shivered, as I imagined that perhaps the mother had died, not from the rigors of a premature childbirth, but from the thing in her shifting belly ripping its way out. I felt guilty about thinking how the couple was better off not bringing that abomination into this world.

Teach must've noticed the look of revulsion on my face. He apologized for not informing me of the addition of the baby for the session. According to him, it had been his brother's idea. He'd tried to talk him out of it, but the grieving man had insisted on a final picture of the family that would no longer be, the infant's appearance notwithstanding.

I reminded myself that I was there to take a picture or two and nothing more. But I have to say, of the dead bodies that I've seen and touched, I don't recall being as repulsed as I was then.

I was in the midst of setting up my equipment when I heard another person enter the parlor.

Standing next to Thomas was his bereaved brother, Arthur. He was a tall one with a slender face and a black, close-cropped beard. Those features, coupled with his gaunt body, put me in mind of Abraham Lincoln, but better looking.

I stood and went to Arthur, extending my hand in courtesy. I introduced myself and told him how sorry I was for his loss.

The bland expression on his face didn't waver, as he ignored my handshake.

"Oh, are you now?" was all he said.

I didn't know how to respond to his lack of manners other than to attribute it to his melancholy and the austerity of which his brother had warned me. I chided myself for expecting the poor man to be in the mood for cordiality.

Thankfully, Thomas broke through the awkwardness by asking me to show him my photography equipment.

Accepting his cue, I said, "Of course."

As we picked absently through the camera's apparatus, Thomas whispered his apologies.

"I'm very sorry for my brother's rudeness," he said. "I'm sure you can understand he's been through a lot recently."

"No offense taken," I assured him. "I'll take my pictures as quickly as I can so your brother can get back to grieving in peace."

Thomas thanked me for my thoughtfulness, then joined his brother. "Okay, Arthur," he said to him. "Let's move you over here in the corner to watch."

Thomas directed his brother to a far corner of the parlor and eased him down into a large wingback chair. It was like watching a store clerk arranging a mannequin.

The solemn man's mouth held its scowl and his eyes their cold emptiness. He said nothing. Didn't move an inch.

Once he'd taken care of his brother, Thomas didn't seem to know what to do with himself, so I asked if I could trouble him for a glass of water.

Once he'd left, I settled in under the black cover at the rear of the camera obscura. Then I inserted the glass plate, focused the lens, and held the flash wand out and up. I was just about to begin the countdown to prepare Arthur for the bright flash when I stopped cold.

On my mother's sweet, green eyes, I swear that devil baby's head was facing me instead of Meg. And if that image doesn't make your skin crawl, Meg's emotionless face was now smiling.

I know what you're thinking, so don't even start. I agree, either I hadn't paid enough attention when I had first seen them or hadn't noticed Thomas or Arthur arranging the bodies in a more suitable pose while I was setting up the camera. But mister, for the life of me, I'm pretty darn certain I would have noticed something as important as that.

Anyhow, I took the picture and a couple more for good measure.

Once I had finished, I quickly packed up my gear and thanked the gentlemen for their patronage and patience. I told them I'd develop the plates back at the hotel, which, thankfully, had an indoor bathroom that would double nicely as a dark-room. I added that the photograph would be ready the next morning. We said our thank yous and goodbyes, then Thomas led me outside.

After paying me, Thomas was kind enough to assist me in loading my gear back onto his wagon before dropping me off at my hotel.

Once there, he thanked me again and was about to leave when I said something I hadn't meant to. Perhaps the disturbing thought, which had been squirming around in my head since I'd left his brother's house, caused it. Before I could catch the words, I asked him about the poses.

"I don't want to keep you from your business, Mr. Teach," I said, "but I have a question to ask you. Did you or your brother rearrange the bodies before I took the pictures?"

He gave me a curious look. "No. I figured you had. Is there a problem?"

"No, sir," I said. "It's merely that I can be a tad forgetful at times. I just want to make sure that you and your brother will be satisfied with the finished product."

He smiled and said, "I'm confident you'll provide us with a quality product, Mr. Leopold. When the picture is finished, leave it at the front desk and I'll retrieve it first thing tomorrow. Do enjoy your stay." Then he was gone.

I had an early dinner, then proceeded to my room to develop the photographs.

Once the pictures had dried, I picked out the better one, set it aside and went to bed (although I don't know how I slept after my scare earlier that day.)

Now normally I would've left the picture to be picked up, paid my hotel bill, and been on my way. But there was something about Whitford that I liked. It felt more like home than my actual home. I figured it wouldn't hurt to stay an extra day. Who knew? Perhaps some more business opportunities would fall my way. As I said, my best salesman has always been word of mouth. And I knew the Teaches would be satisfied with my work.

The next morning, I came back from a pleasant walk through the town and found that Mr. Teach had been by to collect the picture. The desk clerk said that Mr. Teach had been delighted with the product. I was pleased that he was pleased. Another happy customer. Good for both of us.

The following night, I was at the local saloon tipping my elbow and enjoying a steak and potato when Thomas Teach wandered in. I say, wandering, because he looked lost and thunderstruck, shuffling more than walking.

He sidled up to the bar and ordered a double shot of brown liquor. He threw it back in one thirsty gulp, then ordered another.

Thomas Teach had struck me as a man of prominence and refinement, a man not given to frequenting such establishments. His presence and his odd behavior perplexed and concerned me.

I rose from my table and joined him at the bar. He seemed completely unaware of my presence.

"Mr, Teach?" I said.

He didn't answer, but looked ahead at something that only he could see.

"It isn't so... it isn't so..." was what he kept mumbling.

When I touched his shoulder, he yelped like a frightened dog as he teetered on the edge of falling off his bar stool. He was huffing, as though he'd run a mile uphill. His eyes darted around the room before locking with my own. It took him a moment to recognize me.

"Uh, Mr. Leopold," he stammered. "Sorry, I didn't recognize you. I'm quite distressed, as you've no doubt surmised."

"That's putting it mildly," I told him. "Is there anything I can do for you—anything you'd like to talk about?"

He looked down at his shaking hands. "You know, Mr. Leopold, I don't believe I ever want to talk about this to anyone."

I reassured him. "Look, your business is your business," I said. "But I'll be leaving tomorrow. I doubt our paths will ever cross again. Your worry is safe with me. Think about it: who am I going to tell?"

Well, thought about it, he did.

"I suppose you're right, Mr. Leopold. After all, you're the one who brought this about, so I might as well tell you."

That statement brought him my full attention. "How's that again?" I asked.

The next thing I knew, he had me by my collar, panting. His eyes looked desperate and terrified. His face was so close to mine, I smelled the bourbon on his breath.

"Where did you get that camera, Mr. Leopold? Where?"

I told him I didn't know what he meant. "Why is that important?" I asked him.

He let go of my collar, then said, "That's no typical camera, sir. It... it brings the dead to life."

Well, what was I supposed to say to that? The dead brought back from the great beyond? I needed to know more. Where was he going with this? I have to say, he'd piqued my interest.

After all, I'd never talked to a madman before. But I also considered his condition: horrified and confused, with wild eyes like an enraged animal. I felt a bit of guilt for being the source of his anguish, his terror. I figured I owed him my audience, so I indulged him.

I told him I'd purchased the camera obscura a few years back from a reputable seller. I added that I'd taken many photographs and had had no supernatural experiences with it.

Still, he was anxious. He wouldn't stop glaring at me with those wide, frightened eyes. "And you've had no issues with those people after they received their photographs?"

I assured him again that, to the best of my knowledge, none of my clients had spoken of any unusual occurrences.

"You're lying to me! Stop lying to me!" he hollered.

The other patrons were looking at us, wondering what the ruckus was about. I guess Teach realized he was the source of their curious stares, so he settled down.

My interest further whetted, I asked him to tell me what had happened to give him the idea that my pictures had resurrected the dead. What I'm about to share with you is nearly word for word what he told me.

He said, "As you know, I retrieved the photograph you'd taken of my brother's wife and child. I went to the general store, purchased a tasteful frame, and returned to his house.

"Soon after I got there, I tucked the photo into the frame and placed it on the mantle in his study.

"When my brother entered and saw it, he began crying. I've never seen him that distraught, even after he had lost Meg and the baby. I believe that was when he fully accepted that the photograph was all he'd ever be able to see of them. At that moment, I was glad that I'd hired you. I comforted him as best I could, then returned to my home.

"Later that evening, my brother's housekeeper, Carolyn, showed up at my door, visibly shaken. She was pale and quivering, as though she'd seen a ghost. I invited her inside, but she refused. When I asked her the reason for her distress, she said it was my brother."

Teach stopped his story, threw back his shot, then ordered another. He sat quietly for so long, I wondered if he had the courage or the desire to continue. He pulled in a deep, shaky breath before returning to his tale.

"Apparently," he said, "Carolyn had been cleaning upstairs when she heard people laughing and talking. She didn't recall seeing any visitors when she had first arrived, so she was curious.

"As she was making her way downstairs, she said she distinctly overheard my brother and a woman conversing. By the time she reached the door to Arthur's study, she realized to her horror that the voice of the woman was Meg's; she'd heard it a hundred times. Despite her reluctance, she knocked on the door, and the voices ceased.

"She said that Arthur opened the door and demanded to know why she'd interrupted him. She looked past him and saw the photograph of Meg and the baby on his desk. She didn't look at it for long; the mere sight of the monstrous child unnerved her. She mentioned to Arthur that she thought she had heard voices inside the room. Her observation annoyed him, so it did not surprise her when he told her to mind her own business and leave him be. She said he slammed the door so hard the floor shook.

"Carolyn returned upstairs to continue her cleaning. That's when she heard the unmistakable sound of a baby crying. Only it wasn't quite right. 'Abnormal' was how she described it. She compared it to a combination of an infant and a hissing snake.

"Despite her apprehension, Carolyn returned to the study as quietly as she could manage. She was going to knock again, but decided against it. She wanted—needed—to know what was going on in that room. She summoned her courage and eased the door open."

Teach paused a second time, as if he were deciding whether to continue his account or forget it altogether.

"Please, continue," I prodded.

He got that faraway look again, then resumed his story.

"In her effort to recount the event, Carolyn became agitated and increasingly delirious. She vacillated between a childish giggle and the cackle of a lunatic. When she finally spoke, her voice was high-pitched and infantile, a baby's jabber.

"She said that when she stepped into the room, she was horrified at the sight of…"

I was on pins and needles at that point, eager to hear the rest about what the babbling housekeeper had seen. So I asked, "What? What did she see, Mr. Teach?"

The man turned white as sugar.

"Arthur wasn't alone," he muttered. "Joining him near the fireplace was Meg, just as she'd appeared in the photograph, right down to her wide eyes and unnatural smile. The sight had been enough to freeze Carolyn in place. But what had terrified her beyond words was the baby Meg was holding. It wasn't dead, but alive—terrifyingly and inexplicably alive. It peered at Carolyn and licked its purple lips.

"All she remembered after that was fleeing from the house like a horse escaping a burning barn. After telling her story to me, she began weeping and shrieking. I begged her to come inside, so that I might attend to her, but she wouldn't stop wailing. I insisted that she allow me to take her to her home. It was quite some distance, and she was without her horse, which she'd left back in the house's ba rn.

"'No!' she bellowed, then took off running into the night, screaming—my word, the screaming. It was the sound of madness and horror!"

Teach's silence returned. He looked terror-stricken. He waved the bartender over to refill his shot glass. Then he threw back his fresh shot of bourbon and allowed it to calm him before he continued.

"Soon after Carolyn left, I went to Arthur's house and found the front door open, something I attributed to Carolyn's hasty retreat.

"I wandered in and called out to Arthur. When he failed to respond, I called again, this time louder. The house was silent as the grave. Uneasiness blanketed me. I damned the creaking floor, as I ventured cautiously to his study and looked inside."

A statue isn't as still as Teach was in that moment. Peering into that parlor must have been like looking into hell and having hell looking back at you. Judging by his behavior, I couldn't help but think about how fitting it would be if he were wearing a straitjacket. It was as if some terrible force had sucked his soul from his body and tossed it into a hellish hole.

I wanted to know what happened next. What could've brought about this much blind horror to a sane and reasonable man? Once more, I prompted him. "What happened next, Mr. Teach?"

When he continued, I had to lean in close. In a weak whisper, he finished his ghost story.

"I ... I walked into the study. Arthur wasn't there. As I moved further, I noticed the framed photograph resting on the edge of his desk. I went to take it and return it to its spot on the mantle.

Without warning, a cold, phantom wind blew through me. It felt like an icy hand had invaded my stomach, tearing away at my bowels. I inched towards his desk.

"I picked up the photograph and looked at it. I was shocked to see Arthur seated on the settee with Meg and that awful child. I couldn't understand how he could have possibly gotten there.

"As I peered at that frightful photo, I noticed something else. Something less sinister but chilling just the same. Arthur has always been a dour man. But in the picture, he was smiling more brightly than I'd ever seen him do before. So was Meg. You would've thought it a perfect family photo if only the creature cradled in her arms wasn't leering with its bulging white eyes and baring what looked like dog's teeth.

"I was tightly wound like a coiled spring, so it didn't help when I heard footsteps descending the staircase. I had believed that I was the only soul in the house. I called out, "Hello!" But I only heard those slow, heavy footfalls coming toward me. My rational mind told me to investigate the source of the sound, but my deepest instincts sensed danger and horror.

"My primal mind bellowed at me to lock the door to the study. I tried to lock it, but my quaking hands were so slippery with sweat that it took a couple of frantic attempts to engage the lock."

Teach paused, licked his dry lips, then drew in a couple of quick breaths before going on.

"Ominous footsteps shuffled down the hall, stopping at the study's door. I heard high-pitched growling, something between a baby's coo and an angry cat. I was grateful for the door, which was serving as a barrier between whatever horror waited on the other side of it and me. I felt the ghost nearly leave me, as I watched the doorknob slowly twisting.

"I backed away from the door until I bumped into Arthur's desk. The mild force was enough to topple the terrible picture resting on it. Though a large part of me did not want to, I took hold of the frame and lifted it to my face. Something had changed."

Teach closed his mouth so tight, I saw his jawbones clenching through his skin. The words to describe what had happened next seemed trapped in his mouth with fear. I took care not to rattle him, as he was on edge to the point of running screaming from the establishment. Softly, I said, "What was in the photograph, Mr. Teach?"

His head wavered as if it was on the verge of disconnecting from his neck and plummeting to the floor. I've never seen a person's lips turn blue who wasn't at the point of hypothermia. But his were as blue as the sky; they trembled when he spoke.

"Nothing. Nothing but an empty settee," he said. "They all had disappeared. But I knew where they were. They were gathered at the study's door, waiting to be let inside. I have no recollection of feeling my body or emotions at that moment. Then, as if against my will, I stepped to the door and opened it. They were reaching. They..."

Teach said no more. I waited for him to finish, but the look of lost rationality was all over his blank face. He'd said all he was going to say—able to say. We sat there in an uncomfortable silence until the bartender inquired if he would enjoy another drink.

I'll recall for all my days the next moment.

Ignoring the bartender, Teach rose from his seat and turned to me. He was grinning, but it wasn't natural. Human. It was as though Thomas Teach had left his body, bequeathing it to a demonic replica. He lifted his regal chin and said, "Remember, you must die."

Then he casually adjusted his gentleman's tie and plodded solemnly out of the bar, as if he were a pallbearer escorting a casket to its eternal home in the dirt.

The next morning, I took the train back to my home here in Mesa. During that troubling journey, I couldn't get Teach off my mind. I distracted myself: reading, light conversation with my fellow passengers, forcing my thoughts elsewhere. But as night settled over the land, the other folks slept tranquilly, leaving me alone with the frightening memories I had collected in fair Whitford. Here it is, over two years later, and I'm still pondering. Still spooked.

The sheriff of that quaint little town sent me a letter a few days ago. That's why I'm here tonight in this fine establishment, where good times are celebrated and bad ones forgotten. I'll explain.

Morbid curiosity got the better of me one day. I had to know what had happened to Teach after his dance with the devil, so I wrote to the sheriff.

In his letter to me, he shared the details concerning Thomas Teach's state of being.

According to him, Teach had moved into his brother's house, leaving his own to fall into a state of disrepair and decay. Because he seldom ventures out, no one knows how he finds food. He likely lives off the rats, or so they say. Occasionally, he walks the streets of Whitford, whistling an indecipherable tune that has no structure or melody. His meticulously coiffed black hair has grown into a long, unkempt tangle that is now an ebullient white. A stained, matted beard conceals the handsome face that now exists only in my mind's eye. I'm told he still wears the fancy tailored suit I last saw him in, though now it is ragged and filthy. His fingernails are long and cracked; his hands like skeletal claws.

As for Arthur, Meg, and the demon child, no one knows where they disappeared to. And no one ever will except for a deranged housekeeper, poor old Thomas, and me. And now you, I suppose.

The sheriff stops by to check on the property from time to time. He's long since stopped checking on Thomas Teach.

He says Teach is always inside that terrible place, scuttling down the dusty halls like a lost and spider, mumbling that final line over and over: "Remember, you must die... remember, you must die... remember, you must die."

That letter chilled me all right. But it's the last part of it that makes me afraid to be by myself sometimes.

The sheriff told me that whenever anyone walks near the Teach house, they always hear the same things: Thomas's mad babbling and the laughter of other people—that and the bone-chilling sound of something snarling and crying.

Well, my good man, I think this last drink does it for me. I'm sorry if I bored you. My goal was to entertain you. Maybe frighten you a smidge, as well. Either way, thanks for listening to my odd stories. Now if you'll give me pardon, I have to get on home and grab a little shut-eye. I'm leaving for Amarillo tomorrow morning to take pictures for a family whose dog recently recently. You see,

I don't do people anymore. The money isn't as good, but it gives me peace of mind. I've never heard tell of a dog or cat coming back from the dead.

# MADAM ONA'S SHOPPE OF CURIOSITIES: BLAIR'S STORY

## I

"*God, I can't stand this anymore!*"

Blair sat up in bed, wrapping her arms around her middle as if she were keeping her insides from exploding through her stomach. The pain was worsening. Despite the ultrasounds, lab work, x-rays, and countless consultations, there had been no conclusive diagnosis for her searing abdominal pain. No tumors. No tissue scarring. No disease. No luck. By her ninth second opinion, she'd all but given up hope of ever going back to her life as it was, the life before the sickness had ravaged her world. Now, the pain meds were barely working. *Useless pills. I wonder... how many would it take... ?*

There'd been a time in the not-so-distant past when the idea of ending her life would've been unthinkable. Now, it felt like a reasonable option ... an escape plan. *Enough! This ends tonight!* she promised herself. It was a promise she meant to keep.

First, she somehow had to make it to the medicine cabinet for the pills. It might as well have been a hundred miles away. The trip to the bathroom was intolerable when she was having a good day. But tonight, the thought of making the journey bordered on the cruel and terrifying. *One more trip. Just one last try, then it'll be over.*

Blair planned to make the trek in manageable stages. First, she needed to stand up. She inhaled deeply and swung her legs over the side of the bed. The discomfort wasn't as bad as she had feared. Next, she rocked forward a few times and, when ready, stood up straight.

"Oh, my Goood!" She felt as though she'd swallowed a dose of lightning. Her joints stiffened and her teeth gritted so hard that she feared they would splinter. Blair took in short snippets of air through her nostrils, as if they could somehow dilute the agony. After a bit, the pain subsided enough for her to continue. Blair cried as she contemplated the most challenging part of the journey, the walk to the bathroom. "Please, give me just a bit more strength. Just a little more. I'm begging you," she whimpered.

Grunting with each step, she inched closer toward the place wherein her salvation lay.

By the time Blair got to the bathroom, she was exhausted. She placed her hands on each side of the sink, bracing herself up. She gasped when she looked in the mirror. The fit and trim woman who used to weigh a healthy one hundred twenty pounds was now an eighty-pound scarecrow. Her sallow skin sagged as if it were too heavy for her frame to support any longer. Her bulging eyes looked like two grotesque orbs straining to break free of their skeletal cage. Although she grieved for the woman she once was, she simply couldn't cry anymore; she was just too spent.

Blair opened the medicine cabinet and looked at the pharmacy that now inhabited it. She spotted the Hydromorphone and plucked it from the stack of other medications the doctors had prescribed. She looked at the bottle as if it were a loaded gun. Her resolve began to wane. *It's like ripping off a Band-Aid. Just do it quickly and be done with it before you change your mind.* She popped the lid and shook four tablets into her palm, twice the normal dosage. To be on the safe side, she added two more. She filled one of the small plastic cups beside the sink, threw the pills toward the back of her throat, and took the full shot of water.

Blair sat on the edge of the bathtub and waited for the pain to lessen enough for her to return to her bed. Within minutes, she became light-headed. Once the pain ebbed, she got up and plodded back to the place she hoped would be her second-to-last resting spot.

Blair fell onto the mattress, closed her weighty eyelids, and waited for the lightness of death that would allow her to drift away like a wispy, white feather.

# 2

The light pouring through the window of Blair's bedroom the following morning covered her frail body in a blanket of soft gold. After a few tries, her eyes opened and remained so. Her mind was fuzzy, her body limp and heavy. As she became lucid, she realized that she'd lived to see another day. "Oh no, not again," she moaned.

Blair had sat up and gotten out of bed before she realized that her discomfort was somewhat bearable. The extra pills had served a useful purpose, after all. However, experience had taught her that moments such as these were short-lived. Her thoughts taunted her. *I couldn't even catch a break from suicide. The second time's gonna have to be the charm. But first, let's make this last day feel normal, for a little while anyway.*

Blair decided that, more than anything, she wanted to be around people again. She managed to get showered and dressed. When she was ready, she called an Uber to take her to the downtown district. It'd been ages since she'd wandered its streets, shops, and cafes.

Before leaving, she downed a couple of more Hydromorphone tablets to take the edge off, making sure to leave plenty for later.

# 3

The Uber dropped Blair off in front of a coffee shop she used to frequent in the old and better days. The uncomfortable stares from the customers as she entered brought about a swell of embarrassment and sadness. She didn't need a mirror at that moment to remind her of her cringe-worthy appearance; their expressions cut deeper than any cruel reflection could.

Blair limped to a table at the back wall of the cafe and eased into one of its soft, padded seats. Hoping to escape any further scrutiny, she hid behind a menu and waited.

The server's reaction to seeing her was awkward, but expected. Her clumsy attempt at appearing compassionate struck Blair as disingenuous and patronizing. Pushing the unintended offense aside, she relaxed and ordered something. She played things safe, asking for a small muffin and some tea for her breakfast.

The items smelled wonderful, and the very sight of them cheered her. However, the best Blair could manage was half of the muffin and less of the warm tea. Given how much her stomach had shrunk, it was enough to satisfy her.

After leaving the coffee shop, Blair walked along the sidewalk. Her senses absorbed every sight, sound, and smell. Despite the busy life that was swirling around her, she felt a melancholy tugging at her soul. The day's activities would be her last glimpse of real life, a life she'd taken for granted.

Blair knew she was ill, and had for a while. But this was the first time that she felt like a ghost, a stubborn soul that had not yet taken its leave. She decided to walk a few more blocks, then go home, and vanquish the pain for good.

Blair was halfway down the third and final block when she came to a store she couldn't remember having seen before. It was a small, nondescript shop. Its modest appearance was in conspicuous contrast to the more modern, trendier stores. Even its door looked out of date. It was a simple affair—a wood frame with a single large pane of glass in the door's upper half.

Stenciled in old-style calligraphy was the shop's name: Madam Ona's Shoppe of Curiosities.

Intrigued, she turned the door's knob and entered.

*Ring Ring.* The small bell over the door surprised Blair as she walked in; she found it quaint and musical. Despite the foot traffic just beyond its door, the shop was empty of customers. Its interior brought to Blair's mind an eerily lifelike Norman Rockwell painting of a small-town general store. The old ceiling fans, combined with the rough hardwood floors, created a worn, rustic look. The place was full of shelves and glass display cases of mystical odds and ends: jars of colored powders, crystals, incenses, and old books. Blair felt as if she'd stumbled through a mirrored doorway and into a magical lair.

"How may I serve you today?"

Enthralled by the spiritual essence of the place, the woman's voice startled Blair.

"Welcome to my store," said the woman. "I am Madam Ona. I apologize for having startled you." She spoke with a lyrical accent that Blair couldn't quite place. The diminutive woman was dressed in a loose, brightly colored muumuu. She was middle-aged, with piercing gray eyes. Her unkempt mane of bushy, white hair was so bright that Blair squinted at first. Despite the woman's small stature, her presence was intimidating.

"That's all right," Blair said. "My, you have a lot of interesting things here."

Madam Ona swiveled her head from side to side as if she were viewing the setting for the first time. "Yes," she said, "a lot of interesting things." Her eyes locked with Blair's. "Something brings you here today. A worry. A need. Ah, that's it: a need." Her eyes closed, and she tilted her head to one side as if she were receiving an important message from some mystical force far away. "It's a deep, physical pain that modern practices cannot abate."

"That's... right." The woman's intuition both impressed and unnerved Blair.

As if sensing her apprehension, Madam Ona's ominous demeanor changed to a kind and gentle patience. "Fear not, child; I can help you." Her gaze settled on an item resting on a middle shelf to Blair's right.

It was a small glass bottle, not much bigger than a shot glass, sealed with a cork. There was no label of any kind to identify the single ingredient: a black, gray-speckled capsule.

"That bottle there," Madam Ona said pointing, "pick it up." She said it as if she were a teacher coaxing a student into plucking a flower to examine.

Blair pinched the curious remedy between her thumb and index finger. After studying it for a bit, Blair asked, "What is it?"

"What's inside that bottle will devour all your pain. That is your need—your desire—yes?"

Blair was torn between trusting Madam Ona and avoiding being deceived. Such an act seemed cruel and self-serving. After all, she had a bottle full of cure waiting at home in her medicine cabinet. Why should the woman profit from her misery? As far as Blair was concerned, Madam Ona was offering her little more than snake oil. But her anguish was forcing her hand. She wanted so badly to believe that there was hope for herself that she pushed aside her suspicions and allowed herself to be vulnerable.

"Please, don't hold out false hope to me," Blair said. "This is my final attempt before I end this hell myself. So, please, please, don't take this lightly. I'm a human being, and I'm desperate."

Madam Ona smiled at Blair in the way that a mother would behold her splendid child. "I know, I know, young one. Your clear and logical mind is saying, *Oooh, crazy lady. Look at all her shrunk-*

*en heads, potions, and crystals.* But then, there's that part of you that wants—needs—to know that magic exists." She pointed at the jar that Blair was clutching. "That item can erase the agony that the so-called specialists claimed could never be healed. The choice, of course, is yours. But ask yourself: 'After all of the medicines that have been given to me up till now, do I feel better or worse?'" Madam Ona let the question hover for a bit. "As I said, the decision is yours. Either way, thank you for coming in, and be sure to tell a friend." Then she turned and walked away.

"Wait!" Blair said.

Madam Ona stopped. Without turning around, she asked, "Yes?"

"How much?"

Madam Ona turned and walked back to Blair. "Nothing... now. But when the cure has done its work, call me, and I will come to you. We'll discuss a payment then."

Blair's wariness returned. "So, you don't want me to pay you for this today? I can just take it and go? How do you know I won't cheat you?"

"None ever have; I'm sure you won't either." Madam Ona reached into one of her pockets and retrieved a small card, and handed it to Blair. When Blair tried to take the card from her, she held onto its edge tightly. In a sober tone, she said, "Listen, child. You must be patient. You'll need to give the remedy enough of time to do its work—a few weeks and none less."

"I'm sure you won't, child. Now go. Take it, and I will wait for your call."

Going to the front door, it occurred to Blair to ask an important question she'd not thought of before. "Excuse me, ma'am. Should I be concerned about any side effects?"

"Once you take it, you'll experience some tiredness, and your appetite will increase. Anything else?"

"No. Thank you for a—"

Madam Ona was already walking to the backroom, leaving Blair alone with her miracle cure.

Blair didn't want to wait until she got home before taking the capsule, so she returned to the coffee shop she'd visited earlier. She ordered a cup of coffee and then called for an Uber. She took the small bottle from her purse and laid it on the table in front of her. She stared at it, wondering if it would help her if only a bit. *Anything's better than nothing.*

When her coffee arrived, Blair removed the capsule from the bottle and swallowed it with a swig of the coffee. The hot liquid angered her insides.

Thankfully, by the time the Uber arrived, the burning had subsided. Blair hopped into the car and headed straight home, eager to see what would unfold.

# 4

**T**wilight's artful strokes painted Blair's apartment in pastel hues. She was reading as she lay curled up in an oversized leather chair beside the living room window. The growl from her stomach reminded her she had eaten nothing since earlier. She closed the book and set about making dinner.

Blair went to the kitchen, found a small pot, and set it on the stove. Then she opened a cupboard and twirled the Lazy Susan until she found a can of tomato soup. Soft foods and liquids were all she could tolerate. She remembered the woman's promise that her appetite would improve. *I'd give everything I own for a single slice of pepperoni and pineapple pizza,* Blair thought.

Once she had heated the soup to a moderately warm temperature, she emptied it into a bowl and then grabbed a spoon.

Blair sat down at the table and worked up the courage to eat. With hesitation, she spooned some of the soup into her mouth. She braced herself for the first wave of suffering. But to her pleasure and amazement, the tepid liquid made its way painlessly to her stomach. She ate a couple of more spoonfuls—again, no burning sensation. Relieved by the kindness of her stomach, she gulped down the rest of the soup.

Blair stood up from the table so fast that she toppled her chair. "Omigosh! It worked!" She briefly considered rushing back to Madam Ona's store and giving the woman a big hug. But first, her stomach was screaming for another bowl of soup.

# 5

Later that evening, Blair stood before her medicine cabinet, the site she had planned for her suicide. She unscrewed the lid of the Hydromorphone and shook a couple into her hand. She was about to take them, but paused as she noticed the absence of any pain, not even a slight twinge. Blair smiled as she recalled it had only been that morning when she'd planned to swallow the entire bottle of painkillers. Now she was content to skip a dose. She returned the medicine to the cabinet and went to bed. For the first time in months, she didn't need to be drugged out of her mind to fall asleep.

# 6

A strong grumbling in her belly awoke Blair in the middle of the night. Typically, it would've been a twisting pain she had to deal with; now, it was a deep hunger. The welcome return of her appetite filled her with joy and gratitude. She climbed out of bed and headed to the kitchen to appease it.

Blair had a craving for something more filling than soup or jello. Although thrilled to get her appetite back, she couldn't wrap her head around the strength of her gnawing hunger. She kept little in the way of solid food, so she ended up placing a large order from an all-night diner.

As she waited for the delivery person, she walked around her apartment, cramming saltines into her mouth.

By the time the two ham hoagies arrived, she'd consumed a half dozen individual servings of pudding, two cans of soup, and nearly a gallon of water.

When the food was gone, Blair returned to bed. Despite having slept for many hours before her binge, Blair was amazed by how exhausted she felt. She slept for another fifteen hours.

When Blair finally awakened, it was late afternoon. Despite the extraordinary amount of sleep, she was still dog-tired. The only activity she felt any energy toward was eating.

After shuffling around the kitchen in search of something to eat, she found nothing. So, she grabbed a quick shower and headed for the supermarket.

Blair went crazy at the store. She bought so many groceries that she paid the Uber driver an extra ten dollars to help her tote them up to her apartment. Before she could put them away, her stomach beckoned again. An excessive amount of cookies, sodas, and thick sandwiches eventually sated her appetite. Then the drowsiness returned. She slept for seventeen hours.

The cycle continued for another two weeks. By then, Blair had gained forty-seven pounds and was sleeping nearly twenty hours each night. Her desire to eat was relentless. She considered going back to her doctor, but remembered how little he'd been able to help her. Thinking of reaching out to Madam Ona, she remembered the advice: allow a few weeks for the remedy to work.

Within days, Blair had gained an additional fifteen pounds. She hadn't bathed in over a week. Her former physical appearance used to frighten her, but her current state shocked her more. As she stood on the bathroom scale, looking down at the escalating numbers, she became concerned. *It's too far. I'm heading too far in the other direction.*

Sweaty and dizzy, Blair shuffled to the bathroom sink and turned on the cold water. She cupped it in her doughy hands and splashed it on her face. Then she ran her fingers through her unwashed hair. The amount that came out startled her. "Oh, God, what's wrong with me?"

Despite her anxiety, Blair still craved food. As quickly as her bloated body allowed, she waddled to the kitchen. She ate for nearly an hour.

After gorging on everything that was left in the kitchen, Blair plopped down on the living room sofa. Suddenly, it felt like something was sliding around inside her. Indigestion? She lifted her shirt and looked at her abdomen. A small knob pushed outward. She felt nauseous and afraid. She touched the protrusion with her fingertips, and it receded. Blair began panting like a cornered animal as the mass moved up toward her chest cavity. She screamed. Blood dripped from her nose; she could taste its tang in her mouth. Her mind began whirring. *What'd that woman give me? I'm calling her right now!*

Blair staggered to the bedroom. "Where is it? WHERE... IS... IT?" She dumped the contents of her purse onto the bed and pushed the items around until she found her phone and Madam Ona's card. She called and waited. Someone answered on the third ring, but to her, it felt like many more.

"Madam Ona's Shoppe of Curiosities. What is your need?"

Blair recognized the woman's exotic voice. Panicked, she said, "Yes, hello. I hope you'll remember me. I visited your shop a short while back. You sold me a remedy for my chronic stomach pain."

"Why yes, child. I remember you well." Madam Ona sounded pleased, as if she were hearing from an old friend. "How is your health? Are you eating and sleeping well? The pain, tell me of the pain. Is it gone?"

Blair was shivering. "Yes, the pain's gone, but I'm experiencing some serious side effects. I sleep for hours on end, and I can't stop eating. I don't even recognize myself anymore. Now, my hair's falling out and I'm pretty sure I'm hemorrhaging. I'm scared to death."

"Just as I told you, there would be side effects. Are you experiencing any other symptoms?"

"YES! There's something is moving inside me. You didn't say anything about that! Am I going to die? Do I need a doctor?"

Madam Ona snickered, then, in a reassuring tone, said, "You are not going to die, child. The remedy has merely done its job. There's only one last step, and then you will return to normal. No more worries now."

Her sincerity soothed Blair.

"Thank you, thank you, Blair said. "I'm just eager for this to be over."

"And soon it will be. But before I come, I need to know that you will honor your part of the bargain. You must pay me."

"Of course. How much do you want?"

"One thousand dollars."

The price stunned Blair. "Listen, I don't want to seem ungrateful, but that sounds a little steep for a single dose of medicine."

"No, no, the remedy is free. The charge is for the removal."

Blair was confused. "Removal? What removal? What was in that capsule?"

"Oh, my child, that was no capsule—that was an egg."

# REEL

I

It was early summer in 1985. The freshly freed prisoners of the George County Public School System were whirring through the small town of Hanlon with wild abandon. They never wanted summer to end; their put upon parents were counting down the minutes until it did. The local pool was crowded. Drivers took extra precautions to avoid accidentally hitting anyone from the brigade of child cyclists swarming the neighborhoods. Summer blockbusters were in rotation at the town's only movie theater. One of them drew the interest of Katelyn Campbell, a thirteen-year-old, on a secret mission to toughen up her ten-year-old brother, Bryce.

"Please, no! I'm scared, *really* scared!" Bryce pleaded. At ten years old, he had never fully watched a horror movie before. Vampires, werewolves, demons from the dark—they each flooded him with terror. The film, *Fright Night,* the movie they were waiting outside the theater to see, fit that description.

"Oh, don't be such a baby. It's not as if you're gonna die in there," Katelyn teased.

"If you wanna see the movie so bad, go ahead and see it," Bryce said. "I'll wait in the bike store across from the parking lot where Dad dropped us off."

When Bryce turned to leave, Katelyn took hold of his wrist. "Oh, no you don't. I'm doing this for your own good. You'll thank me later."

Bryce squirmed, as if he were struggling to break free from the jaws of a ravenous crocodile. "No fair, Katelyn; you lied to me. You said that we were gonna see *The Muppet Movie.* I'm gonna tell Mom and Dad."

Katelyn let go of Bryce's wrist and switched to her nurturing big sister's voice. "Look, Bryce. You've got to learn how to conquer your fears. When I was your age, I was terrified of the water. I hated going to the pool with my friends. I knew they'd figure out that I couldn't swim, and then they'd make fun of me. Well, they did. I ran the whole six blocks home, crying my eyes out. You're probably old enough to remember what Dad did about it."

Bryce nodded. "Yeah. Dad took you back to the pool after most of the people had gone home and tossed you in the deep end."

"That's right. At first, it horrified me that he would do something like that. But guess what? I was able to tread water. Within an hour, I could dog paddle and hold my breath underwater. If I hadn't faced my fear, I never would've learned how important it is to be brave. For the rest of the summer, I hung out with my girls down at the pool, whooping it up, and flirting with boys. Ever since then, I've faced my fears and worries head on. You can do it, too. If you're afraid of bugs, let a caterpillar crawl up your arm—they're harmless. Afraid of heights? Climb a tree. Afraid of scary movies...?"

"Watch a scary movie," Bryce finished.

"You got it, Hercules," Katelyn said.

"But the rating says we're not old enough to watch it," Bryce reminded her.

The corner of Katelyn's mouth curled with mischief. "Not to worry; I have a plan, mah man. I'll buy a ticket to *The Muppet*

*Movie*, then I'll blend in with the people who are going into the theater where *Fright Night* is showing. You walk around the corner of the building over there. Give me about ten minutes; I'll open the exit door and let you in. Then it's easy peasy, lemon squeezy, George Jefferson married Weezy."

The saying always stole a giggle from Bryce. But that was Katelyn: fearless and peerless, but most of all, funny. "Okay, then. I'll try to be brave," he said.

Katelyn smiled and playfully punched Bryce's shoulder. "That's my baby brother. By the time we leave here, you'll be a fan of these kinds of movies. Now go on around and wait for me. I'll buy the ticket, snag a soda and some popcorn for us to share, then I'll let you in. We good?"

Bryce forced a weak and insincere smile. "We're good, I guess."

"Okay, let's get moving," Katelyn said, then made her way to the box office.

Bryce watched Katelyn walk into the theater, then trekked around the side of the building and to the exit door, uncertainty and trepidation nipping at his heels.

According to the plan, Katelyn made the purchases. Then she insinuated herself within a group entering the auditorium, hoping she wouldn't be noticed by a blabbermouthed adult.

Katelyn entered the large, weakly lit area and took a seat up front. The irresistible aroma of theater popcorn and Coka Cola filled the air, creating a perfect cloud of delicious scents. She was relieved that only a handful of people had shown up for the early afternoon screening. *Fewer witnesses,* she thought. Most of the people were engaged in private conversations. One young couple was doing an enthusiastic lip press in the back row, making Katelyn giggle. With the stealth of an assassin, she continued to survey the semi-dark auditorium, waiting for the opportune moment to act. When she was satisfied that everyone's attention was fixed elsewhere, she rose from her seat and began creeping toward the exit doo r.

When Katelyn got there, she turned one last time to make sure no one was watching her—the coast was clear. She took a couple of breaths to steel herself, then pushed on the narrow bar that opened the exit door. She was relieved to discover Bryce standing in front of her. She grabbed the collar of his Star Wars t-shirt, yanked him inside, then closed the heavy steel door before anyone noticed anything awry. "Follow me," Katelyn whispered. With Bryce in tow, she settled him in the front row, strategically placing him close to the screen for an up-close and chilling experience.

Fear-induced adrenaline rushed through Bryce's nervous system, leaving him wobbly and breathless. Sweat wetted his forehead and palms. "Why do we have to sit so close?" he whimpered.

"Look, Bryce," Katelyn said, "this experience is like getting on a roller coaster: It's scary as all get out, but deep down, you know you're gonna come out at the end safe. Do you want your buddies making fun of you because you're scared to watch cool movies like *Alien, Halloween,* or *Friday the Thirteenth*?"

"No, I suppose not," Bryce sheepishly muttered.

"Okay, then. Just cover your eyes if it's too much to take in at once."

"But what about the sound? It's gonna be super noisy. It might hurt my ears."

"Close your eyes if it's too scary, and cover your ears if it's too loud."

"How come I feel like I'm gonna be doing a lot of closing and covering during this movie?"

"Trust me. At some point, you won't feel so scared. You've got this, little brother. Don't underestimate yourself."

"Okay, if you say so." Bryce jerked when, without warning, the auditorium went full black and the front row speakers erupted in a shrill cacophony of earsplitting noise. After some genre related trailers (something that Bryce also found terrifying) the thin curtain on either side of the silver screen pulled away and the feature began.

Bryce dreaded the nighttime scenes when the vicious, undead monsters exsanguinated their victims with violent fervor. He took advantage of the daytime scenes to catch his breath and uncover his eyes. *It isn't real, it isn't real…* he reminded himself. But as the plot progressed, he gradually became accustomed to the building tension. His uneasiness dissipated as his curiosity about the direction of the movie grew within his newly opened mind. By the middle of the film, his faith in Roddy McDowell and William Ragsdale to save the day surpassed his fear of the vampire played by Chris Sarandon. Near the end of the feature, he was cheering on the protagonists who'd found a courage they did not know they possessed. And whom, despite overwhelming odds, had vanquished the evil vampires. When the film came to its exciting and satisfying conclusion, Bryce surprised himself by applauding. He felt exhilarated.

Katelyn leaned over the armrest separating her and Bryce. "See? You did it. I told you that you'd end up liking the movie."

As the lights came up, Bryce and Katelyn left the way he'd entered earlier and stepped outside into the everyday world of sunlight and normalcy. Bryce understood what Katelyn had been getting at: Fear plus victory equals courage.

"So, how do you feel?" Katelyn asked, as they walked to the parking lot where their father would pick them up in the hideous yellow station wagon that was part eyesore and part embarrassment.

Bryce grinned with giddiness. "I have to admit, you were right. That was really cool! The special effects were amazing, and the actors were terrific. They had me believing that vampires are real, which, of course, they aren't. I'm glad you dragged me here. This was awesome!"

Katelyn beamed, proud and tender. Knowing she had helped her little brother overcome his prepubescent phobia warmed her spirit. "Didn't I tell you? You've gotta stand toe to toe with your fears. Think you'll be watching any other horror movies, maybe with your buds?"

Bryce puffed out his chest. "Let 'em bring it. I can handle it. I am *invincible*!"

Katelyn laid her arm around Bryce's small shoulders. "Now that's what I'm talking about... Hercules."

Bryce grinned broadly. He was proud that he'd overcome his fear. But he was also happy that he'd pleased his big sister, whom he adored. He felt taller, older, and tougher. He no longer feared fictional monsters. At least for now.

# 2

The day after conquering the vampire flick, Bryce was shooting hoops in his driveway. It was early evening, the time when he took advantage of the low summer sunlight, so as not to get overheated.

He wasn't surprised to see Jack Miller, the town's sheriff, pull into the driveway. He and Bryce's dad, Wes, had been friends since childhood and remained close. Jack was a common sight across the dinner table and at the occasional backyard barbecue. Bryce waved at the sheriff as he left his police cruiser and joined Wes, who was clipping the hedges along the edge of his property line.

Jack waved back, yelling, "It's Bryce Campbell! He shoots... he scores!"

Bryce returned his focus to his game as the two men talked. Despite the thudding of the ball on the concrete driveway, he overheard Jack talking about a dead man who'd been found near the local graveyard.

"I tell ya, Wes. Not only have I never seen anything like this, I've never even heard about anything like this," Jack confided.

"So what happened?" asked Wes.

Jack looked off into the distance and sighed, hesitating to share official information. But he'd known Wes long enough to know that he could keep his mouth shut, so Jack began his story. "This is just between you and me. Understand?"

"Absolutely," Wes said.

"Okay then. Walter, who's one of my deputies, went with me to respond to a call from a lady who was out walking her dog around ten o'clock Tuesday morning. The dog was getting into firing position, and she didn't want to leave a mess on the sidewalk, so she took him into that small grove of trees next to the cemetery. You know the place I'm talking about, right?"

Wes nodded. "Yeah, I know it."

"Well, she discovered the man's body sprawled on the ground."

"Whoa! She must've freaked out," Wes said.

"That's putting it mildly," Jack said. "It's quite a creepy coincidence that he died so close to a graveyard, don't you think? Anyway, Walter and I drove over with the meat wagon in tow. By the time we got there, the woman was hysterical. Walter ushered her away while the paramedics and I checked out the body. Wes, I've seen a few corpses in my career; they're still, they're stiff, and they're pale. But this guy was beyond pale; he was chalk white. There were two small holes in his throat over his jugular. There should have been blood everywhere, but aside from a bit around his shirt collar, there wasn't a drop to be found."

"Geez, Jack. Do you think Dracula's responsible?" Wes joked.

"I don't know about that," Jack said. "But I've got to admit, this case has given me the same chills I got when I saw my first vampire movie."

Upon hearing Jack's account, Bryce stopped practicing, his spine turning into an icy rope.

*Katelyn's wrong*, he thought, trembling. *They're out there. I knew they were out there.* The fear that he thought he'd shed like on outgrown skin reappeared. His body was so tense he could no longer move.

The silencing of the basketball drew Jack's and Wes' attention. They turned to Bryce, whom they didn't realize had been listening in.

"Bryce, are you eavesdropping?" Wes asked.

"I only heard the part about a man losing blood," Bryce said, hoping not to be shooed away.

"This isn't anything you need to be hearing," Wes told him. "Go back to playing basketball. Your jump shot could use some work."

"Sure, Dad. I'll butt out." Bryce went through the motions of practicing while listening to the rest of Jack's story.

When Wes felt confident that Bryce was occupied, he resumed the conversation with Jack. "Sorry about that, Jack. So what happened next? "

"I checked the body for ID, but he didn't have any. Still, I felt like I'd seen him someplace. It was dark, so it took me a minute to recognize him. I've chased him out of the park a couple of times. He's homeless and harmless. I let the paramedics take him away while Walt and I hung around the crime scene and searched for clues. We were there for a good bit, but we didn't find anything—no weapon, no blood trail. Fast-forward to the following afternoon. The coroner called to confirm what I already knew: someone had drained our John Doe like a diabetic camel."

"Have you at least figured out who he was?" Wes asked.

"Unfortunately, no. We checked missing person files from around the state, but found bupkis. I visited a dumpster behind the bakery where I recalled he'd been living, if you could call it living. There was a garbage bag there full of dirty clothes, a half-empty fifth of whiskey, a few non-perishable foods, and a winter coat. Poor guy had very little in the way of personal possessions."

Wes sighed sorrowfully. "So, what happens to him now?"

Jack grew glum. "In situations like this, we fingerprint the body, send their picture to statewide law enforcement, and then cremate them."

"Ashes to ashes," Wes muttered.

"And dust to dust," Jack finished. "Well, I better get back to it. Somewhere out there is a murderer."

"Listen, if there's anything I can do to help, just say the word," Wes said.

"Help me keep a lid on this," Jack replied. "This is a tight-knit community; we don't need anyone panicking. I'll let you know how things are going. Probably be a good idea to make sure that you're locked up tight till we find the culprit or culprits."

Before leaving, Jack waved at Bryce. "See ya, little man. Keep working on that jump shot."

Bryce stopped and returned the wave. "Yes sir, Sheriff Miller. I'll do that."

"You still coming by Friday night for supper? It's Lasagne Night," Wes reminded Jack. "Ever since Angie moved out on you, Karen worries that you're lonely, drinking, and not eating right."

Jack grinned, shaking his head. "Come on Wes; you guys could see this one coming from a mile away. Angie hasn't been happy for a long time. She never liked sharing me with the job. To tell the truth, I think we could use a break—give ourselves time to figure out what's most important to us. Tell Karen I'll be here with bells on. I know you aren't a big fan of your wonderful wife's cooking, but her lasagna is to die for."

"It's a date then," Wes replied.

Jack climbed into his cruiser and went on his way.

Wes' thoughts left the Jack and Angie saga and returned to the chilling murder. "Ta hell is this town coming to?" he mumbled to himself. He finished the hedges, then made his way toward the house. As he passed Bryce, he said, "Don't stay out here too long, kiddo."

*You better believe I'm not,* Bryce thought. He felt something like dread slithering its way through him, unsettling him further. *Katelyn's right about one thing,* he thought. *Those movie vampires are nothing to be afraid of—it's the real ones that terrify me.*

# 3

"Man, oh man, Karen. That was some awesome grub," Jack said, rubbing his full belly. He laid his fork down, reclined in his dining room chair, and cradled the back of his head on his interlaced fingers.

Karen smiled at the compliment. "You keep saying that, Deputy Dawg, and I'm gonna start believing you. Maybe you can convince my husband with the sophisticated palette that not all of my cooking sucks."

"Hey!" Wes said with mock indignation. "I love your cooking—tastes a lot like food."

"Screw you," Karen shot back with humor.

Bryce's eyes widened, and his mouth fell open. "Dad! Dad! Mom said, 'Screw you!'"

Katelyn felt compelled to chime in. "Yeah, Mom. That was highly inappropriate."

"Speaking of inappropriate," Wes said, giving Katelyn his patented glare of disapproval. "I'm sure you know all about how Jack and I went to high school together. Well, there was this really cute girl named Anna Ferrington in our chemistry class. Very smart girl. I remember I was so surprised when she didn't apply to any colleges. No, she wanted to stay here in Hanlon, maybe meet a nice guy, get married, and be a housewife. Nothing wrong with that. Well, the husband never appeared, the bills were piling up, and she needed a full-time job. She found one down at the Avon Theater working the concession stand, and within a few years, had worked her way up to manager. I still run into her every now and again. In fact, I ran into her at the supermarket a couple of days ago. She told me this really funny story about how my thirteen-year-old daughter sneaked into an R-rated horror movie. I seem to recall that said daughter was in charge of taking her little brother to a family film. I wonder where he was while my *responsible* oldest child was sneaking into a movie geared towards adults. Care to share?"

"Buuusted," Karen snickered.

Guilt filled Bryce. "Dad, she was only trying to help me get over my fear of—"

"I don't want to hear it," Wes interrupted. "Katelyn, either I can trust you to show good judgment, or I can't."

"But Dad," Katelyn pleaded, "it wasn't even that scary. There was no nudity, or a ton of curse words, just monster violence. I only wanted to show Bryce that monsters are fake—that they can't really hurt you."

Her words caused a silent exchange of worried looks between Wes and Jack.

Wes took his time piecing together his concerns, hoping not to alarm Karen and the kids. "I appreciate what you were trying to do for your brother, Katelyn. But there are still some very real and scary people out there. I'm not trying to frighten either of you, but I don't want you to stop being cautious, particularly of strangers. I'm just looking out for you guys. I love you. You both know that, right?"

It was time for Bryce and Katelyn to exchange worried looks.

"Okay, Dad," Katelyn said demurely. "I'll be more responsible. *We'll* be more responsible. Right, Hercules?"

Bryce took Katelyn's lead. "Yeah, Dad. We'll both be more responsible."

"Good," Wes said, the happy dad part of him returning. "Take your dishes to the sink and get your homework knocked out."

"Yes, sir," the two chimed in unison.

Once Bryce and Katelyn had gone upstairs, the conversation took on a darker tone.

Karen started. "Jack, Wes told me there's been a murder in town. I read about it in the paper, but Wes said there might be more to it than what was reported. Should I be scared?"

"I don't know, Karen," Jack confessed. "This case is so strange; it gets stranger by the day. Fact is, I suspect it may be tied to another case."

"What do you mean?" Wes asked.

"This hasn't been leaked to the papers yet, so mum's the word, all right?"

Karen and Wes looked at each other, as if for permission to agree.

"Yes, of course, Jack," Karen answered for the two of them.

"All right, then," said Jack. "You guys probably don't know them, but there's a married couple named Cheryl and Hal Mabe. They have—had—a little girl named Callie. She passed away last week. Apparently, she developed some kind of virus that the doctors couldn't identify. Within a couple of days of going into the hospital, she died."

"Oh my God," Karen said, pressing her hand to her mouth.

"I know," Jack said. "It's awful."

Bryce was heading downstairs to ask for help with his math homework when he overheard the adults speaking in hushed, serious voices—the *Don't let the children hear* voices. He crept to the top step, where he sat and listened.

"What's that got to do with your dead John Doe?" Wes asked.

"The Mabes buried Callie this past Saturday morning; that's three days before we found our John Doe," Jack explained. "Sunday morning arrived, and the little girl's parents went to visit her grave. Don't ask me who, what, or why, but someone had dug a two-foot wide hole in the hump of earth she was buried under. Obviously, the Mabes were distraught."

"Well, I would certainly think so," Karen said.

"Anyhow, Mr. Mabe called it in and I, along with Walt, went out to the cemetery," Jack said. "Just as we'd been told, there was a hole. I can't say how far down it went, but it looked fairly deep. Thankfully, no other part of the grave had been disturbed. I asked Mr. and Mrs. Mabe if they could think of any reason why someone would be digging in their daughter's grave. They told me there were no valuable possessions buried with Callie that would tempt someone to break into the casket. I promised them I'd get to the bottom of it, then sent them home.

"Walt and I searched the immediate area, but aside from Callie's grave, nothing else seemed out of the ordinary. We chalked it up to a case of cruel vandalism and had a groundskeeper fill in the hole."

"Could it have been an animal that dug the hole?" Wes asked.

"Don't think so," Jack said. "There aren't any animals in this neck of the woods who'd dig that kind of hole. And if there were, why that one grave? Like I said, neither I nor Walt found any other graves disturbed."

Bryce's heart plummeted to his stomach, making him feel like he was on an elevator that was heading downward at a quick clip. The details were all too familiar to him. *I don't like this story,* he thought. *I wish that I'd stayed in my room.* But it was too late; he'd already heard too much. He knew he should leave his place on the staircase and return to his room, but he wanted to know how the story ended, assuming it had. *Please let there be a reasonable explanation,* he inwardly pleaded. He stayed put, listening. Hoping.

Jack continued his story. "Mr. Mabe revisited the grave the next morning to make sure that it hadn't been vandalized again. When he saw the hole had returned, he was furious. He was about to call the Sheriff's Office when he observed several small human footprints leading away from the grave and further into the cemetery.

"He followed them to a thin crop of trees located beyond the headstones—the spot where we would soon discover our John Doe. Mr. Mabe must've been horrified when he found Callie laying there dirty and wet, clutching the remains of a dead dog."

Karen hugged herself, attempting to control her shivers. "I'm not sure that I want to hear any more of this. You guys talk. I'm going to straighten up the kitchen." With unsteady hands, she gathered and stacked the dirty plates and silverware from the table, then hurried to the kitchen.

Jack waited until Karen was out of earshot before speaking again. "I'm sorry, Wes. I didn't mean to upset her. Maybe I should go. Fact is, hearing myself talking about this case makes it seem more outlandish."

"No need to apologize, Jack," Wes said. "She'll be fine once she settles down. Tell me what happened next."

"We get there to find the girl and this poor dog with its throat torn open," Jack said. "Then we observed something more unsettling: the blood around Callie's unwired mouth. What the heck was I supposed to make of that? I did my best to calm Mr. Mabe, but you can guess how that went. I walked him back to his car, where I assured him I'd keep him apprised of any progress that I made on the case, and that Callie would be respectfully and immediately returned to her casket."

"And did that satisfy him?"

"For the time being. I went by the cemetery's office and explained the situation to the site manager. I asked him if he or any of his staff had seen or heard anything unusual. He claimed that, aside from having the previous hole filled in, this was the first he'd heard about any new incidents. He assured me that nothing like it had ever happened before. I told him I needed to have the body put back and reburied. He said he'd get two of his guys over to the grave ASAP.

"I stuck around and waited for the grounds crew to show up. I'm not sure why. I think maybe I wanted to make sure they did the job properly. I could tell they were aggravated as soon as they got there. With no funerals scheduled for that day, I figured they were looking forward to an easy shift. But despite their annoyance, they re-dug the grave as instructed. When they were just about down to casket level, I left them to their work and headed toward the parking lot.

"I hadn't walked more than thirty yards when one of the men yelled after me to come back. I ran to the gravesite, wondering what in the world they'd come across. I have to say, it was not what I expected. Not even close."

Jack paused and took a sip of his tea. He hesitated before speaking. "There was a jagged hole in the upper lid of the casket, about the same size as the one in the dirt," he said.

Bryce sat spellbound by the horrible tale. *Please don't let this be real... please don't let this be real,* he repeatedly thought.

Wes' wooden chair squeaked as he leaned forward. He looked toward the kitchen, making sure Karen wasn't near. He was relieved to see that she wasn't. "What do you think caused it? Did someone break into the casket or not?" he whispered.

"Through a small hole? Why not dig up the entire grave? And, too, why would they have punched a hole in the upper lid, rather than lifting both parts of the casket? And why remove the girl and drag her away? And the dead dog—why would they kill it and leave it near the body?"

"This is some weird stuff you've been dealing with, Jack. But I'm curious. You said you thought this case might be somehow connected to the murder of the homeless man. How so?"

"Because, just like the man, someone had drained the dog of all of its blood. And then there's the proximity of the bodies. I can only find one common denominator: the cemetery. Maybe it's all coincidental. At least that's what my rational mind tells me."

"I can't believe I'm saying this, but keep going." Wes said.

"After some discussion, Walt and I decided that it would be in the best interest of the parents not to mention the damage," Jack said. "A guy on the grounds crew went to a supply shed on the back nine of the cemetery and found a piece of press board that was big enough to patch the hole. Once he completed the repair, he and his partner placed Callie's body back in the casket and refilled the grave."

"Let me back us up for a second," Wes said. "You said that your rational mind provided you with a theory. What was the other one?"

Jack sat silently. His attention appeared to waver, as if his mind was caught between the facts and the frightening alternatives.

"Jack?" Wes said, breaking the trance.

Jack looked at Wes with haunted eyes. "This is going to sound morbid and crazy, but there was another thing I noticed about that casket. The lid wasn't pushed in... it was pushed out. And then there were the scratch marks around the edges of the hole. I'm getting chills just thinking about it."

Bryce felt the same chills as he sat frozen at the top of the staircase. A big part of him didn't want to stay there. But another part needed to know more, no matter how disturbing.

"Later that evening, I paid a visit to the Mabes, you know, just to let them know I'd taken care of the matter," Jack said. "Mrs. Mabe had drunk a bottle of wine and gone to bed. Mr. Mabe was pacing back and forth in the driveway, chugging a bottle of his own liquid solace. I tried talking to him, but the man was out of his mind. He told me that he feared one of two things was true: enemies unknown to him were defiling his daughter's grave or... that part, he wouldn't say.

"I left the poor man in peace and returned to the station to finish up the paperwork on the cemetery incident. Then I went the heck home, cos I was tired, and I had personal matters that were weighing on me just as heavily.

"Now here is where the story got even stranger. Later that night, while Mrs. Mabe was snuggled in her bed sleeping it off, Mr. Mabe got busy. For reasons known only to him, he gathered some items from the kitchen and the garage, then went back to the cemetery."

"Good grief," Wes said. "What did he do there?"

"I'll explain the rest as best I can. Mrs. Mabe came to around three in the morning to discover her husband was missing. She went through the whole house calling his name, but he wasn't there. Then she checked the garage and…"

The fine hairs on Wes' arms and neck bristled as he watched Jack blanch. "Jack? What did she find there? Was the husband… dead?"

"No, Wes. The husband wasn't dead—he wasn't there at all. But what *was* there were some small, muddy footprints that led to the vacant spot where Mr. Mabe's vehicle had been parked.

"I don't know what made her think to do it, but Mrs. Mabe drove to the cemetery and went straight to Callie's grave. That's where she found her husband playing in the dirt and babbling like a lunatic. She said it was difficult to make out what he was saying, but it sounded like, "Stay there, Daddy's girl… Stay there, Daddy's girl.'

"How'd you find out about all this?" Wes asked.

"It'd been a long day, so when I got home, I went straight to bed," Jack said. "The stupid phone rang and woke me up. I almost ignored it, but something told me it might be important. Why else would they be bothering me at that hour of the night? I took the call. Linda from Dispatch was calling to inform me about trouble at the cemetery. It could only be one thing, so I threw on my uniform and went straightaway to the office to grab a deputy to accompany me.

"It was one hot mess, let me tell ya. The missus had requested an ambulance before notifying our office. By the time my deputy and I got there, two paramedics were preparing Mr. Mabe for transport to the psyche ward at the hospital. I put Tim, my deputy, in charge of checking out the gravesite. I helped Mrs. Mabe to the ambulance so she could accompany her husband.

"All of a sudden, Tim starts hollering for me.

"When I got to the gravesite, he was on his knees moving around some of the loose soil.

"'What do you make of this?' he asked me. He opened his palm to reveal a clove of garlic.

An uncomfortable thought blossomed in my mind. "Dig a little deeper," I told him.

"He dug a few more inches and removed another garlic clove from the earth. He looked perplexed, then asked me if he should go down any further.

"I said, 'Yep. Go down as far as your arm will reach.'

"He did as I told him. By the time he was shoulder deep in the dirt, he had removed close to a dozen garlic cloves. Poor Tim likely wondered how deep Mabe had gone with the things. Then he looked up at me and said, 'Sheriff, you don't think he might've believed that Callie's been digging out of her—'

"I stopped him right there. 'Not another word, Deputy,' I told him. 'This stays with us. That family has gone through enough.'

"Then he asked me what he should do with all the garlic.

"I took a moment to think about it. I could tell that something about the whole affair spooked him; it sure spooked me. 'Put 'em back,' I said. 'Maybe it'll give her father and us some relief.'

"Tim put the cloves back and refilled the hole, then he and I headed back to our cruisers. As we neared the cars, a terrible thought hit me, and I stopped. Tim asked me if something was wrong.

"'You go on to the squad car,' I said. 'I just need to take care of one more thing.' I waited for Tim to get to his car, then I pulled a small, silver cross from my pants pocket. Whenever I'm tense, it calms me to know that the cross is close to me. It's like its touch is holy—protective.

"I went back to Callie's grave, scooped out a shallow trench with my fingers, and placed the cross inside. Then I pushed the dirt back into the fresh hole and left. I hoped that I'd never have to return."

"And you think that all this ties in with our John Doe? How?" Wes asked.

"Right after they brought him in, I asked the coroner for an approximate time of death," Jack said. "She said it was hard to be exact, but his death had likely occurred late Monday night—the night before we discovered him. The night I think Callie Mabe was laid to rest for the last time."

Goosebumps covered Bryce's body in a cold wave.

"Have there been any other incidents involving Callie?" Wes asked.

"No," Jack muttered flatly. "Not since we buried the garlic and cross."

Bryce listened for a while longer, but there was no further discussion about the awful incident. He imagined the look of confusion and fear on the faces of the adults. Confusion about what they were unwilling or unable to accept, and fear of what they dreaded: that vampires might exist. What was left of Bryce's newly found courage evaporated under the glare of that possibility.

# 4

*Bryce found himself in the eerie local cemetery, where the echoes of recent terror still lingered among the tombstones. The sight before him was chilling—rotting corpses clawing upward through the softened soil that covered their grave like an earthen blanket. The fetid smell of wet earth, coupled with the stench of decayed flesh, infiltrated his nostrils, making him retch. Bryce wanted to move, to scream. But the ground tethered him, preventing him from running or looking away from the horror unfolding around him.*

*After several graves had regurgitated their dead, four remained intact. Then, the dirt from those graves began to shift and rise. Bryce stared on in helpless horror as each tenant pulled themselves free from their mahogany cell. In minutes, all four corpses were standing within yards of Bryce, peering at him through worm-eaten eyes. They encircled him, then shuffled toward him. As they closed in, he was able to make out their identities: his father, mother, sister, and*

*Jack. The quartet opened their mouth, revealing long, sharp incisors. Finally, Bryce found his voice and screamed long and loud.*

Wes burst into Bryce's bedroom and flipped on the light.

Bryce was sitting up in his bed, wailing in terror at the invisible monsters that only his wild eyes could see. His skin was so pallid that his veins and arteries stood out like a network of blue rivers.

"Bryce! Wake up!" Wes hollered. "You're having a nightmare!"

Karen and Katelyn rushed into the room, panting like a couple of panicked horses.

Bryce became lucid. "Oh my God… oh my God. That was awful."

Wes went to Bryce and sat down on his bed, brushing the rumpled hair away from Bryce's sweat-soaked forehead. "Easy son. Try to relax and catch your breath."

"What the deuce, Bryce? I was sound asleep," Katelyn said, rubbing her sleep-reddened eyes.

"Baby, are you okay now?" Karen asked Bryce.

Once Bryce's heart settled back into a normal rhythm, he looked at Wes with eyes that belied his embarrassment at the ruckus he had caused. "I'm okay. It was only a nightmare. I'm better now."

"What kind of nightmare did you have?" Wes asked in a voice full of fatherly concern.

"If I tell you, do you promise not to get mad?"

"Why would I get mad?"

Bryce hesitated.

"Bryce, tell us why you woke everyone up," Karen urged, her tone a mix of curiosity and frustration. "You scared the bejeebers out of me."

Bryce knew he would have to come clean. "I had a dream about vampires crawling out of their graves to attack me. Some of them were you guys."

"I knew it," Wes growled. Then, turning his anger on Katelyn, asked, "Are you happy now? This is what happens when you act irresponsibly. You knew good and well that your ten-year-old brother wasn't ready for horror movies, but you forced him into going to one, anyway."

Wes' harsh tone scared Katelyn. She moved behind Karen, using her as a human shield.

"Dad, Katelyn didn't force me," Bryce said, coming to his sister's defense. "It was my idea, too. Besides, I heard you and Sheriff Miller talking downstairs after dinner."

"Bryce, what did I tell you about listening in on private conversations?" Wes asked heatedly.

"But Dad, I was only coming downstairs to ask you or Mom to help me with my homework. I couldn't help overhearing about what happened in the cemetery."

"Wait a minute. What happened in the cemetery, Wes?" Karen asked.

"We'll discuss it later," Wes replied. Then speaking to Bryce said, "As for you, I want you to try and forget about what you heard. There are no such things as vampires. They only exist in movies that careless sisters drag their little brothers to."

"I'm sorry, okay? Totally my bad," Katelyn said.

"All right, I want all of you to listen to me," Wes said. "Jack's on top of everything. There's nothing to be concerned about. Now then, let's all get some sleep."

"Night, sweetie," Karen said to Bryce in a soothing voice. "I'm going to turn off the light, but I'll leave your door open in case you need anything."

"Thanks, Mom. I think I'll be okay now," Bryce said.

"Night, Hercules," Katelyn yawned, before heading back to her own room.

Wes tousled Bryce's hair and smiled. "I'll see you tomorrow, son. Sweet dreams, okay?"

Bryce returned Wes' gentle smile. "I'll do my best. I really will."

"Okay, then," Wes said. He rose from the side of Bryce's bed and joined Karen at the bedroom door. "We love ya, kiddo," he added, just to make things right. He flipped off the light and left with Karen.

Bryce lay down and pulled the covers to his chest. Seeking calmness, he shut his eyes and immersed himself in the peaceful silence of the house. But despite his dad's reassurances, he couldn't shake the uneasiness that clung to his mind like sticky oil.

# 5

A few months later, October rolled in with its usual crispness. The sweet autumn air smelled of bonfires and seasoned meat cooking on outdoor grills.

As soon as Bryce and Katelyn returned home after a Halloween trek through the neighborhood, they entered the kitchen to drop off their bounty for its requisite parental inspection. No one had yet debunked the old urban legends about razor blades in apples and needle marks in candy bar wrappers.

Wes and Karen were in the middle of a discussion, but stopped when the kids walked in.

"Ready for inspection, officers," Katelyn said, laying her bag on the counter. She noticed the conspicuous pause in her parents' conversation. "Are we interrupting you guys? Are you exchanging juicy gossip?"

"Ooh, can we listen in?" Bryce asked excitedly.

Wes grinned. "Apparently, your mom's sister has gotten in a motherly way, courtesy of a wayward biker."

Karen issued Wes an icy glare. "Keep it up, Wes, and I'll tell them what your mother caught sweet ole Grampa doing."

Wes' grin drooped as a look of embarrassment and panic connected on his face. "You heard your mother, kids! Off you go!"

"Come on wittle baby bwother," Katelyn said in an infantile manner. "Us baby-wabys are too innocent to hear about a pwegnant aunt."

Bryce and Katelyn slipped past Wes and Karen, and solemnly plodded into the den as if they were pallbearers carrying a coffin.

They dropped onto the sofa, flipped on the television, and turned to channel seven. The station was showing *Night of the Living Dead*.

"Yee haw," Katelyn squealed. "This here's a good 'un."

After the vampire incident, Bryce wanted nothing more to do with horror movies. "No thanks, Katelyn. I'm done with scary pictures."

"Oh Bryce. Really? Are you still worrying about some freaky happenings in the graveyard?

That was over three months ago. There's been no more reports about murders and dead girls. If there had been, Sheriff Miller would have said something to Mom and Dad. Besides, this one is a classic zombie movie—no vampires here."

"Gee, I don't know," Bryce meekly muttered.

"It's one of the first zombie movies. It's not nearly as bad as the ones that are out now. Come on, Bryce. It's time to grow back your spine."

Bryce pouted, as he decided what to do. "Okay, I'll watch it. But I better not hear about any zombies walking around town."

Katelyn snuggled into the sofa and pressed her lips to Bryce's ear. "They're coming to get you, Barbraaa," she moaned, chuckling at his discomfort.

They had gotten to the part where the zombies were outside of the old farmhouse devouring human flesh when Wes waltzed in.

"Katelyn, what is wrong with you?" Wes hollered.

"It's okay, Dad. I wanted to watch it," Bryce said.

"Yeah, Dad," Katelyn whined. "Let us watch it. It's really dated and cheesy. The zombies look fake and so do the rubber guts. Besides, Bryce knows monsters aren't real. Ain't that right, Hercules?"

"You're going to have to give me a better reason than that to get out of the trouble you're in," Wes said.

"Well, we could do you a favor and clean out the garage. Say, isn't that something Mom asked you to do a while back?" Katelyn asked with a sly grin.

Wes smirked conspiratorially. The task had been on his honey-do list for a while, and he was seeing an opportunity to cross it off. "All right, you little hustlers, but not a word to your mom.

This is a win-win for all of us, so don't blow it."

With a duet of, "Aye aye, Daddy," Katelyn and Bryce returned to the carnage.

After Wes left the den, Katelyn asked Bryce, "You're not gonna freak out again like last time, are you?"

"Nah. I get that it's just a movie," Bryce assured her. "I'm old enough to know that monsters don't live in the real world." At least, that was what Bryce was telling himself.

# 6

Bryce kept his lamp on for a few nights after viewing the zombie film; the movie stayed with him longer than he anticipated. He questioned the decision he'd made to watch another creature feature after the chilling vampire episode. *Guess I'm not old enough to know better after all,* he thought. Now his frightened imagination had him worrying about a zombie invasion.

It didn't help that his parents were having deadbolts installed on the main doors of the house because of what they had recently heard from Jack, as well as from what the local news had reported.

Investigators had discovered the ravaged corpses of three individuals—two women and a man. Something had eaten parts of their bodies, including their entrails. Things got even creepier when the bodies mysteriously disappeared from the coroner's lab. Some unnamed witnesses claimed to have seen the reanimated victims, who were naked and nearly hollow, roving through the streets the night after the authorities had stored them.

One of Karen's friends told her she'd heard gunfire later that same evening. She didn't know what to make of it.

The next morning, the local news reported that a couple of deputies had recovered the missing bodies. Also, the thieves who had stolen them from the morgue were still at large. That was the official report, anyway. There was no mention of shootings.

Also not reported was that the two deputies involved resigned the next morning. They packed up their families and left town quickly and quietly.

Soon, a rumor circulated the way most rumors do. Someone who had spoken to someone else who knew the janitor at the county morgue revealed that the coroner deliberately omitted an important detail from the report. The three corpses had gunshot wounds to their head.

Sheriff Miller didn't come by to share the details, something that troubled Wes. As far as he knew, Jack hadn't discussed the incident with anyone, and Wes didn't press him about it.

Bryce contemplated the potential correlation between the movies he had watched and the bizarre and violent incidents that had occurred in his town. *This is too much of a coincidence,* he thought. *Vampire movie... dead bodies with no blood. Zombie movie... dead people walking the streets after being half eaten. Have I been causing these terrible things to happen?* Bryce felt sad and guilty. But mostly, he felt horrified. Horrified by a power he'd received from God knows where. He made a pledge to himself that he was going to lie off horror movies for a while—perhaps forever.

That pledge ended as soon as his best friend, Harrison, told him about a movie his parents had rented from the video store.

# 7

"It's called *Halloween*," Harrison told Bryce. "My old man rented it for him and Mom to watch. They thought I was asleep, but I was beatin' it to the rhythm of Penthouse, if you get my meaning."

"Ooh, gross," Bryce said, cringing. "I could've gone all day and not heard that."

"Aw, like you've never done it," Harrison haughtily replied.

"As a matter of fact, I haven't. Where'd you get the girly mag, anyway?"

"Same place I got the video: on the top shelf of my old man's closet, under some sweaters. That's where he usually hides things he doesn't want me to find."

"So, have you watched it yet?"

"Oh yeah. I didn't want it to get returned before I checked it out."

Bryce's curiosity swelled. "Well?"

Harrison grinned wickedly. "Let's just say it will freak you the heck out. This psycho breaks out of a mental institution, see? Then he finds an old mask to disguise himself and starts roaming around town, slicing and dicing up everybody with a big butcher's knife."

Bryce felt his stomach tighten. "Is there a lot of blood?"

"Yeah, but it's all fake. You should see the kill scenes; they so look real. It's a lot of fun to watch. Come on, let's go over to my house. We've got a few hours before my folks get home from work."

"Gee, I don't know, Harrison. I don't think it's a safe thing for me to be doing."

"What's that supposed to mean?"

"If I tell you, you'll think I'm crazy and make fun of me."

Harrison flashed the wicked grin again. "Okay, now you have to tell me. How weird are we talking?"

Bryce lightly bit his top lip, deciding whether to tell Harrison about what he thought were connections between the movies he had watched and the violent acts that had occurred near their neighborhood. *If I don't tell someone, I think I'll go bonkers,* he thought. "Okay, I'll tell you. But you have to give me your solemn promise to never tell another soul for as long as you live. I haven't even told my family about this. My folks are already upset with me for watching horror movies, and Katelyn will tease me about it."

Harrison snapped to attention and held up the Boy Scouts' hand gesture. "I promise I'll never tell anyone that you're a total whack job who hasn't learned to jerk off."

Bryce felt frustrated. "I'm serious, Harrison. You're the only person I'm going to tell about this. Can I trust you or not?"

"Okay, okay. It'll stay between us."

Despite his lingering skepticism, Bryce told Harrison his story.

Harrison did something that he'd seldom done before: He sat still and listened. Once Bryce finished, he exclaimed, "Man, oh man, that's intense. You're not yanking my chain, are you?"

"On my mother's eyes, I am not making this up," Bryce said. "You believe me, don't you?"

"I've heard about stuff that's a lot weirder."

"You have?"

"Of course not, you dweeb," Harrison chuckled.

Bryce's chin fell to his chest. Embarrassment consumed him, as did his disappointment in his best friend. "I knew I shouldn't have trusted you."

Somewhat guilt-ridden, Harrison offered his support. "You say that whatever horror movie you watch, the creatures in it come to life, right?"

Bryce nodded yes.

"So then, how about a little experiment? Let's watch *Halloween* and see if anything happens. That would be the best and only way to prove to me you're not making this up. Besides, don't you wanna know if you're causing this? Come on, let's go to my house. I promise you: You're going to love this movie."

Bryce considered Harrison's words. He still didn't find the idea convincing.

Sensing Bryce's hesitation, Harrison put forth his own theory. "What if the reason those monsters came to life is that they're imaginary? You know, something that doesn't exist in real life. Michael Myers, on the other hand, is a flesh and blood character. It's possible for someone like him to exist in the real world—just read the papers! Let's watch the movie and see if a human killer comes to life. Come on, dude. Don't you wanna know for sure? I would."

Bryce thought the idea made sense. "Okay. Let's get this over with."

Harrison pressed his palm against Bryce's back, guiding him to where he wasn't sure he wanted to go. "Mmm-haha! We're off to the la-bora-tory!" he chuckled.

# 8

"Turn it off! It's making me sick!" Bryce pleaded.

"Come on, Bryce. We're more than halfway through it. Don't forget that all this is made up," Harrison assured him.

"The other movies were supposed to be pretend, but look how things turned out. I can't take a chance on Michael Myers. Look, if you want to keep on watching this gore fest, have at it. I'm going home and try to forget that I ever watched it."

"Okay, okay," Harrison said, stopping the video. "Don't get your panties in a wad. How about we find something different to watch?

Bryce relaxed. "Fine, as long as it's not another horror movie."

"No worries. We'll see what's on HBO. They're still showing Halloween movies; that includes mysteries and science fiction."

Harrison perused the offerings, steering clear of any that Bryce might deem too scary. He came across some current and older science fiction movies that looked interesting. Stopping at one, he said, "Say, how about this one? It's an oldie but a goody. I've watched it before with my parents; it's pretty tame."

Bryce decided that he'd been too much of a buzz kill already. He didn't want to ruin any more of Harrison's afternoon, so he agreed to view the picture. "Yeah, okay. I've heard about this one. You're right; it's a classic."

When the movie ended, Bryce said his goodbyes to Harrison and headed home. He felt better about his decision to disconnect from the slasher film.

The bright afternoon sun was now a hazy orange as it began its descent into night. The tall trees that had earlier sheltered Bryce were forming large, crooked shadows. He sped to a trot, hoping to get home before his imagination overtook him, leaving him vulnerable to the dark and lurid things that lurked within the deep, twisted shadows.

# 9

An ominous feeling overtook Bryce as he walked through the open kitchen door. *Who left the door wide open?* he wondered with unease. Dusk had settled over the room, making it gloomy and unfamiliar. He felt around for the nearest light switch; he was relieved when his fingers grazed it. He flipped the switch up and down a few times without effect. He listened for movement, but the house was eerily quiet. *Where is everybody? What's going on with the house lights?* he wondered. Something felt off.

A kitchen window allowed enough light for Bryce to find the drawer that housed a flashlight. He flicked it on and directed the yellow beam around the room. As he cautiously moved forward, his foot unexpectedly collided with an object, startling him and prompting an instinctive leap backwards. The metallic object spun swiftly across the linoleum, its gleaming surface catching the ray from the flashlight. With a gentle whir, it gradually came to a halt. The glint of a sharp butcher's knife, its stainless steel blade shimmering against the cold, tiled floor, left him momentarily breathless.

"Is anybody home?" Bryce called out, but no one answered. He looked at the oven clock. The time was approaching 6 pm. Typically, everyone would be in either the den or the kitchen discussing their day. But the house felt empty. Lifeless.

A terrifying thought shot through Bryce's frenzied mind like a bolt of electricity. Had he watched enough of the slasher flick to create a knife-wielding lunatic? *Don't think that,* he warned himself. But recent events had taught him better—taught him that, by now, it was likely too late.

"Mom? Dad? Katelyn? Are you guys here?" Bryce yelled with urgency. Again, total silence. He trembled. *I don't know what's going on here, but I have a feeling that it might be something bad,* he thought. A part of him wanted to leave the foreboding house, yet there was a bigger part of him that insisted on securing his family's well-being. Because he heard no movement downstairs, he decided to begin his hunt with a cautious search of the upstairs area.

Bryce stealthily moved to the hallway from the kitchen, delicately placing each foot in front of the other, attempting to avoid being overheard—by what, he didn't know. He poked his head into the hall, looking in both directions. Clear.

He quietly hung a right out of the kitchen, his stomach churning with nerves, and carefully made his way to the staircase, each step muffled and filled with apprehension. With great caution, he ascended the stairs, working to avoid the creak of the three telltale steps, as if he were serpentining through a minefield.

Once Bryce cleared the stairs, he soundlessly made his way to Katelyn's bedroom. The door was ajar, allowing him a wide view.

His eyes crisscrossed the night-blackened room, but detected no one.

Next, Bryce slinked to his parents' bedroom and peeped inside. The room was dim and still. The furniture appeared as vague, looming figures that gave off an eerie presence. He made his way across the room and peered out of the bedroom window at the empty patio below.

Bryce attempted to rationalize the disappearances. *Where the heck could they be? If they all left the house together, why'd they leave the kitchen door open? Why's there no electricity? And why's there a big knife laying on the floor?* The knife troubled him the most. His anxiety returned.

"Hey guys!" Bryce called out in a soprano shriek. A deep silence filled his eager ears; a thick sob formed in his quaking chest. *They're dead... I just know it!* he thought. Bryce wanted to be wrong. He wanted to find Katelyn and his parents alive and well, proving how silly his suspicions had been. But based on recent happenings, he now knew that monsters were real, and that they existed around him. "Save your family, you big baby," he muttered to himself. Refusing his panicked mind's desire to shut down, he fought to pull his scattered thoughts together to form a plan. *If this were a real horror movie, where would everyone be?* He almost vomited from tension when he realized where he needed to check—the dreaded basement.

Bryce gathered himself and went downstairs to the basement door in the part of the hallway that connected the foyer to the dining room at the rear of the house.

The door was closed, so he turned the knob, and then forcefully yanked it open. The depth of the darkness overwhelmed him. He pressed hard against his urge to flee. Bryce worked up enough breath to talk. "G-g-guys? H-hello?" He heard something skittering in the blackness. Perhaps it was the spiders that inhabited the dark, damp corners. Perhaps not. His voice tremoring, he asked the question that he'd heard a soon-to-be movie victim ask: "Is anybody down there?" When no one responded, he knew he had an important decision to make. *Do I run to a neighbor's house and call the cops, or do I venture into the unknown?* He recalled that in the movies, it was typically the latter option. But this wasn't the movies. He was a grade-schooler who was terrified beyond belief, so he chose the former.

Bryce bolted from his house, screaming like a broken soul damned to hell. He quickly dashed across the street, desperately seeking safety.

# 10

Mrs. Selby, the neighbor across the street from Bryce, called the Sheriff's Office.

Within minutes, two tan cruisers pulled in front of Bryce's house. He did not know who most of the people were, but he recognized the man pushing his way to the front: Sheriff Miller.

Three deputies followed him into the house, guns drawn. Bryce waited on the Selby's front porch, feeling trapped in an episode of *The Twilight Zone.*

After about ten minutes, Sheriff Miller walked out of the house and sat on the porch steps. He ran his fingers through his thinning hair before lighting a cigarette.

*Here it comes,* Bryce thought. *He's thinking about how to tell me that my family's been murdered by a psychopath.* Trepidation roiled his stomach like a whirl of acid. He wasn't going to wait a second longer.

Bryce ran from the Selby's porch, across the street, and straight to Sheriff Miller.

Bryce figured he must have startled the sheriff because his head jerked up, revealing sad, red eyes. He locked eyes with Bryce, who was hysterical.

"Tell me! Tell me what's happened to my family!" Bryce yelled.

His insides melted when Sheriff Miller looked at him and said, "Son, I need to tell you something."

"What? What do you need to tell me?" Bryce begged, his voice cracking from grief.

Howling laughter erupted from the house. The deputies walked out and onto the porch, followed by Wes, Karen, and Katelyn.

Bryce's eyes brimmed with hot, heavy tears. He couldn't move or speak.

Katelyn looked at Bryce and chuckled. "I'm sorry for going along with this, but when Mom and Dad told me about the prank, I just couldn't resist. Hey, at least you know now that monsters aren't real, right?"

When the feeling returned to Bryce's body, he whizzed past Sheriff Miller, up to the landing, and hugged his father as though he hadn't seen him in years. Then he tightly embraced his mother. He buried his face into her stomach, desperately attempting to hide his tears from everyone.

"Oh, fine," Katelyn said sarcastically. "Nothing for me?"

The hug Bryce had given his beloved parents paled compared to the one he lavished on his big sister.

"Now do you get it?" Wes asked Bryce. "We told you about watching all those horror movies. Harrison's dad called and said he found a copy of *Halloween* in the VCR. When he threatened to ground Harrison, your best buddy ratted the two of you out."

Bryce's cheeks reddened with anger, not because of Harrison's betrayal, but because of how callously his loved ones had tricked him. "How could you guys do this to me? I was terrified that I'd never see you again. Thanks, everyone—now I'm scarred for life."

Wes looked into Bryce's wet eyes. "I'm sorry we upset you so much. We just wanted to show you that no good will ever come from watching those outlandish horror flicks, especially at your age. Now then, no more scary movies until you're old enough to process them. Deal?"

After his terrifying experience, Bryce readily agreed to the decision. "Deal," he said. After a moment, he relaxed, accepting that his young mind had simply overblown the isolated incidents. *Nothing to see here, weirdo,* he thought.

Wes thanked Jack for his and the deputies' roles in the ruse.

"Don't thank me, Wes," said Jack. "All of this is my fault. I shouldn't have gotten you guys worked up over things. I wasn't very professional, I guess."

Karen walked over and rested her hand on one of Jack's slumping shoulders. "Don't worry about it, Jack. You were just trying to protect us."

Jack's face belied his nagging guilt. He glanced at Bryce. "Hey, little man, sorry for upsetting you. No hard feelings?"

Bryce forced a smile; he didn't feel right about hurting Jack's feelings. "It's okay, Sheriff Miller. We're good." Looking across the street, he saw Mrs. Selby angrily marching toward them. "I wish I could say Mrs. Selby found everything as funny as you all do. But judging by the look on her face, I don't think she does."

Mrs. Selby, dressed in her bathrobe and slippers, stomped across the yard to the front porch, her eyes blazing with rage. She crossed her arms over her chest, as if restraining herself. She fixed her fury on Wes first. "The next time you pull a stunt like this, I'm calling Child Protective Services!" Then, turning her ire to Jack, said, "And as for you, Mr. Public Safety, I ought to report you to—"

The screech of tires drowned out her voice, as a cruiser skidded to a stop at the curb. A deputy sprang out and galloped toward the group.

"What's up, Del?" Jack asked his deputy.

The deputy whispered into Jack's ear.

Jacks's calm expression turned to one of abject terror.

Wes noticed the change in Jack's demeanor. "Jack, is something wrong?"

Jack stood stiffly, no readable expression on his pale face. "Gotta go, guys," he muttered in a chilling, empty voice. "A call came in.

A man discovered his elderly parents lying on their kitchen floor skinned like rabbits."

Karen clamped her hands over Bryce's ears. "Jack, we just finished talking about sharing too much information."

"Sorry, Karen. I better get going." Jack and the deputies jogged to their cruisers, jumped in, and left in a whir of shrill sirens and strobing blue lights.

Just then, dozens of large, glowing streaks of reddish light streaked across the night sky. A series of loud, earth-shaking booms followed, causing the porch to rumble beneath everyone's feet.

"What was that?" Mrs. Selby yelped.

Cold realization encompassed Bryce's mind, petrifying his body. He wanted to admit to what he'd done, but horror trapped the words in his throat. If he could've spoken, he would've shared the name of the science fiction movie that he had watched after the horror flick: *War of the Worlds.*

# PITY THE LIVING

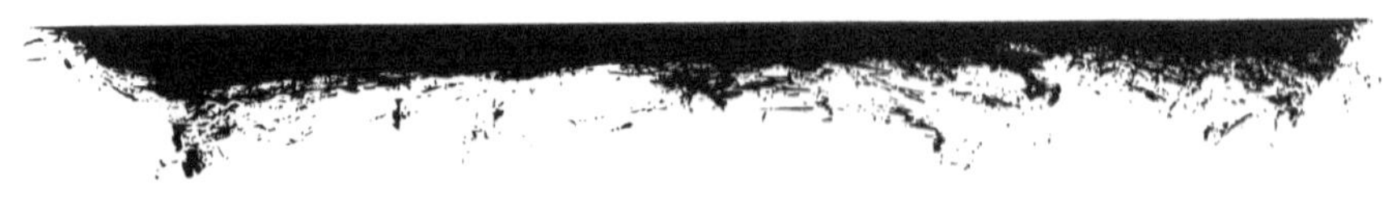

I think it's the stench of the dead that attracts them. Or maybe it's the moaning of our older and more vulnerable ones. Whatever the reason, they are driven to us. The thing that once made them civilized has long since abandoned them. These days they wander, foraging for food of any kind: human and animal, young and old, man and woman—they are not discriminating.

When we first learned of the new disease, we were caught up in the banalities of everyday living: driving to work, watching television, going out to movies and restaurants, and living until death took us. And we stayed dead. Most of us don't remember when people were finite. The dangerous ones aren't able to remember much at all.

At first, their kind went after the plentiful creatures: dogs, cats, rats, or other animal life. I've even seen them eat bugs and spoiled food. But as the months passed, their hunger evolved and became more insatiable. They turned their attention toward something larger that held more meat and muscle. They began coming for us.

The pack mentality is how we survive. No one ever goes out alone; there are far too many of them. We need to eat; however, that is more difficult when you are avoiding being eaten.

Their bodies have become unhealthy and unclean. I smell them even in a slight breeze. I experience melancholy and disgust when I think of the victims, whose neighbors and family have killed them for the bountiful harvest that their bodies presented. In exchange for maintaining their basic survival, they've jettisoned mercy, compassion, and simple human decency.

Even after all this time, my mind is still intact. I remember who I used to be, even if my memories are not clear. However, this ability has its downside. I suffer the overwhelming loss of my family, whom the authorities took away not long after the disease began sweeping across the country. I miss them. But God help me, I'd rather they had died, and their bodies burned before becoming like the others.

I also reminisce about the things the others have taken from me, as well. I can't help but wonder if they, too, ever think of their previous lives. Even if they can think and feel, they stifle those longings to focus on what's coming tomorrow or the next day. Like mindless crocodiles, the roaming predators only possess the instinct to survive. To eat.

I don't sleep anymore; neither do they. They stalk their quarry and destroy the city 24/7. Even the bitter winters can't deter their mounting destruction. I once saw a teenager trudging through the snow, half-naked, for reasons known only to him. I wondered about the series of horrendous circumstances that might have befallen this teenager, whose once biggest concern in life was winning at video games or daydreaming about buxom girls. I am saddened, but that is the reality now.

I question whether there's that much difference anymore between the destitute survivors and the famished zombies. We both suffer and yearn. We both do whatever it takes to keep going. If need be, don't we devour our own in some form or another? Hasn't our evolution led us to a new form that erases our understanding of humanity and all it once meant?

My group and I are poking through the wreckage of a once-bustling street, searching for anything we can use or eat. We need to hurry; staying in one place too long can bring about a nasty end for some or all of us. I hear the marauders clawing their way through the rubble and hiding behind long-dormant cars. Their kind is stealthy and creative. As they attempt to surround us, I can smell their stained and ratty clothes, their desperate sweat. We have only seconds to flee; I hope we can move fast enough. The slowest among us often serve as a distraction in these situations. They're brought down by the violent cannibals, eviscerated, and then consumed, providing the rest of our pack with a small window of escape. I fear the day when I stumble and fall. Being eaten alive is an excruciating and terrifying way to die.

Even in my darkest moments, I can't help feeling sorry for them. They once shared common dreams: walking their daughter down the aisle, achieving fame and wealth, or sharing a dance and a kiss at the Senior Prom. But that's all gone. Their former selves are not what they are now. They search, they kill, they ravage, and devour. They are little more than animals now—humans who've morphed into monsters.

If you've ever read a book, seen a movie, or watched a TV show about the undead, you've rooted for the living. But life is not a work of fiction. In this reality, there are only survivors.

Now, I see the world through a unique set of eyes. They are milky and sunken. One of them feels loose and will pop out soon—the putrefaction process is cruel and horrid.

This is the new order. Those who were victims of the brutal disease continue to walk this waning earth, dying but never dead. The uninfected hunt us. Among themselves, they mistrust, quarrel, and murder one another. They've chosen to divide themselves up into small tribes bent on destroying what's still left to them. Owing to the desolate landscape and decimated livestock, their food sources have dwindled to nothing. When our kind is gone, they will have to consume each other—some already are.

I hope my family has joined the company of the non-living, the in-betweens. Our unique lives are simple: we walk, dream, and work in teams to attack and defeat those who represent the worst of us. And yes, we eat as many of them as they do of us. They're faster and more cunning than we are, but that doesn't make them wiser.

Once most of them are gone, the wretched few will pray for death, and they will find it. But for them, their passing will be permanent.

Although I covet the things they take for granted—the ability to love, laugh, and be mortal—I prefer this existence to the so-called living. They are the ones who became the worst monsters. With what little thought or emotion that I possess, I will fear them. I will loathe them. But most of all, I will pity them.

# DIRTY HAT

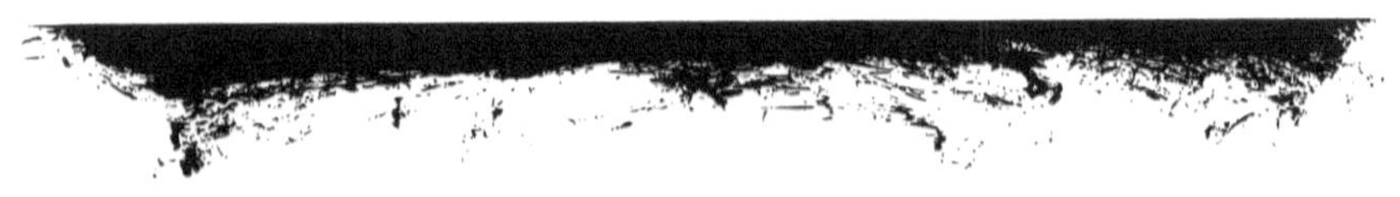

"Wow. Wow. Wow," the homeless man kept whispering to himself, as he peered into the dirty hat resting on his lap. He sat in a grimy alley, leaning back against a folded-up cardboard box. The transient was a disheveled black man with a scruffy beard dotted with flecks of gray. He was of an indeterminate age, his years obscured by filth, hardship, and time. A look of amazement encompassed his unkempt face. His delight was that of a child's who had just discovered a grand and shiny object.

Derek and Pauly were out prowling the nighttime streets again, fanning out like a dank mist from a sewer grate. It was as if someone had stamped the word *FAILURE* on their head at birth. As they walked past the alley, they heard a voice softly repeating, "Wow." They stopped, backed up, and peered down the narrow corridor. Someone had busted out most of the overhead security lights positioned at the backdoors of some businesses, adding to the lane's dinginess.

"Wow, oh, wow," echoed the nearby voice.

"Where's that comin' from?" Derek asked.

"Probably some homeless piece of crap sleeping behind one of them dumpsters," Pauly replied.

"Wow. Wow," the hidden voice continued.

"Let's go check it out. Find out what he's wowin' about,' Pauly suggested.

"I don't know, man, he might be hopped up on somethin'. Might take a knife to you."

"C'mon, D. Let's go mess him up, burn off a little jet fuel. Wanna?"

"Man, I'm just out to score some weed. Ain't no old, homeless man gonna have no money or drugs."

"Let's go find out what's got him worked up. 'Wow, wow, wow,'" Pauly said mockingly.

"Nah, I ain't about none of that. I'll catch you at Javon's later."

"Fine, you puss. I'll catch up to you then."

"Suit yourself." Resigned to his friend's blatant stupidity and lack of human decency, Derek went on his way.

"'Kay, my man," Pauly said to the shadow in the alley, "let's see what's got you *wowin.*"

He took his time approaching the man, who was too fixated on the rumpled fedora to notice him.

"Wow! Wow! Wow!" the man kept repeating with increasing excitement.

"Whatcha got there, street trash?"

"Wow!" was all the man would say.

"Let me see that lid for a second." When the man didn't respond, Pauly snatched the hat from his hands. "What's got you trippin' over this thing, fool?"

"Look and see," the man said through a broad and toothless smile. "Just look and see!"

Pauly sniffed contemptuously and peered inside the fedora.

His eyes bulged with terror, and he screamed as if he'd just awoken in hell. Half blind with madness, the now white-haired youth threw the hat down and turned to run away.

Scaly arms sprang from the fedora. Their mottled, six-fingered hands grabbed Pauly's ankles, causing him to crash face-first on top of the ragged asphalt. He yelled continuously, as the monstrous arms dragged him backward. His fingernails splintered and became useless anchors in his vain attempt to break free. His ear-splitting screams morphed into an inhuman howl as the creature yanked his cracking frame into the fiery pit inside the hat. The last thing Pauly's broken mind registered was the peaceful countenance of the vagrant, who ignored his panicked pleas for help.

Then there was silence again, where fruitless cries to God had echoed just seconds before.

The man picked up the fedora and placed it on his unwashed head. Then, his raspy voice pierced the thick quiet as he smiled and said, "Wow."

# WHAT'S HAPPENING TO MRS. STROBEL?

*I wonder how the poor dear's getting along,* Ellen wondered. Her sympathetic heart broke a little more each time she thought of the elderly widow.

Mrs. Strobel had recently lost her husband, Joe, to cancer. They'd lived together in their modest and beautifully maintained home on the corner for nearly fifty years. But what the Lord giveth, He also taketh away. Now, the old woman had only scrapbooks of monochrome memories to keep her company—those, and her small, wiry-haired pooch, Buster.

Unfortunately, Joe, a retired blue-collar man, hadn't been able to leave her much in the way of money. And with his pension coming to a close, she had to learn how to get by on less.

Ellen didn't know the Strobels very well. Neither did the other neighbors. In fairness, the old couple had lived on the block before many of them were born. She figured today's crop of suburbanites didn't busy themselves with their neighbors' lives the way the older generation had. They were too busy with work, soccer, or taekwon-do to notice what was going on down the street. They had their own crap to deal with.

Ellen used to glimpse the couple as they doted on their front yard: he with the push mower, she with her garden trowel. After Joe passed, weeds and tall grass overtook the yard, and the once vibrant flowers faded and wilted. It was as if they all had died along with him.

For weeks after Joe's death, no one on the block saw much of Mrs. Strobel outside of her daily trips to the mailbox. It pleasantly surprised Ellen when one day, while sitting on her front porch, she saw the widow walking Buster. *Well, would you look at that?* she thought. Mrs. Strobel smiled and waved as she passed by. Ellen was happy to return the courtesy. However, her smile dropped like a stone when she noticed Mrs. Strobel was missing her right-hand fingers. *Judas on a pogo stick! What the heck happened?* Ellen wondered. She reasoned that whatever had taken place must've transpired inside the residence. As long as she had known the couple, they'd seldom ventured far from their property. Despite her misgivings, Ellen let the matter go.

A few days later, she saw Mrs. Strobel and Buster again. Her eyes immediately zeroed in on the widow's hand. Ellen was aghast—Mrs. Strobel was missing the entire appendage. In its place was a crimson-dotted bandage. *Oh, God, when did that happen? Ellen thought. What's going on in that house?* She thought about dropping by to check on her, but that seemed nosy. "Maybe it's time to call the authorities." But she wondered what they'd think if she said, "Uh, hello there. I'd like to report some missing body parts from my neighbor." Against her instincts, she decided not to get involved just yet.

A week passed with no sign of Mrs. Strobel. Ellen was chatting with Ben, her next-door neighbor, when the old woman—or rather what was left of her—strolled past them with her beloved pet in tow. The conversation came to an abrupt halt when they observed that she no longer had an arm below her elbow.

"Oh my gosh, Ben," Ellen said. "What's happening to Mrs. Strobel? Each time I see her, there's less and less of her.

"I've noticed that, too," replied Ben. "But have you noticed anything else unusual?"

"Like what?"

"As she gets smaller, the dog gets fatter."

# LATE NIGHT LISTENER

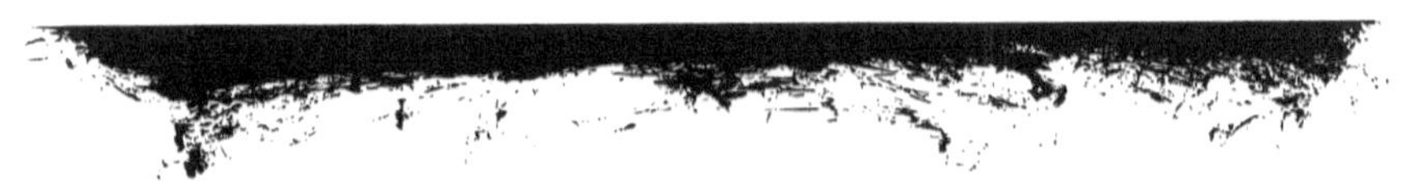

It's my first night working as a janitor at the Milton Building downtown. The place is kind of creepy this late, so I put in my earbuds and turn on some music as a distraction.

A few hours in, I sense someone behind me. I spin around to look, but there's no one there. I shake it off and get back to mopping the floor.

A short time later, I happen to glance up and catch a fleeting glimpse of someone crossing the long corridor several feet down from where I'm working. I turn off my I-pod and shout, "Is anyone there?" There's no reply.

My shaky nerves need some assurance that I'm truly alone, so I work up the courage to venture down to the hall's end, where I thought I saw the motion. I look both ways but observe no one. Chalking it up to the willies, I turn the music back on and continue cleaning.

Almost immediately, I get an uneasy feeling that someone is watching me—sizing me up. I turn off my I-pod again and yell, "Where the heck are you?"

That's when the low, scratchy voice comes through my earbuds and says, "Right behind you."

# LITTERBUG

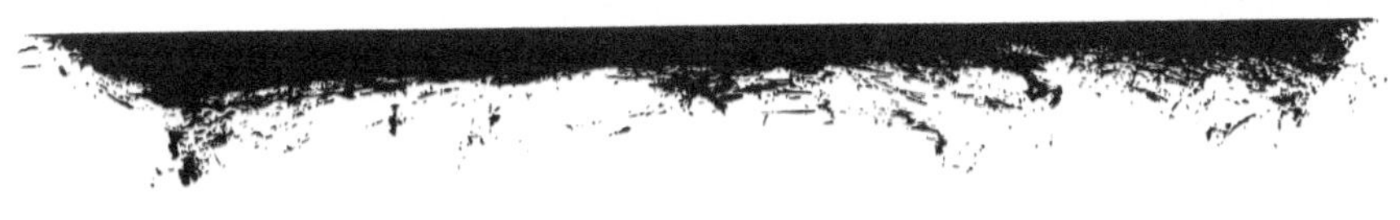

"**D**ammit! He did it again!" Nancy shrieked. "With Howard J. God as my witness, I'm gonna kill that little jackass one day!"

"Old Crazy Nancy," as she was known on the block, was a recluse. She routinely hurled stares at all of her neighbors through eyes so cold they could drop the outdoor temperature by fifteen degrees.

Phil, a.k.a. "Jackass," moved into the neighborhood just a few months prior. Although he quickly ingratiated himself with the small community, he found no purchase with Nancy. While everyone else was friendly, she barely acknowledged his existence, the exception being the occasional dress-down he got for his leaves blowing into her yard. *Good lord*, he often thought, *as if I can control the wind*. But the one thing that really drew her ire was whenever one of his used gum wrappers landed over there as well.

Phil liked to go for a jog in the afternoon just after work. The jogs helped him to decompress after a stressful day at the insurance office. On these runs, his mouth always got dry, so he chewed some gum to keep it moist. His preferred product was Juicy Fruit; had been since he was a kid. *Ought to try another flavor for variety's sake*, he thought. *It might even keep Madea's stunt double off my back.* He would sometimes toss the empty wrappers in the gutters along the road. The trouble-making wind took care of the rest.

This practice upset Nancy so much that she had started collecting the discarded wrappers. She put each in a small Ziploc bag, along with a piece of paper with the word "litterbug" and the day's date written on it in bold print. The bag was then placed in a desk drawer that contained all of the other incriminating evidence she compiled. Her well-thought-out plan was to have enough goods on Phil to report him to the police. She wasn't sure what the legal ramifications were. She was holding out hope for a nude public flogging or, her preferred choice, lethal injection... while sitting in an electric chair... in the rain.

Nancy was very particular about the appearance of the neighborhood. She had grown up in a small, Norman Rockwell sort of place. Early on, this neighborhood had the same sensible appeal: plastic covers on all of the furniture, a birdbath in every meticulously mown lawn, an oil painting of Jesus hanging over every mantel. Everything had been sunshine and fairy tales around this neck of the woods.

But as older residents passed on to Glory, their kids unburdened themselves of the piece of real estate they'd been bequeathed by selling it to home-flippers. The home-flippers would come in and start working their magic: They'd clean the carpets, slap some fresh paint on the walls, and *voila,* you had a rental property that catered to people like Jackass with his stupid Juicy Fruit wrappers.

As the months passed, Nancy became increasingly stressed: annoyance became frustration, frustration became anger, and anger became a smoldering rage. The grenade in the campfire moment finally came when another of Phil's gum wrappers blew onto one of her decorative bushes and lodged itself there, looking like a cheap Christmas ornament. Nancy, who had stepped out to check the mail, noticed it immediately.

"That's it, Jackass!" Nancy said through gritted teeth. Driven by the indignance that served as a strong tailwind at her back, she marched across her yard, then her next-door neighbor's yard—*What a crappy edging job around that sorry flower bed*—then across Phil's yard and up to his front stoop. Nancy stomped up the steps and beat on the door as if it owed her money. There was no answer.

"I'll fix you, Jackass! I'll fix you good!" she declared.

Nancy went home and retrieved the accursed wrapper from her violated shrub. She went into the cramped kitchen, which had never been updated from its original early-60's look. Nancy opened a low cabinet door and began spinning the Lazy Susan shelving unit until the sandwich bags box showed itself. She yanked a fresh one out, unfolded the wrapper, and started to put it inside the latest evidence bag, which would join the others in the desk drawer. She noticed that this particular wrapper was not from a Juicy Fruit, but a Wrigley's Spearmint.

"Well, aren't we a clever little monkey?"

Utilizing her cunning Sherlock Holmes-ian gift of keen observation, she deduced that Jackass Moriarty had changed his M.O. to throw her off the scent. "If that's the way you want it," she sneered, "then I guess it's gonna be a good old-fashioned butt whompin' for you. One more wrapper, Mr. Smart Aleck, and I'll shut you down faster than a brothel in the Bible Belt."

Despite not having seen Phil out for one of his usual jogs over the last few days, Nancy continued her vigil. She sat in the worn medical lift chair that she turned to face the large picture window that looked out at the street. From the outside, Nancy looked like a life-sized, framed portrait of a pissed-off Mona Lisa. She had sat there for the last three afternoons, red-eyed and angry, her nicotine-stained fingernails tapping against the hammer's wooden handle. By the fifth day, Nancy had all but given up catching Phil in the act of pre-meditated littering.

She stepped outside on a warm Saturday morning, eager to collect her daily paper at the end of her recently poured asphalt driveway. It was then she caught sight of it. Balled-up and taunting her, at the end of her drive, lay a single nugget comprised of the devil's two favorite playthings: paper and foil.

Nancy stared at it as if she'd stumbled across an insect from another dimension, before slowly walking over, bending down, and picking it up. Her face registered no expression, as she unfolded it as if it were part of a pirate's dried-out treasure map. She examined it. He'd attempted to confuse her again by disposing of the same brand of gum wrapper as last time.

"How dumb do you think I am? As if I don't know it's you. Okey Dokey. Let's get 'er over with."

Nancy, dressed for battle in her floral bathrobe and lime green slippers, stormed back into her split-level fortress. She secured the latest evidence in a baggie that she slipped into her robe's pocket and returned outside with the claw hammer.

Bob Hankton, who lived across the street from Phil, had stopped trimming his hedges long enough to shoot the breeze with his next-door neighbor, Roy Roebuck. He was a couple of minutes into the conversation with Roy when he detected someone walking up the street. He stopped mid-sentence. "Oh, Lord. Roy, you better check this out."

Eyes widened, and mouths dropped open as they watched Old Crazy Nancy making her way

up Phil's walkway and toward his front door with a large hammer in her hand.

Saturday was always Phil's "cheat day" when he didn't work out, ate what he wanted, and slept in late. The sleeping-in-late part was interrupted by a barrage of earth-rattling bangs on his door. He rolled out of bed, shook some alertness into his groggy head, and shuffled to the door, ready to cuss out a Mormon. He opened the door and looked at the elderly lady standing there in a grungy bathrobe. It took him a second or two to recognize her as the weird old bat who had told him off more than once about dropping gum wrappers on the street's side.

"Look, lady. Before you unload on me about the dopey wrappers, you should know—"

"Just so *you* know," the woman said, "this is what you wanted."

The first three blows with the blunt end of the hammer were enough to render him dead. The next fourteen were administered with the claw end of the weapon. Nancy enjoyed the wet, crunchy sounds as she pried and yanked away eye sockets and cheekbones from Phil's unrecognizable skull.

It was Bob Hankton who called the police. Roy was too busy puking and hyperventilating to be of much help. When the police arrived, Nancy was sitting calmly on the curb in front of Phil's house. Her demeanor was a stark contrast to the circus that was beginning to swirl around her. The street quickly became lined with additional police cruisers, gawking neighbors, a CSI unit, and an ambulance (though Phil was far past needing it).

After reading Nancy her rights, the detective in charge walked a short distance away and lit a cigarette. He was approached by one of the uniforms.

"She tell ya why she did it?" the female officer asked the detective.

"Not yet. She seems shell-shocked. She mumbled something about her neighbor jogging recently, but the poor guy's been out of town all week, according to the captain of the Neighborhood Watch."

As the female officer lifted Nancy by her elbow and led her away to the police cruiser, Nancy dropped something. The officer picked it up. It was a clear bag containing an inner and outer gum wrapper and a small piece of white paper with some scribbling on it.

"What the hell is this?" She stuffed the bag into her pants pocket for later inspection by the detectives.

Bob and Roy stood on the front edge of Bob's lawn. They watched as the police and coroner's vehicles drove away.

"You believe that mess?" Roy asked.

"Never in my lifetime," Bob whispered, pulling a pack of chewing gum from his left breast

pocket.

"Want one?" he asked Roy.

"What?" Roy replied.

"Gum. Want some? I'm trying to quit smoking again. Gum helps. Just started chewing it last week."

"What flavor is it?"

"Wrigley's Spearmint; want one?"

"Naw, I'm good."

"Suit yourself. Might get the taste of that vomit out of your mouth," Bob advised, as he slid a stick of gum into his own mouth. Then he twisted the foil and paper wrappers together and tossed them on the road, where they blew a few doors down, across the street, and into the neighbor's yard.

# FLOATING

The young girl screams. Her high-pitched cries assault my ears, making me grimace. I want to speak to her, calm her, let her know I mean no harm. But I can't seem to form the words, much less release them. Her small face is unfamiliar to me. I watch her, hoping for recognition on her part or mine. But she only gapes at me, round-mouthed and trembling; harsh wails rush from her slender throat like a song of terror.

A masculine voice travels from another room. "Katie?"

At least, I think that's what he calls her; the walls and distance make it indistinct.

"What's going on in there?" he asks.

In between deep pants, the child yells, "Daddy, come quick!"

"Katie, go back to sleep," he says. "Remember: Bad dreams can't hurt you."

Is that what he thinks is going on in his daughter's shadowy room? He should check, but then, that would ruin everything.

She continues staring at me, her gaze so intense that it penetrates my form. Her wide, wet eyes are broad with a horror that can only be generated by terrible things seen and unseen. She rolls her delicate hands into tiny fists. She doesn't move—does she dare?

I swivel my head, taking in the full view of the room. The dolls and stuffed animals that adorn this dark space seem familiar to me somehow. Disjointed thoughts coalesce into opaque memories. But memories of what? I will the scattered images to come together like pieces of a puzzle, but they resist.

The girl—is Katie her name?—looks as if she's trying to make sense of me. I do the same for her. She reminds me of someone. But whom? A thought enters my head.

Another little girl slept in this room, but no longer. Where did she go? What was her name? The answer hovers in the ether.

Katie raises her head from her pillow. The images are sharpening, each visceral picture lining up in sequence to tell the story.

A woman is packing up toys and clothes... she leaves with a child... someone remains... deep despair... a pop of noise... then lightness.

Oh, my! Bella! That was her name! That was my little girl's name! The child here now is not Bella. But where did she go? Please. *Where's my Bella*?!

The girl screams again.

I hear shuffling in another room, a creak of bedsprings. This time, a woman calls out. Unlike the man's voice, this one is patient, warm with love. "Baby, is it the same dream?"

"Yes," says the frightened child. "It's the man floating on my ceiling."

# MADAM ONA'S SHOPPE OF CURIOSITIES: BRODERICK'S STORY

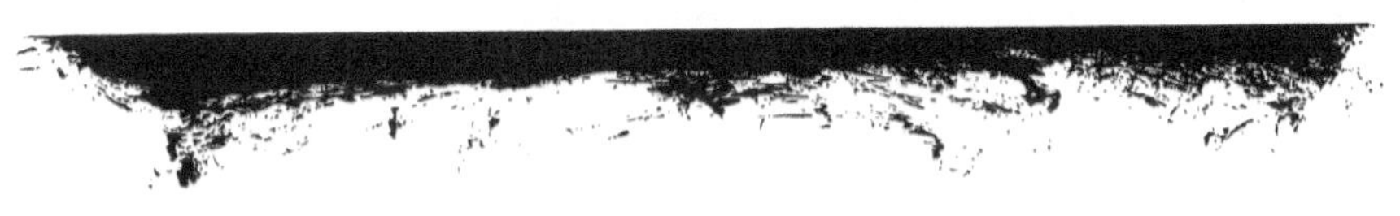

## I

There lurks within each of us a haunted house inhabited by the ghosts of our worst mistakes.

Broderick O'Connor was no exception.

Broderick was an ass-hat, plain and simple. He was all sunshine and bunnies, as long as everything went his way. You were the love of his life, his bestest bud, or a job that was enjoyable and satisfying. That is until you crossed the line. Oh, yeah—that line. Once you crossed it, there was no chance of going back. You were now excommunicated, dumped, despised, scorned, or, in extreme cases, dead to him. Ex-friends, jilted lovers, aggrieved parents, and unfortunate food servers littered the desolate highway of his icy heart.

When it came to women, Broderick found attraction in those who possessed beauty, intelligence, and emotional dependence. He viewed them as drinks he could pull from the fridge any time he was thirsty for a particular flavor. It was anyone, anytime, anywhere, for tall, handsome Broderick. God, life was good!

But Lilah was a different scenario altogether. She was sharp-witted, pleasant, and self-aware, qualities that Broderick lacked. Her attraction to him mystified her friends and family, perhaps herself a bit as well. She had the pick of the lovesick man-puppies who followed her around with their tongues hanging out, hoping to catch her notice.

This only made Broderick more determined to woo her, to have her. Control her.

But while he plucked others with ease, Lilah's roots went deep. She was hip to his jive, and she let him know it. Broderick realized, perhaps for the first time, that *he* had become the clingy lover. But he was okay with that. He reasoned that eventually a wild stallion would be corralled. Now was simply his time.

However, as in many relationships, needs and wants change. After two blissful, Hallmark movie, pass-the-Kleenex years together, Lilah made her new needs known. She desperately wanted to get married. Broderick did not want her to.

Lilah had never misled Broderick and had been telling him for months that her once stormy passion for him had been downgraded to a localized, lets-be-friends drizzle.

It never crossed Broderick's mind that she would tire of his temper tantrums and selfishness. But boy, did he get his mind around reality when she packed up, kissed his cheek, and wished him well.

Broderick moped for weeks. It didn't help that on the few occasions his friends dragged him out of his lonely, cluttered apartment, he would run into Lilah and her fiancée, Ted.

If Broderick went to a movie, they were there.

To a bar? There.

At a concert? Four seats down on the left.

*Hell,* Broderick thought, *"if I moved to the middle of the Gobi Desert, they'd come by on a flowery float, with the USC Marching Band out front passing wind to the tune of 'Livin' La Vida Loca.'"*

Broderick's emotional stability vacillated. He hated her. No, he still loved her. No, wait, he hated her and wished her butt would break off. Yet he desired her—he *neeeded* her!

During one of his brief moments of introspection, Broderick pummeled himself with the truth. "I was a complete tool," he said to himself. "It's time to take yourself in hand and admit you were a jerk. She was always giving, and you were always taking and asking for a receipt. Sorry, dawg. This one's all on you."

Every time Broderick called to apologize, Lilah would accept. Each time he called and begged for another opportunity, she would kindly ask him to be happy for her and move on. And when he called and yelled threats at her, Ted had a few threats of his own.

So, Broderick lived alone, unloved, unwashed, unshaven, and unhappy. Except for work, he never left the apartment. However, that changed one mild sunny Sunday, when he talked himself into venturing outdoors.

Broderick called an Uber and went for a ride that had no set destination. When he was tired of riding, he paid the driver, got out, and started walking.

During his long and aimless trek, Broderick made only three stops.

The first one was to eat a hot meal at a downtown café.

The second stop was to check out his reflection in a large shop window (sure, he was full of angst. But OMG, did he still look hot or what?).

The last stop was impulse or destiny. He couldn't be sure which, and he didn't much care.

A small, unremarkable shop was tucked between two downtown businesses. Its outdated appearance suited a small town better than bustling Boston. There was a stenciled sign on the glass door that read Madam Ona's Shoppe of Curiosities. *Ya gotta love originality,* Broderick thought. He was about to give the store a hard pass when he felt an unseen force—was it fascination—drawing him to it. He paused, staring at the door, deciding if he should enter. *What else do I have to do today?* he thought. With his decision made, he entered the curious shop.

A small, delicate bell over the door dinged, annoying him. Broderick sauntered through the front of the store, taking in the atmosphere and wondering, *The hell kind of crap is this?* The simple, rustic appearance of the store, along with its odd collections of bottled powders, trinkets, and potions, struck him as hokey. A sweet smell of strawberry incense permeated the air. Aside from him, the place was empty, making him uneasy. Still, his curiosity led him to venture further into the store.

Caught up in the shop's intrigue, Broderick moved from aisle to aisle, inspecting the various items for sale. The only sound was his feet tapping against the wooden floor like the slow clippity-clop of a horse's hooves on a cobblestone street. The silence of the store seemed to deepen until...

"How may I serve you today?" the unexpected voice asked, startling Broderick.

"Wow!" Broderick snapped. "I almost made mud in my shorts!"

"I apologize for having startled you," the small, thin woman with bright white hair said. "I'm the proprietor, Madam Ona."

"Congratulations," Broderick said, catching his breath. He touched some items with his index finger, assessing their interest. "You've got a lot of interesting stuff here."

"Yes, a lot of interesting things. Perhaps I possess something you desire... need."

Broderick continued picking through the merchandise as though he hadn't heard her. After a moment, he absentmindedly responded. "Lady, I don't see anything I want, much less anything I need."

The mysterious woman scowled, her eyes a hard, steely gray. "Really? I'll be the judge of that."

Broderick's eyes widened as the diminutive woman quickly closed the distance between them. "What the...?" he mumbled.

Once Madam Ona was face-to-face with Broderick, her ominous demeanor diminished and she became a sales clerk again.

She looked at an item on the middle shelf to Broderick's left. It was a grayish-colored stone, roughly the size and shape of a spearhead. It was cushioned on a bed of black velour cloth. It looked old, but clean. It bore an unusual symbol: an oval at the top, connected to a jagged line running to the bottom, with a short arrow jutting out at the end like a kickstand.

"Pick it up," Madam Ona said invitingly.

"This?" Broderick asked, pointing to the stone.

"Yes, that one."

"Why this one?"

"I sense you have a need. This item could be helpful."

Broderick inched his hand toward the stone as if it were a snake he was attempting to grab without being bitten.

"BOO!" Madam Ona shouted.

Broderick again thought he might require some absorbent underwear.

"Just kidding," Madam Ona said with a hearty laugh. "Seriously, though, pick it up and look at it."

Broderick, more irritated than amused, relaxed and took the stone. Although it was small, it had a dense and heavy feel, measuring only four or five inches in length and a couple of inches at its widest point.

"'Kay, what now?" Broderick asked disinterestedly.

"Look at the symbol. Feel the weight of the stone in your hand."

Broderick started playfully tossing it from hand to hand. "So, what is it?"

"A talisman," she answered.

"What's it go for?" he said, as he continued playing with the piece.

"Ten thousand dollars."

"*WHAT*?" Broderick screeched in surprise, losing his grip on the stone. He resembled a man trying to hang on to a flopping fish, as he hilariously attempted to grab it. Recovering his grip on the talisman, he asked, "Why the heck would you have a ten-thousand-dollar item just sitting out here like this?"

"Easy, easy," Madam Ona said in a calm, measured tone. "I wouldn't... if that were the real price."

As Madam Ona chuckled again at his expense, Broderick's facial expression conveyed a tandem of relief and hostility.

After enjoying her cruel trick, Madam Ona became serious again. "As I said, I suspect it is a need that brought you here today."

"Nah, I'm pretty sure it was boredom and an Uber," Broderick retorted sardonically.

"I guess it's your turn to make jokes," Madam Ona said good-naturedly. "That's fair. Now, let's return to our initial discussion. I sense you are a person burdened with guilt and regret: zigging when you should have zagged, saying no when you should have said yes, or saying yes when you should have said no. Your ego has been the cause of all of your significant relationship failures. Like countless other shattered spirits, you long to rewind time and make different choices with the knowledge you possess today."

With his smarmy veneer melting away, Broderick felt the shame of a man who had been caught red-handed and who must now accept judgment. "That's right," he whispered. He realized that the intuitive woman wasn't prepared to buy any of the B.S. he regularly sold at rock-bottom prices in volume, volume, volume.

Leaning in, Madam Ona grinned at Broderick. "What if I told you there is a way to fix something you broke? Would you grab that chance? Your clear, logical mind may think I'm a crazy lady with crystals, potions, and shrunken heads who believes in magic. But what if time and space were nothing more than a human construct, man's vain and futile attempt to bring order to chaos? And what if I told you that there are some things that exist beyond our mortal boundaries?"

"Go on," Broderick said.

"That object in your hand is a key to the door that opens up to that plane."

Broderick broke away from his trance and snapped back to the reality he believed in. "Are you trying to play me?"

"Play you? No. I'm attempting to offer you a different past for a different, personal future—a new trajectory, if you will."

"Oh, I see. And this wonderful opportunity costs how much? Ooh, if I act now, will you send me a second stone at half-price?"

"It will cost you nothing," Madam Ona replied.

"Nothing?" Broderick asked suspiciously.

"That's right. Well, nothing at first."

"Oh, here we go," Broderick said, rolling his eyes, mocking her.

"Hear me out," Madam Ona said. "I'll let you borrow the talisman and try it out for a few days, free of charge. But first, you must master how to skillfully and safely use it. For that, I'll send you on a trial run. Think of a time that might be fun to experience: a moment from your early childhood, your first kiss, or even an important moment in history. Interact with the past, but change nothing yet. A benign visit will teach you how to be gentle with the talisman until you learn to control its power. Only then will you be competent enough to make the change you want."

Broderick was skeptical. "Tell me something. If this rock works so great, how come you haven't already sold it?"

"Because the borrowers only needed to use it once. The people who've used this talisman have suffered about the same number of regrets as anyone else. But for them, there was always the one wound that refused to heal. They felt no obligation to fix the world, nor did they possess the ability to do so. Their needs were personal. Painful. All they wanted was to go back, make a smarter investment, and prevent bankruptcy for their family. They wanted to save their brother from suicide, or step to their left instead of their right to avoid tripping an I.E.D. Once the talisman served its purpose, they brought it back, and went on with their happier lives."

"And what happens if I don't return it?"

"The stone works its own type of magic; it always finds its way home."

"Spooky. All right, how does it work?"

"Hold the talisman tightly between your hands and close your eyes."

Broderick squinted as tightly as he could manage.

"Not so tight," Madam Ona said. "Relax your eyes, as if you were taking a nap."

Broderick complied.

"Very good," Madam Ona whispered. "What is your name?"

"Broderick O'Connor."

"Broderick O'Connor, I need you to listen very, very carefully. You must follow my instructions to the letter. Take a few deep breaths, hold each one briefly, and then gently blow on the talisman three times."

Broderick continued to listen intently.

"First, as you feel yourself going deeper into a relaxed state, imagine the period you want to return to. When you experience sounds, tastes and smells from that location in time, open your eyes and you'll be there. Make the most of your visit because the talisman will not allow you to return to that event again; it's a one and done proposition. Lastly, ensure the talisman is protected, perhaps by placing it in a pocket, to avoid losing it."

At that point, her voice shifted to a somber tone.

"Now, Mr. O'Connor, you really have to focus here, because this part is the most critical. Do not remain anywhere for too long—ten minutes at the most. To return, have the talisman firmly clutched again between your hands. It can't be in your pocket or in one hand. If you don't perfectly repeat the ritual, you will be a prisoner of that moment, condemned to an eternity where you'll play out the same scene over and over again. A world without end, amen. Once you're satisfied with the stone's authenticity, bring it back to me. At that time, we can negotiate a fair exchange."

Broderick was nervous. However, the power to say or do things differently also excited him. Demonstrating to Lilah that he could change and become the man she yearned for was his immediate thought. *But what if goof up? I can't go back and try it again*, he worried.

Broderick turned his attention to successfully completing the test run. He took a couple of beats, then said, "I'm ready."

"Then let's begin," Madam Ona said.

With the talisman still grasped in his hands, Broderick blew three gentle breaths over it. He contemplated time-traveling to the 1980s, a decade of eclectic fashion and the birth of music videos. However, he recalled the 80s were also filled with undeniable unpleasantness: Iran Contra, AIDS, Huey Lewis & the News. *Let's move a lil' further back*, he thought.

Broderick formed a strong mental vision of the Viet Nam protests back in the 1960s. He thought about a history class in high school where he'd learned about the turbulent era. He recalled viewing old black and white footage of war protests, soldiers in jungles, and the assassination of influential people.

Soon, Broderick experienced a surge of fear and exhilaration, as he felt himself being pulled backward, then fired forward as if he had been launched out of a giant, invisible slingshot. As he was propelled forward, he heard music and vocals. "Hey now, what's that sound? Everybody look what's goin' down." Broderick recognized the lyrics from a song that his grandfather used to play on his stereo. He recalled that the title of the song is "For What It's Worth" by a band called Buffalo Springfield.

Broderick detected the pungent smell of sweat and hot asphalt and felt the summer heat. Behind the music, voices were shouting. When he opened his eyes, he was marching with a mob of angry, young protesters. Many of them were carrying anti-war signs. A long-haired, shirtless twenty-something man handed him a sign that read, "1, 2, 3, 4, you can shove your stupid war!" Broderick slipped the talisman in a pocket of the faded, tattered jeans he was now wearing.

He soon regretted his hasty choice of locations. *Why didn't I choose Woodstock, for pity's sake?* he wondered. *It's where you learned that the best things in life are free, especially hippie sex.*

Broderick was overwhelmed at first. But when his mind accepted that he was actually taking part in a 60s protest, he became enlivened. For the next few minutes, he marched, yelled, and gave the finger to some anti-protesters lining the sidewalks.

He was enjoying the experience until the group rounded a corner and met with a brigade of ticked-off police. The protesters were armed only with signs containing crappy poetry. The cops had tear gas, fierce dogs, and fire hoses.

"Yep, seen enough," Broderick spat out. He dropped his sign and removed the talisman from his pocket. Thankful for having paid attention to the shopkeeper, he held the stone relic in both hands, closed his eyes, and blew three light breaths over it. His thoughts were solely on the store he came from. Soon, his ethereal body was flying through space again.

Broderick smelled strawberry incense and felt the wooden floor beneath his feet. Relief washed over him as he opened his eyes and realized he was back in the present.

Madam Ona sat near the front door behind a glass counter, leisurely reading a copy of *Glamour Magazine*. "Welcome back," she said nonchalantly, as if Broderick's trip was an every-hour-on-the-hour occurrence.

"How long was I gone?" Broderick asked breathlessly.

"I cannot say for certain. Perhaps a few minutes," she said.

"Did I disappear?"

"No. You stood there with your eyes closed, as if you were dozing, then you jolted awake. Where'd you go?"

"The 60s. A Viet Nam Protest March."

"Seriously?" Madam Ona looked befuddled, as if Broderick had selected a stupid and unusual destination.

"It was just an arbitrary time that popped into my head!" Broderick said defensively.

"'Kay," she replied.

"Oh yeah? Well, where the heck would you have gone?"

"How should I know? It was your space trip, Major Tom."

Broderick looked in awe at the wondrous, magical stone still clasped in his hands. "I'll take it!" he shouted exuberantly.

"Don't get ahead of yourself, Broderick O'Connor. As I said, I'll allow you to try it. But it's also a trial period for the talisman to test you. You have to demonstrate responsibility and respect."

"Respect for what? You?"

"No. For the talisman," Madam Ona said cryptically. "Borrow it. Use it wisely. Fix your problem. Don't lose the talisman. Return here with it, then we'll see if you still want to own it."

Broderick absorbed her words for a moment. "Deal," he said.

He went to the entrance and stopped. "See ya soon," he said over his shoulder. Then his face became stern, a glint of menace in his eyes. "Be warned; it'll be sooner if this thing doesn't work again." Then he left with the stone.

"Whatever you say, Mr. Broderick O'Connor," Madam Ona muttered before returning to her magazine.

# 2

The talisman was lying on the glass-topped coffee table. Broderick was orbiting around it as if it were the sun. He gnawed on his thumbnail, a habit he had whenever he was perplexed or had a good idea (which was seldom).

"Do it. Do it. Just do it," he kept repeating. This had been going on for nearly an hour. "Can I do this? I need more time to think. I've only got one shot. I can't afford to screw this up."

Broderick was circling the coffee table again when an idea struck him.

"I'll need to take another test run. I'll try going back in time a little farther than before. Now, how far back do I want to go? That graduation trip to the beach with my buds? My first frat party? Nah, let's really see what this bad boy'll do. Go big or go home, Broddy."

No one could accuse Broderick of not being creative. For him, it was an essential building block in the art of lying with ease and plausible conviction.

After thinking it over, Broderick impressed himself with a bold and brilliant decision. It came to him while he was looking at a painting that his parents had given him as a house-warming gift.

It depicted a Revolutionary War battle. Smoke billowed from cannons and muskets, men fearlessly charged at each other with bayonets at the ready, and horses reared on their hind legs in the ethereal battle mist.

"Let's get *it ooon*!" Broderick shouted like a MMA fight announcer. He picked up the talisman, held it between his hands, and began the well-rehearsed rite.

Everything around him faded, as his mind thought of nothing but the battle scene. Broderick again felt the sensation of propulsion through time. He tasted the metallic tang of spent ammunition and warm, squishy mud under his feet. He heard the sounds of victory yells juxtaposed with the screams of the dying and wounded.

When Broderick opened his eyes, he was in the scene depicted in the painting. The soldier's attire he wore revealed his status as a member of the Continental Army. He tucked the mystical stone inside one of his jacket pockets. Holding a musket, it occurred to him he'd never shot a gun in his life. He had certainly never taken a life before, unless you counted his pleasant daydreams regarding the twit in the cubicle next to his own; the loser never stopped talking. Bringing a violent end to the dunce's incessant droning filled Broderick's heart with sweet contentment.

All Broderick could think to do was to run around yelling, hoping he didn't get plugged by a round bullet or lanced with a British bayonet. When a whistling cannonball vaporized the head of the soldier a few feet to his left, Broderick was ready to bring the experiment to its necessary conclusion. He ditched the rifle, pulled the talisman from a top pocket of his grimy, ragged coat, and headed for home.

# 3

Broderick arrived back at his apartment, standing in the spot from which he'd left. He was pale and shaking. Once his nerves settled, he roared in the triumphant manner of a successful scientist, as he confidently concluded, "And thus it is proved!"

Broderick planned on sleeping on it for a night, but decided he was as ready as he'd ever be to visit Lilah. The results of his experiments confirmed his capability to regulate travel distances. In light of this, he reasoned that if he made a mistake during his first visit to Lilah, he could continue to regress in their relationship until he achieved his objective.

*Remember*, he instructed himself, *don't rush it. Begin with how sorry you are for being selfish and insensitive. Keep it simple. Keep in mind that if necessary, you can go back as far as you need to and take another stab at this.*

That last thought, "stab at this," reminded him of how close he had come to being the marshmallow portion of some Redcoat's cosmic S'more. He shivered and swallowed a thick gulp of spit.

"All right, let's do this," he said.

Broderick lowered himself onto the plush, comfortable couch that Lilah had generously, or possibly accidentally, bequeathed to him. He relaxed and recalled the vivid memory of the day Lilah had left him for Ted. His focus momentarily trailed off as he caught himself humming the song, "Livin' La Vida Loca." He swiftly managed to get re-centered.

Following the prescribed ceremony, Broderick felt the soft embrace of the couch give way to the hard metal chair of the coffeehouse that he and Lilah had frequented. He inhaled the scintillating smell of freshly brewed, and unconscionably over-priced, coffees. He heard acoustic Americana music coming through the shop's sound system, as well as the undecipherable chatter of the surrounding patrons.

Broderick didn't open his eyes right away. A great sorrow weighed heavily on his heart. He felt a lump forming in his throat and the beginning of tears in his eyes. He hadn't considered what his reaction would be when he opened his eyes and saw the love of his life sitting in front of him. He braced himself, as he felt the comfort of her small, delicate hand gently touching his own, and her captivating, mellifluous voice.

"Broderick, are you okay?"

Broderick opened his eyes and did his best not to appear overly emotional. "Yeah, babe," he said, "I just blanked out there for a minute."

"You looked like you were napping. I thought that maybe I'd bored you to death."

"No, no, I'm good. I need to say something to you. I need to tell you I realize that I've been a total jerk. I've taken you for granted for too long. I—"

"Broderick, there's something I need to tell you, too. And based on where I think you're about to take this conversation, now should be the time."

His heart plummeted to his churning stomach. "No, angel, don't. Please, Lilah."

"Babe, this just isn't working out. I know you're trying to make things right, but even if you'd been perfect, this would still be the end for us. Thing is, and it's taken me a while to figure out how to do this without coming apart, I'm in love with someone else. This isn't a spur-of-the-moment thing. I've known it for a while now."

The bravado that Broderick brought into this failing plan was being supplanted by a complete sense of vulnerability. His mouth was thickening with nervous spit while the tears he was fighting threatened to reveal his pain. Gone was his pride, his dignity. He didn't care about the indifferent looks that some of the nearby coffee-swillers were shooting at him. Realizing that this trip was doomed to failure, he felt hopeless and broken. Despite his cleverness, planning, and cockiness, he was going to lose her, anyway.

Desperate, Broderick used the only tool he had left: pleading.

"Tell me what to do," he begged. "Whatever it takes to make you happy, I'll do it. Whoever you need me to be, I'll be that. Lilah, this isn't an infatuation; I need you. I know this guy says he loves you, but my hand to God, he can never love you as much as I do. Please, babe. Please give me a little more time to show you I can change—that I can make you happy."

"Broderick, if you really want to make me happy, then you need to let me go, so I..."

*Oh, crap!* Broderick realized. *I'm taking too long. If I don't leave, I'll be stuck here listening to The Indigo Girls and having my heart ripped out with an ice cream scoop forever.*

"I gotta go, Lilah," Broderick blurted.

"What?" Lilah asked with a look of mild confusion and annoyance.

"I'll come back. I'll come back for you, but it's gotta be later. I mean, earlier. I mean... oh, Judas on a triscuit with cheese... I'll be back."

"Be back for me later? Earlier? What are you even talking about?" Lilah asked angrily.

Broderick realized he had to leave things where they were for the time being. He lifted the talisman he'd been holding under the table and did the dance.

"Broderick, what is that thing? Are you conking out on me again? So help me God—"

Broderick began the jaunt home.

# 4

Soon Broderick felt the warm embrace of the sofa. He heard the hum of the air conditioning forcing its way out of the floor vent. Once Broderick knew he had successfully completed the journey, he opened his eyes. The melancholy at his failure melted under the brightness of his knowledge that he could cheat time and head back to Lilah again.

Broderick understood and accepted that he was only allowed one opportunity to change an event, but what he was talking about was changing the outcome under different circumstances, different times. He'd already shown the ability to go back in time as far as he wanted. But first, he needed to lie back, pull himself together, and carefully plan his next attempt. This time, he'd arm himself with something that he'd neglected to bring along on the initial trip: an unbelievable amount of B.S.

Broderick dug up his daily planner from earlier in the year. After some effort, he finally secured the date he wanted: the night he asked Lilah to move in. It had taken some coaxing at first, but she relented. Broderick wanted to eliminate any of the doubts she'd had. He concluded that those doubts were probably the cause of all the subsequent pain.

Broderick's plan was to adopt a new persona, one in which he was patient instead of pushy; a listener instead of someone who dominated the conversation; and sophisticated instead of crass. He hoped that Lilah would love him more deeply and accept this new version of Broderick as the soulmate she had dreamed of. And most importantly, *no Ted*!

Broderick practiced his lines, body language, and facial expressions in front of the mirror. To enhance the experience, he imagined himself in a stylish brown sports coat, crisp white shirt, well-fitted blue jeans, and clean dress loafers. It wouldn't do to show up this time in a Green Day t-shirt, with wrinkled jeans, and some grungy white sneakers.

Broderick was preparing for take-off when it occurred to him that some cologne might help to complement his image. The problem was, he'd never worn any because he'd never owned any. When it came to his personal hygiene, he figured a morning application of deodorant fulfilled his part of the social contract. He also flossed three times a week. Surely, that counted for something. Broderick grinned broadly as a brilliant flash of ingenuity hit him.

He went to the laundry closet, grabbed a dryer sheet that contained a fragrance called Lemon Meadow, and used it to wipe down his entire body.

Once the stage was set, Broderick plopped onto the sofa, took the talisman in his hands, and pulled every memory of that night into his mind's eye. Then...

# 5

"Why, thank you. You look quite nice yourself," Lilah said from her side of the table. "You know, I don't think I've ever seen you this spruced up. You really clean up nice, kiddo."

"I did it for you," Broderick cooed with the sliest of smiles, as he placed the talisman in his pants pocket.

Lilah leaned forward over the restaurant table and sniffed. "Did you put on some cologne for me as well?"

"Why, yes, I did. Do you like it?"

"I guess so. It kind of makes you smell like a lemon tree... or dryer lint. I can't tell."

"Lilah, I want to talk to you about an idea that I have. I can only hope that it will excite you as much as it does me."

Broderick began his carefully crafted speech. He laid out an eloquent, statesman-like soliloquy about the importance of commitment. His lawyerly summation concluded with his asking Lilah to share his life, his love, and his home. Broderick delivered the seemingly heartfelt appeal with a robust, theatrical style reminiscent of Sir John Gielgud in a Shakespearian tragedy, with just a hint of Tom Cruise in *Jerry McGuire*.

After he completed his sales pitch, Broderick gave himself a mental pat on the back. *Boo-yah!* his inner voice cheered. *Drop the mic, cue the sunset, and roll the credits, baby, cuz Daddy, just put it to bed!*

With the best fake tears he could muster, Broderick took Lilah's hands in his and leaned in. "I'll make you happy for the rest of your life and any to come."

Lilah, a soft twinkle in her eyes, waited for a moment to take everything in before replying. "Nah, I don't think so."

Broderick's fawning eyes and cherub-like facial expression didn't change as he asked, "Wait. What?"

"Look, Broderick, I thought you were a man who's comfortable in his own skin. Sure, you can be a bit short-tempered, immature, and narcissistic. But you come here tonight looking and smelling like a metrosexual who got lost in a lemon orchard and talking like a drippy romance novelist. You look like you're so emotionally fragile that you might start crying at any second. I'm just not ready to make the kind of commitment you're asking me to make. I'm sorry, Broderick, but if this is really who you are, then it might be better just to give each other some space for a while. Besides, it's not like you'd notice I'm gone. You barely acknowledge me when I'm here."

Broderick felt like the north end of a southbound mule. *How the heck did this plan fail?* he wondered. *The clothes. The tender, caring person. The stupid, lemony fresh dryer sheet, for God's sake!* The futility of everything he'd done to change this one thing enraged him.

Broderick sprang from his chair and allowed Lilah, the waiter, and the other proud Americans in the establishment to be sucked into his profanity-laced, red-faced, lost-the-case, swirling vortex of shame and fury.

By the time he finally ran out of steam, all the cowardly patrons had evacuated the scene. The braver ones who'd remained disregarded Broderick's outburst as nothing more than dinner and a show.

Lilah, who'd sat through the entire performance, with eyes as wide as the Rio Grande, began clapping slowly and unenthusiastically. She stood and announced to the whole room, "And now, ladies and gentlemen, fresh off his Tony Award-winning role for Best Actress in a Comedy or Drama, it's none other than Broderick, the lemon-scented monkey's ass." Far from done, she added, "Thank you, Broderick, for all of the good times, along and tonight's stirring performance. Now, if you'll excuse me, I'm calling a friend to pick me up. Someone who's a little bit more mature than you—and I might add better smelling."

"Lilah!" Broderick yelled as she began walking toward the entrance of the shop. "After everything I've done to make you love me, don't you have one kind thing to say to me?"

Lilah stopped short and turned. "Yeah, Broderick, here's some kind advice. You know that recipe you concocted for your world-famous Oyster and Raisin Casserole? Well, it's an abomination before the Lord—burn it!" Lilah turned her sights back to the door and did the rest of her talkin' with her walkin'.

Broderick was numb. He couldn't think, couldn't speak. Most importantly, he thought she loved his Oyster and Raisin Casserole. If he thought this moment was the zenith of his humiliation, he would've been wrong. Very wrong.

When Lilah got to the door, before she could push it open, a handsome, young man with a square jaw, crystal blue eyes, a thick head of wavy brown hair, and movie star good looks pushed it open for her.

"Saw what happened," said the lean, tanned, and effortlessly charming young man. "Actually, it was probably picked up by the International Space Station."

At that, Lilah's rage-hardened face softened, and she laughed.

"Anyhow," the young stranger said, "I was just heading out to meet some friends who are having a small rooftop party. I could give you a ride home on the way, if you want."

"Sounds great," Lilah said coquettishly. "But that party sounds a little great, too."

Broderick stood there dumbfounded as they walked through the door together. The café was still and quiet, so he was able to hear their last exchange.

"I'm Lilah, by the way."

"Well, hi, Lilah-by-the-way. Pleased to meet you. I'm Ted."

# 6

Broderick didn't sleep much that night. He was sad, angry, and out of ideas. He remembered a quote by Soren Kirkegaard: "There is no more pitiful state of being that comes about than when one has to let go of a future that will never be." No matter what he did, or how far back he went, there would never be a future with Lilah. It hurt.

By the early afternoon of the next day, Broderick's growling stomach outmatched his martyr's desire to starve to death, so he ventured out. Besides, his limited trial time with the talisman was almost up. It was time to return it.

Broderick took an Uber to the diner he'd eaten at prior to his first visit to Madam Ona's Shoppe of Curiosities. He ended up being more of a martyr than anticipated, leaving half of his Turkey and Havarti sandwich uneaten. He paid the tab and set out for Madam Ona's.

When Broderick entered the store, he saw Madam Ona seated behind the counter, perusing a magazine. Without looking up, she asked, "Oh, hello. Back already?"

The store was still as empty as the tomb on Easter morning. Broderick shuffled over to the counter. He took the talisman out of his pocket and laid it on the glass countertop. "Didn't work," he said solemnly.

"Of course it did," Madam Ona said. "I saw you take your first trip." Then she sniffed the air. "Do you smell that?"

"Smell what?"

"Lemons and dryer lint."

"Oh, that'd be me. No, I meant that it didn't help me do what I wanted to do. I lost Lilah anyway. I should've listened to you. I only had one chance to fix things. Getting creative with the rules to cheat the talisman is a fool's errand; it won't stand for it. I suppose that's fair."

Madam Ona got up from her metal stool and walked from behind the counter to Broderick.

"You're not the only person who's had an important moment slip through their hands," she said soothingly. "As you learned, you're not allowed to try more than once. What you get is what has to be. At least you had the presence of mind not to stay there for too long. You didn't get stuck reliving that bad moment for all of eternity; that would've been the real hell. Now, you can move on with the knowledge that you've done all you could to erase your pain. It seems like you've let the stone teach you the importance of boundaries, humility, and respect. Do you still want the talisman?"

Broderick thought for a bit. "I don't know," he replied soberly. Then a mischievous grin spread across his face. "Maybe... yeah, why not? Unlike the others, I could use it to bounce around history. Maybe I can sell the stone myself. That's quite a piece of magic you have there."

Broderick snatched the talisman from the counter and began flipping it in his hand like a coin.

Madam Ona's hand shot out and seized it from the air, just before he could catch it. "No!" she said defiantly.

"I'm sorry. Did you say no?" Broderick asked.

"This talisman is a sacred artifact, not a toy for your amusement. I thought that it might change your cavalier, impertinent attitude, but apparently, even it's not powerful enough. It has been used countless times throughout history, in spans too long to even fathom. Like you, there have been others who have demanded to possess it, no matter the cost, even after they proved themselves unworthy. I've only offered the talisman to a select group of people: those who mourn; those who've wronged others through cruelty or personal gain; and those who yearn to gain back something precious that's been lost."

"Well, if you've found worthy people to sell it to, then how does it always end up back here with you?" Broderick asked indignantly.

"As I've already explained to you, when the need was no more, they returned the talisman to me. Mr. O'Connor, instead of, as you put it, bouncing around in time, this talisman can provide you with something more meaningful and keep you from living a self-centered existence. You could use it to help the people in your life who have also known regret. Or, you could use it to inhabit your own personal universe, in which you always profit and never lose. Have you ever stopped to consider that sometimes it's the hardest lessons that shape us into becoming who we are meant to be?"

Broderick felt the same old ferocity rising in him. His evil, inner demon encouraged him to put his foot down and demand his own way, lest there be consequences. He bent his head down until it was nearly touching the small woman's forehead.

"You said you find me cavalier and impertinent," Broderick hissed. "You left out a couple of other descriptions: determination... and wrath. You told me not three days ago that if I was satisfied with the stone that you'd work out a fair price for me. I think now is an appropriate time for that. See, like me and that rock, you need to learn about boundaries, humility, and respect. Here's what I know and what I don't know: I *know* you're gonna sell me that stone. What I don't know is what's gonna happen if you don't. That talisman isn't a sacred artifact; it's a total screwup. It had one task to accomplish, and it couldn't handle it. But I'm a creative guy. I can come up with some adjustments. I think you've figured out that I can take this rock if I want to, but I believe in being fair. Sell it to me, and I promise that I won't go back in time and murder your pregnant whore of a mother. What say you, all-powerful soothsayer?"

Madam Ona's eyes never left Broderick's. When he finished his blatant threat, she allowed a mischievous grin of her own to paint her face.

"All right, then," she said. "You drive a hard bargain, Mr. O'Connor. I suppose it was always going to pass to another owner at some point. I told you I would sell it to you for a fair price, and so I shall."

Broderick smirked. "That's more like it. Well? I'm listening."

"I'm a purveyor of unusual objects, but I'm also a business-woman. How else could I afford to keep this shop open? After all, you can only make so much by selling healing crystals and love potions."

"Aren't you the little hypocrite?" Broderick asked mockingly. "I'll bite. You said the price would be fair and would include a final transaction?"

"And it will," she promised. "I want you to use it one more time for me. There's something I'd like from the past, something I'd really love to add to my inventory."

"If you want it so bad, why haven't you gone back and gotten it yourself?"

"Sorry to say I'm not as adventurous as some people. Besides, if I didn't make it back, who'd feed my cats?"

"How many cats do you have?"

After an awkward pause, Madam Ona said sheepishly, "Crap. I didn't expect you to ask. All right, all right, I don't have any stupid cats. I'm just cowardly. Sue me."

Broderick snickered, shaking his head back and forth in disbelief. "'Kay... what is it you want?"

"A sliver of wood from the cross of Christ," Madam Ona said matter-of-factly.

"You mean Jesus Christ?"

"No, Carl Christ. Yes, I'd like you to travel back to the day of the Crucifixion and bring me back a small piece of the cross."

"That's it?" Broderick asked with a sigh of relief. "Nothing else, like maybe a Roman toga, or 10 dollars' worth of shekels? Nothing like that?"

"No. Just the one bit of wood. I have a use for it."

Broderick clapped his hands together and again used his booming announcer's voice. "Let's get it *ooon!*"

"Okay," Madam Ona said. "Come, look at this."

She turned and walked across the sales floor at a quick clip, her purple muumuu billowing behind her.

They ended up in front of a tall, glass display case.

The unique and disparate items intrigued Broderick. "Now what have we got here?" he asked, as his eyes swept over her collection of valuable relics. His eyes settled on a button. "Where's that from?"

Madam Ona enjoyed the look of genuine fascination on Broderick's face. "I had that button taken off the coat of George Washington during the winter of 1777 at Valley Forge."

"That's the real deal? Seriously?"

"Seriously."

"Get outta my room!" Broderick exclaimed with an air of excitement. "And that?" he asked, pointing at an ornate dagger.

"That's an actual sacrificial dagger from about 2000 B.C. that was retrieved by one of my travelers. It belonged to a Mayan tribal chief."

"Is that what I think it is?" Broderick pressed his forehead against the front of the glass case to confirm what he thought he was seeing.

"That's right," Madam Ona said. "That is the crown of thorns worn by Christ, and those are the three nails used to hold him on the cross. As you can see, they're large and slightly bent—definitely post-crucifixion. And by the way, stop steaming up the glass. I have to clean these things, you know."

"I said it before, and I'll repeat it now," Broderick chuckled. "You are one careless, clumsy, and irresponsible person. What is it with you and leaving expensive stuff sitting out for someone to just grab and run?"

"First off, Mr. Know-It-All, they'd have to know what it was they were stealing. Secondly, I store these, as well as my other rare items, in a large, secure vault."

"Really? Is it inside a bank or hidden behind a secret wall?"

"Actually," Madam Ona confessed with some embarrassment, "I keep them locked in an old freezer in the back. But it *is* locked!"

Broderick looked at her with pity and incredulity. "Does the Federal Reserve know about this kind of cutting-edge and possibly advanced alien technology?"

"Well... it's a *huge* padlock!" Madam Ona was eager to change the subject and get back to the matter at hand. "Here, look at this." She took a key from a lanyard around her neck and used it to unlock the front of the case. She removed a small, wooden figurine that depicted the Crucifixion. A Roman soldier was piercing Jesus's side with a long spear. John, the disciple, Mary Magdalene, and Jesus's mother were staring on in disbelief, an expression of palpable despair etched on their upturned faces. The center of the figurine displayed an image of Jesus on the cross. His was a look of intense sorrow and utter anguish.

"A marvellous piece, no?" Madam Ona asked. "What I'd really like is the wood from the actual cross of Christ to form a set with the bloodied crown and the nails. That would really bring together the touch of authenticity that I'm hoping to convey. This figurine will better ensure your effectiveness. I need you at the foot of that cross, not a yard away."

She held the object up to Broderick's face.

"Now then," she said in a low and severe tone, "Focus on Jesus as He hangs on the cross.

Imprint the image into your mind as indelibly as possible. When you get there, don't get overwhelmed by what you are witnessing. It'll be hard, I know, but I need you to collect what I asked from you. Are you ready to do this?"

"Yes," Broderick said with the cocksureness that only a arrogant bully would wield. "But remember, if you screw with me, I'll make good on that threat. In fact, if your mom's still living, you might want to call her. You know, just in case you both disappear into the ether."

"I'll remember, Mr. O'Connor. I assure you, it is at the forefront of my mind."

Madam Ona handed Broderick back the stone. "Now then, close your eyes and hold the talisman between your hands tightly. Likewise, you'll need to be holding it in your hands to return here. I'm sure you know the rest of the drill."

"Ready or not," Broderick said. Then he started the process.

Broderick pushed aside everything that was cluttering his mind and focused all of his energy on the wooden figurine.

It wasn't long before he sensed dry and dusty air. The mix of soldier mockery and grieving women's wails echoed in his ears. He kept his eyes closed until he felt ready to act.

From a distant place in the recesses of his mind, Broderick heard Madam Ona's heavy voice.

"Keep your eyes closed a bit longer, Mr. O'Connor. Reach out. Can you feel the wood? Touch the wood of the cross and feel a connection to it."

Broderick took her instructions, sightlessly reaching until he felt hard wood.

Soon, a burning, crushing, and indescribable pain blanketed Broderick's entire body. A sensation of sticky wetness was rolling down on him. A profound sadness gripped him so tight that it squeezed his soul.

Broderick snapped his eyes open, expecting to look up at the twisted body hanging horrifically from the cross. That was not what he saw. Rather than looking up, he glanced down at a man comforting a distressed woman. A younger woman, with tears and dirt smearing her face, was also present. To his left and right, he saw broken men on crosses.

Breathing became difficult. Every time Broderick slumped, his lungs compressed. Despite his efforts to straighten up, the thick nail securing his feet to the small platform only made him cry out louder. His confused and horrified mind understood what was happening.

When Broderick looked down again, his torment and terror intensified as he saw a Roman soldier standing next to his cross with a long spear, gazing up at him like a vulture.

"Oh, God," Broderick said in a gasping, hoarse voice, saturated with raw fear. "What did you do, woman? What did you do? I gotta get back!"

Broderick didn't remember stowing the talisman. Dressed only in a bloody, ragged loincloth, he wondered how he could've secured its safety. Was it still on him? "The talisman. Where's the damned talisman?"

Broderick's gored hands were riddled with so much pain that he couldn't feel anything else. Screaming, he twisted his hand open to check if he still had the life-saving artifact. It wasn't there. "Please, God. Let it be in my other hand." He agonizingly spread some of the fingers of his left hand and saw that they were loosely grasping his ticket from his awful fate.

"Screw your wood, you piece of filth," he snarled through gritted teeth. "If my hands are not ripped to shreds when I get back, I'm gonna bitch-slap you to another hemisphere. Oh yeah, and there's that party with your big, sweet momma to enjoy as well."

Broderick's sense of hope and relief at having the talisman back soon turned to wide-eyed delirium, as he remembered the most fundamental rule of teleportation: You must hold the stone with *both* hands, not one.

He became a wild and helpless animal, thrashing and howling. His vain attempts at ripping his right hand free so he could reach the talisman proved futile.

The full weight of his predicament hit him squarely in his face when he realized he had overlooked yet another important rule: If you fail to return promptly, you will be trapped in the moment forever. *A world without end, amen.*

With a high-pitched wail that would've brought a grand feeling of pleasure to the stone's owner, poor Broderick hollered, " *NOOO!*" But not for the last time.

Back at the store, Madam Ona stared at the wooden figurine in her hand. Broderick's crucified image was forever etched into it, his contorted face a rictus of misery and excruciation. A look of sublime satisfaction spread across her own face as she began flipping the figurine from one hand to the other, just as Broderick had once done with the talisman.

"Yes, Broderick O'Connor, this piece will add considerable worth to my collection. It was carved from a one-of-a-kind slab of wood from a specific cross. Whoops! And to think I sent you back there for nothing."

Madam Ona carried the piece to the glass display cabinet, where she kept the other priceless artifacts. She was removing the key from her lanyard when a thought made her stop. "I understand how valuable and rare you are, so I should place you under lock and key. But you did say that I was careless, clumsy, and irresponsible. You did say that, right? Now let's see... where to put you... where to put you."

Madam Ona pouted in concentration as she began surveying the sales floor. Once she settled on an appropriate spot, she sashayed to it and stopped. It was the shelf where she had originally displayed the talisman.

"I think you'll go perfectly with some other items that I've sent some cunning folks back for.

You should all get along fine; you have so much in common."

Madam Ona smiled as she positioned the figurine alongside some other items on the shelf.

One of them was a framed, 5X9, black-and-white photo of a desperate man, inches away from the dorsal fin of a gigantic shark. The image of a sinking battleship in the background called the U.S.S. Indianapolis was visible in the distance.

Next to the photo was a small porcelain piece depicting a woman writhing in agony within Dante's Inferno. And like the 30-ish, short-haired man in the wooden figurine next to hers, she, too, was screaming.

# WREAKAGE

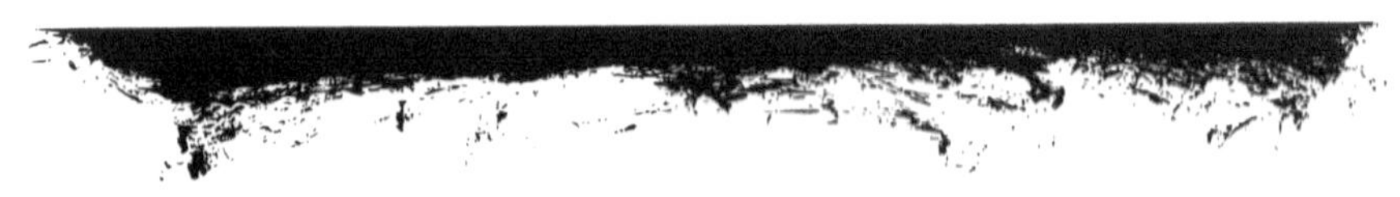

"**S**ing it, girl!" Friday at Five on WZMX had arrived. The heavy bass beats were pounding their way out of the Lexus' high-end sound system. Madison's head bobbed along as her fingers kept time on the rim of the steering wheel. Her mental starter's pistol had fired, propelling her toward the long-awaited weekend.

Madison had eased her way through the sloth-like traffic downtown and was now flying down the interstate, Dua Lipa's soaring voice riding shotgun. She had been making speedy progress until the traffic slowed to a painful crawl a few miles before her exit. "Come on, people. You're standing between me and an ice-cold margarita. Are you sure that's where you want to be?"

The traffic in the lane next to Madison began moving. "God! How come the traffic in the other lane is always faster?" As soon as she saw a space between the two vehicles to her left, she darted in. Predictably, she'd only gotten about ten yards when her current lane came to a stop and the one she'd abandoned started moving again. She remembered an Eagles song with the line, "Life in the fast lane... surely make you lose your mind." Her frustration became hostility; hostility became impatience. *Some people drive defensively*, she thought, *but I drive competitively!* As soon as she saw an opening in the right lane, she whipped in.

Ed Sheeran was crooning an R&B ballad through the speakers, the smooth melody washing away Madison's tension. She took a deep, cathartic breath and let her mind wander toward the evening out she'd be enjoying later with her boyfriend, Todd. She could almost hear the laughter and music in the bar, the tastes of craft beer and high-end cocktails, and the scent of expensive perfumes. She smiled at the sensory explosion... she glanced up at the rearview mirror... she saw the grill of the eighteen-wheeler; it was literally closer than it appeared. In the blink of an eye, the accident occurred: metal crumpling, glass exploding, and then nothingness.

The first sensation Madison experienced when she became conscious was confusion—*What just happened?* The second was intense pain—*How bad is this?* The third was terror—*Am I gonna die?* She heard the sounds of heavy traffic around her: horns bellowing, people yelling. "Oh my God—is she still alive?..." "Somebody call 911..." "We need to get her out of there..." "Stay back, it might blow up!" The pungent odor of charred rubber and steaming radiator fluid attacked her nostrils. As soon as she could think clearly, she went through a mental checklist of physical assessments. *Wiggle your fingers and toes.* She couldn't tell if they were moving. *Try speaking.* The best she could manage were choked gasps.

There was movement around her, feet scurrying over the asphalt. She tried to move, but felt pinned in by the metal enclosure. Her thoughts bounced around inside her head like a pinball. In order to calm herself, she imagined her activities after the nightmare ended and life resumed its normalcy. Thoughts of her mom and dad, two sisters, her many friends, and, of course, Todd comforted h er. *I'm not gonna die here. I'm comin' home as soon as whatever comes next happens*, she promised herself. Nausea filled her stomach; she was blanking out again.

Sometime later, her mind reawakened. Madison struggled to open her eyes. It took her a moment to recall the accident and its aftermath. She felt numb with cold. She had no sense of time.

*What am I still doing here? Why am I not in a hospital?* Again, she became aware of the tight metal enclosure in which she lay motionless. She attempted to cry out. Her thoughts became words, but her throat would not release them.

Finally, she felt some movement of the vehicle. Something lifted the wreckage and moved it forward. Her thoughts became hopeful. *They must be moving me off the interstate, where it'll be safer to work. I just need to hang on.* She patiently waited for the first responders' tools to free her from the mangled car. After a short time, she could distinguish faint words nearby. *What are they discussing?* she thought.

Then she experienced the sensation of being lowered. *Okay, here we go,* her mind told her.

She heard something soft raining down on top of the metal trap, followed by a profound silence. *What's happening? Where are they?* she asked herself.

Todd wept as he and Madison's loved ones left the cemetery.

# FIVE SECONDS OF TERROR

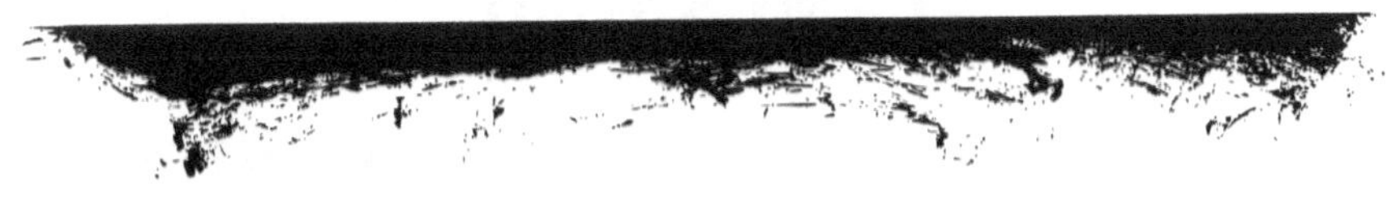

I enjoy looking at statues. That is until they start moving.

I've always been comfortable in my own skin. I'm even more so in other people's.

I love hearing my wife laugh. I only wish she'd put down the bone saw and untie me.

I slept with one eye open. The kidnapper had removed the other one.

I asked the organist to turn down his volume, but he didn't. I don't think he can hear me from my casket.

Who's the creepy old woman smiling and waving at me? And why is she in my bedroom this late at night?

I kissed my wife on her way out the door and told her to have a great day. Then she came downstairs and asked me whom I was talking to.

I played my dead girlfriend's favorite album today. When it finished, she asked me to play it again.

We stood together solemnly, as Uncle Larry's casket was lowered into the dusty earth. It was a shame Uncle Larry marred the moment by screaming to be let out.

# MADAM ONA'S SHOPPE OF CURIOSITIES: JIMMY'S STORY

## I

The stroll downtown to relax was having the opposite effect on Jimmy. It was loud, busy, too bright. It made it hard to breathe and think. The heavy weight of his career and personal obligations had beaten him down to a throbbing nub.

Jimmy's sales job was sucking his soul dry. His first year as a rep for Tannen Windows had been daunting but exciting. Because he was a rookie, they'd set the bar low. He could have coasted along, only meeting the expected sales quotas, but Jimmy had always been ambitious. Driven. The first year, he achieved double the number of sales he had been assigned. Impressed, his bosses upped his sales quotas the following year. Again, Jimmy slayed them, and again, the bosses increased his sales quotas. It was an endless cycle. Now, in year five, he struggled to meet the sky-high numbers. He had no social life, private life, or any other kind of life. *If it didn't take so much effort, I'd throw myself in front of a bus,* he often thought.

It was these worries that led him downtown on a simple Sunday morning. Jimmy meandered the bevy of Boston businesses, looking for what he didn't know. He just needed something to take his mind off things.

Soon, he saw a small shop that stood out in the bustling marketplace. It gave the impression of being older than it likely was. Something about it beckoned him, as if it were whispering, *You'll find peace here.* The etching on the door introduced it as Madam Ona's Shoppe of Curiosities.

Jimmy went to the door and peered inside. The store had no customers, just several short rows of items he couldn't make out from his vantage point. He looked at the store's sign again, but with more interest. *Curiosities,* he thought. *I'm curious all right.*

Jimmy entered and heard the delicate ding of a small overhead bell greeting him. He let his eyes check things out before allowing his feet to continue their journey further into the store. The sales floor was small but not cramped. The merchandise—a mingling of candles, figurines, powders, and elixirs—adorned the wooden shelving units in a neat arrangement. A pleasant mixture of strawberries and old wood drifted through the air like a fragrant breeze. He took a few steps further into the shop, but stopped when he detected a figure emerging from a back room to his left.

"Welcome," the woman said. "I'm Madam Ona, the proprietor. How may I serve you today?"

Madam Ona's smile conveyed graciousness and warmth, something that Jimmy appreciated. Needed.

"It's very nice to meet you, Madam Ona," Jimmy said. "I was just admiring your shop. It's unusual in a good way. Is it always this quiet?"

"Not always, but not busy, either. I get the feeling it suits you."

"You're very observant. I much prefer the quietness of your store to the craziness in the rest of this district. Fact is, I appreciate silence and calm wherever I can find it."

"I see," Madam Ona said, joining Jimmy near a rack of assorted jewelry beside the front counter. "I sense you have a need. You have an aura of weariness and despair. You feel overwhelmed, disheartened, and defeated. Would this be so?"

"You can tell all that by looking at me? How do you—"

"Everyone has a need, a desire. Some hide it so deep within themselves they aren't aware of it. But there are others such as you that carry so much pain and unhappiness that it seeps from their soul. What is your name, child?"

"James Louder, but everyone calls me Jimmy."

Madam Ona reached out and took Jimmy's hands in her own, her soft fingers wrapping around his in a soothing, motherly embrace. "Jimmy, what if I could free you from your burdens? I can, you know."

Jimmy was interested, but dubious. "And how would you do that?" he asked. "I've tried meditation, yoga, and creative self-medication. But then the alarm goes off the next morning and I'm right back where I started: a soul-crushing job that's taking away the best of me."

"That's a lot of strain for one man to bear alone. You probably wish there were another Jimmy to help out."

Jimmy sighed. "If only, Madam Ona... if only."

Madam Ona let go of one of Jimmy's hands, then tugging on the other said, "Follow me, child." She led him down an aisle stocked with unusual artifacts and jars of colorful liquids and jellies. She stopped halfway down, then turned to face Jimmy. Letting go of his hand, she picked up a small bottle of light blue liquid. "This is it."

"This is what?" Jimmy asked.

"What you need... desire. It's called Calaya. When used properly, it will remove stress from your busy life."

Wariness remained with Jimmy. "Have you sold many of these?"

"Quite a few, actually. A month ago, I sold a bottle to a young woman about your age. She was struggling to balance her life and her family's needs. Like you, she felt overwhelmed. I sold her some Calaya, and she became a new person. You, too, can become a new person. Will you take the cure? Will you become a new person, Jimmy Louder?"

"First, tell me how it works. Do I drink it?"

Madam Ona snickered. "Only if you want to get sick and throw up. The elixir doesn't work on the inside; it works on the outside."

"I don't understand."

"Right before bedtime, fill a bathtub full of warm water. Pour the liquid in and mix it well. Soak for at least twenty minutes. When you are finished, *do not* drain the tub—this is vital. By the next morning, the problem will be solved."

Jimmy felt like laughing at Madam Ona's claim, but her earnestness kept him in check. "What's going to happen overnight?" he asked. "Is this elixir some kind of hallucinogenic? How does this solve my problems?"

"Oh, so many questions. I understand your doubts. But ask yourself how far you'd go to bring peace and contentment back into your life? I am offering you a cure. Either you are interested, or you aren't. What is your decision?"

Jimmy compared a mental list of pros and cons.

Madam Ona shifted her weight from foot to foot, as her patience with Jimmy dwindled. "Perhaps I mistook your need. Thank you for dropping by. Please tell your friends they are welcome to visit as well. You do have friends, don't you, Jimmy? Or are you too busy and depressed to care?"

*Touche',* Jimmy thought. "How about this: If I buy a bottle and it doesn't work, I get a full refund. Can you live with that?"

"I can make a better deal. I will allow you to take the elixir without payment... for now. I am positive you will get the result you are looking for. When that happens, you can return to make payment.

"And the price is…"

"Five hundred dollars."

"And what if I don't return?"

"I trust you, Jimmy Louder. I believe that when you see how much better your life has become, you will pay what you owe. Is my trust misplaced?"

Her faith in his honor moved Jimmy. "No, ma'am. I always keep my word."

Madam Ona gave him the bottle. "Very good. I'll see you soon, Jimmy Louder." She turned and walked to an adjacent aisle, where she straightened some macabre figurines.

Jimmy placed the small bottle in his jacket pocket and headed home. Suddenly, he was in the mood for a nice, warm bath.

# 2

It was close to bedtime. Jimmy swished the bath water around, checking its temperature for comfort. He grabbed the bottle of cure from the counter and removed the cork. He sniffed the contents, hoping it didn't smell like a vulture's anus. "Not too bad. Smells like… cotton candy," he observed. He added a bit of the mixture to the water and stirred it until the water was pale blue, then he disrobed. "Here goes nothing."

Jimmy stepped into the bath, eased himself into the murky water, and reclined. The mixture was sticky, as if it were coating him, rather than cleansing him.

After soaking for twenty minutes, he climbed out and toweled off, something that was uncomfortable given the tacky residue covering his body. "Yuck. I look like a Smurf."

Jimmy wrapped the towel around his waist and went to his bedroom. He didn't want to stain the sheets, so he dressed in sweatpants and an old T-shirt. Lying in bed, he binge-watched the ceiling, attempting to relax enough to fall asleep. Tomorrow was going to be another hectic day at work, accompanied by trips to the dry-cleaner and gym, so he needed rest.

After an hour of tossing and turning, he still felt anxious. He waited for something—anything—to happen. *When am I going to feel different? I still feel like a stretched out pair of socks,* he thought. He felt the weight of disappointment resting on top of him like a wet quilt.

At last, the sleep that was so elusive began taking hold of him, making him drowsy. As he gave into the gentle tug of sleep, his last thought was of Madam Ona and her fervent promise. *Did you play me, Madam Ona? Will tomorrow really be any different from the last thousand or the next million hopeless days?* Soon, he'd have his answer.

# 3

The dream about still being at work roused him. It was the sound of movement in the bathroom that made him sit up.

*Swish, swish, splash*

Someone was in the bathroom.

Jimmy eased his legs over the side of his bed. His pulse quickened, and he remained as still and quiet as he could. His senses intensified with the sound of his pounding pulse, the cold sweat on his trembling body, and the raw smell of his fear.

Bare feet slapped against the bathroom's tile floor, then slid wetly to the door. The knob turned, and the door creaked open. Footsteps dragged past Jimmy's room, bringing about a fight-or-flight panic on him. The phantom footfalls traveled to the kitchen, followed by the sucking sound of the refrigerator door opening. He heard the intruder rummaging through its contents.

Jimmy's scared mind attempted to make sense of what was happening. He remembered the blue potion. Was it causing him to hallucinate, hear things that weren't real? Who or what might he encounter if he entered the kitchen? *I better go now while I still have the advantage of surprise,* he thought. He crept to his bedroom door and opened it with muted caution. Glistening, blue footprints trailing down the hall caught his eye.

Jimmy inched toward the kitchen, using the noises of the intruder's rustling, grunting, and chewing to conceal his presence. He stood still at the entrance, preparing himself to run if he had to.

The naked stranger had his back to Jimmy, cramming food from the fridge into his hungry mouth. The same residue that Jimmy had toweled off himself earlier coated him.

"Did... did Madam Ona send you here?" Jimmy asked, his voice quivering.

Upon hearing Jimmy's voice, the stranger froze. He didn't turn or answer. He looked like a mannequin that someone had dipped in blueberry jam.

"How did you get in here?" Jimmy asked. "Who are you?"

The man turned around and faced Jimmy.

Jimmy gulped, his spit thick as syrup. His body trembled and his breath came in shallow hitches, as he fought to keep his terror at bay. He recognized the stranger. He was looking at himself.

# 4

Jimmy helped the stranger clean up, then dressed him in a robe. "Let's have a chat, shall we?" Jimmy said, leading the stranger to the living room.

Once there, they sat across from each other, staring in curiosity and disbelief.

Jimmy jumpstarted the conversation. "How is this even possible? You look exactly like me.

Where did Madam Ona find you? I've gotta say I'm very impressed."

"Who's Madam Ona?" the stranger asked.

"She's a store owner," Jimmy explained. "She sells odd, mystical things. She lent me a bottle of potion that's supposed to relieve my stress. I poured it into the bath earlier, as she told me. I soaked for a bit, then went to bed. I heard you coming out of the bathroom and followed you to the kitchen."

"Yeah, I was hungry and thirsty. All I remember is waking up in a tub of water. I felt disoriented, wobbly. Somehow, I knew where to find food and drinks. And even though I've never been here before, I know every inch of this apartment. I think I'm supposed to be helping you. Trust me, I'm as confused as you are. Maybe together we can sort this all out."

After a moment of thought, the answer came to Jimmy, amazing him. "Oh, my gosh! I understand now. You're right about having a purpose. You *are* here to help me. My life has been a tangle of stress and responsibilities. There's been times when I thought about how terrific it would be to have a twin who could sometimes take my place. Madam Ona knew this; she sensed it right at the start. She said that I'd become a new person. I didn't think she meant it literally. This is going to be great! You're the answer to my problems!"

The stranger pinched the bridge of his nose and winced. He looked as if an immense headache had overtaken him.

Jimmy was concerned. "Hey, are you all right? You're not about to melt, are you?"

The stranger pulled in a few deep breaths and relaxed. Then his face displayed the same excitement as Jimmy's had when everything fell into place for him. "You're right. I can see it all. I'm here to share your burden. I know where you work and what you do there." He closed his eyes. Emotions immediately enveloped him as images of the past rushed through his mind in a blur of mental photographs, leaving him breathless. "I remember growing up as you. I see my first bike and my years as an Eagle Scout. I remember losing my virginity in college. Whoa! Was Mary Beth a tiger, or what? I see Mom and..." Tears rolled from his eyes; heartache slinked through his soul. "Dad," he choked. "God, how I miss him."

Jimmy felt the same haunting ache, barely managing to push it away. Once it subsided, he focused on ideas about how the new relationship could work. "Okay, we need to figure out a plan. How can we pull this off without getting caught?"

The new Jimmy gave it some thought. "Walk me through your typical day. I just need some details. I can handle the rest."

The doppelgänger listened to a thorough description of a day in the life of Jimmy Louder, only interrupting a few times with questions. The briefing ended a short while later.

"Thanks, Jimmy," the twin said. "I think I have enough information. Do you have any questions or suggestions?"

"What should I do while you're being me?" Jimmy asked.

"I don't know. My purpose is to give you some freedom. Take in a movie, go to the gym, become a couch potato. You officially have a thousand days off. Nevertheless, you should keep your phone handy, in case I need to ask you anything else."

The possibilities that his newfound liberty afforded him excited Jimmy. But his old friend/foe, known as practicality, barged through the door of his well-ordered mind. As a thinker and planner, he knew it was the little things that could send you sprawling face first onto the concrete, especially something that appeared too good to be true. His eyes squinted and his lips tightened, his facial expression belying his concerns.

"Something still bothering you?" his twin asked.

"Something's always bothering me," Jimmy moaned. "For example, do you know how to drive?"

New Jimmy leaned forward, a knowing grin on his face. "Jimmy, how many times do I have to explain to you that if you know how to do it, then I know how to do it? Not only can I drive that sad Kia, I can have its oil changed. It's not like you're ever going to get around to it. Maybe I can take care of that tomorrow after work."

"Whoa there, chief," Jimmy said, lifting his hands in a warding off gesture. "Who said anything about you taking over for me tomorrow? Don't you need some time to adjust?"

The doppelgänger smiled. "Jimmy, I'm fresh out of the box, and the batteries have been loaded. Now flip the on switch and let me get to it."

Jimmy had to admit he was eager to get started with the wild experiment. "Okay, then. Let's do this thing. First, you're going to need some work clothes and a few other items. Wait here."

Jimmy went to his bedroom, collected clothes, socks, underwear, and shoes, and took them to the living room, laying the items on the coffee table. "This should get you started. Will you need help to get ready in the morning?"

"No, but thanks anyway. Obviously, I know where the food and shower are, so I should be good to go."

"I can't believe this is actually happening," Jimmy chuckled. "My friend, I think this might be the start of a beautiful relationship. 'Course, this means I've got to double up on groceries and utilities."

"Hey, you're the one who gets to goof off every day," the double said.

Jimmy yawned, his drowsiness returning.

His double mirrored the yawn.

Jimmy rose from his chair. "I've lost track of time. We need to get some sleep. You get the couch. You don't snore, do you?"

"I don't know," said his double. "Do you snore?"

"How should I know? I'm always asleep. Extra blankets and pillows are in the hall closet. Knock yourself out."

Jimmy yawned again, scratching his sleep-tousled hair.

His twin did likewise.

*Creepy,* Jimmy thought. Then he said, "Okay, I'll see you tomorrow. Help yourself to whatever; just keep it down. Sleep well."

Then he returned to his bedroom, leaving his double to fend for himself.

As Jimmy slept, his double laid awake, ideas and memories flowing through his mind like an endless river. Then the dark thoughts came, and he grinned.

# 5

The ringing of his cellphone awakened Jimmy. He hadn't bothered setting his alarm, seeing as how he had no work to attend to. He looked at the wall clock and noted that he'd slept well into the afternoon. He answered his chirping phone. "Hello?" he asked, his voice slow and groggy.

"Hi there, brother," the doppelgänger said. "I wanted to touch base and let you know that, so far, everything is going great here at work. I was deliberately rude to that jerk, Larry, who works in H.R. But I was super nice to Ella from Accounting—you do like her, right?"

Jimmy rose and rested on an elbow. He liked what he was hearing. "That's great..." He paused, as it occurred to him that his double needed a name. It seemed silly calling him Jimmy Two or Mirror Man.

"Is something wrong?" the twin asked.

"We need to give you a name—nothing too far out there."

"I agree. Say, how about James? That's close enough for government work, don't you think?"

The thought of such little separation between them left Jimmy ill at ease. Still, he had no better idea. "Sure, that'd work fine—James, it is. But everywhere else, you're Jimmy, understand?"

"Understood," James said. "Listen, I have an idea about you hooking up with Ella. I know you're nervous about asking her out, but I'm comfortable handling it."

"Gee, I don't know James. It might not be wise for me—I mean you—to rush things. I'm not comfortable having you write checks that I can't cash. Besides, I want to be the one who starts things off with her. She's important to me."

"Gotcha. But if you change your mind…"

"I'll let you know," Jimmy said, before adding, "Don't you have some work to do? My boss wants those sales reports done by—"

"Already done," James said.

Jimmy imagined James smirking as he said it. "Good, because the next thing hanging over our heads is—"

"… putting together the flow charts for your presentation at Friday's meeting," James finished. "I completed them half an hour ago. Oh, and forget about those emails you haven't had the opportunity to reply to—your inbox is empty. All I have left to do is to set up the zoom calls for the Branski and Lillard accounts. We've gotta close those deals, and I know just how to do it. Can you smell those outrageous commissions yet?"

Jimmy was wordless and impressed. Then the old, familiar doubt reared its head. "Are you messing with me?" he asked. "You've accomplished all that since eight o'clock this morning?"

"No, that's what I've accomplished since I rolled in at six a.m." James gushed.

Jimmy grew concerned. "Look, James, I appreciate your conscientiousness, but you're making it hard for me to maintain that rapid pace when I get back to work."

James chuckled. "What do you mean by 'get back to work'? Jimmy, you don't ever have to come back here to this pressure cooker. Leave everything to me. I'll make you look like a rock star."

Jimmy had to admit that James was lifting a great weight off his shoulders. Still, it felt too good to be true. He looked at his bedroom clock. 4:07 p.m. His day was beginning while James' had not yet ended. He felt a brief twinge of guilt.

James interrupted his thoughts. "Yo, Jimmy—you there?"

"Yeah, I'm here. So this means I can read a book, take in a movie, or go back to sleep?"

"That's what I'm saying, Jimbo."

Jimmy grinned at the possibilities until he realized James had the keys to the apartment and Kia.

James sensed the shift in Jimmy's mood. "What's wrong now?" he asked.

"I presume you drove to work this morning?" asked Jimmy.

"Oh, I see where you're going with this. Don't worry, I didn't leave you stranded. I grabbed enough for bus fare out of your wallet. I locked the doorknob instead of the deadbolt when I left, so I didn't need house keys. There you go—no more excuses."

Jimmy felt good again. "Well, in that case, you better get back to work. If I head out for a while, I'll leave a key under the welcome mat. Just make sure to put it back for me so I can get in."

Jimmy felt good again. "Well, in that case, you better get back to work. If I head out for a while, I'll leave a key under the welcome mat. Just make sure to put it back for me so I can get in."

"Sounds like a plan, Jimbo. Have a great afternoon."

The phone call ended, and Jimmy went back to sleep, feeling lighter than air.

# 6

Jimmy returned home from his excursion around ten o'clock that evening. He let himself in, then threw his keys on the kitchen counter and sorted through the mail that James must've brought in when he had returned home. He looked for James, but didn't see him. He wasn't in the living room or the kitchen. Jimmy was about to call out for him when he heard the distant splashing of water coming from the bathroom. He went there and rapped on the door. "Hey, James, you in there?"

The splashing stopped, but there was no reply. James tapped on the door again. "Are you okay? James?"

The twin's voice floated through the door. "I'm fine. Don't come in here," he groused.

Jimmy was surprised by James' ill temperament. "Why not? It's not as if I haven't seen myself naked before."

"Does this mean I'll have no privacy?"

James' petulant tone was unexpected. Something was off; Jimmy felt it in the trepidation that had come over him. "Of course not," he said. "After all you're doing to help ease the load, I'm sure I can afford you some time for yourself."

"Thank you, Jimmy. I appreciate that."

The matter being settled, Jimmy went to his bedroom to undress and settle into something comfortable for the night.

When he came out, James was sitting on the sofa in his robe, staring ahead at nothing. His face was expressionless, his body still, as if he were in a trance.

"James?" Jimmy asked, his voice tinged with wariness. "How ya doin', buddy?"

There was no response at first. Then all at once, James broke free of his reverie and smiled at Jimmy, as though someone had flipped his happy switch. "I'm doing great. How was your day off, Ferris Bueller?"

"What do you think? It was fantastic, thanks to you, my industrious friend. But listen: Take things slower at work. Part of the reason I'm stressed is that I got off to too fast a start and closed a lot of sales. Now, my bosses expect me to build upon that every quarter. Don't give them a reason to put more work on you. If you're not careful, you're going to hit the same wall I did, and that doesn't help either of us. Do you understand where I'm coming from?"

James considered Jimmy's concerns. "I see your point, but you have to accept that this version of you *can* handle the increased responsibilities. I can make you such an indispensable part of the organization that they'll have no choice but to move you upstairs. From what I heard from the watercooler trolls, there's not a lot of work going on up there. Their idea of improving the company is to play golf with ritzy clients, attend junkets in Las Vegas, and yell at their subordinates. I'm here to help you, Jimmy, not make your life worse. You need to get onboard with that, or else why did you bring me here?"

James had made a good point. Why had he given James a life if he didn't want to improve the quality of his own? "Okay, you win," Jimmy said. "I'm going to let go and trust you to be the better version of me. Just keep me in the loop, okay?"

James shifted in his seat, embarrassment registering on his face. "Uh... about that..."

"What did you do?" Jimmy asked with concern.

"Well, remember when you said not to interact with Ella?"

"Jaaames..."

"I kind of—sort of—asked her out."

Anger converged with panic. "Oh, come on, James! I told you to leave that to me! See? This is what I meant about taking things too fast and keeping me informed. What were you thinking?"

James stood and stepped closer to Jimmy, locking their gazes, and speaking in a commiserating manner. "Jimbo, you deserve to be happy. I knew you'd never get around to asking her out; you're afraid to take chances. And let's face it: You're not exactly suave and sophisticated. Besides, I didn't completely disobey you. I'm only teeing up the ball. She agreed to meet me for drinks tomorrow night at Nightingales. Trust me, Jimbo—I'm gonna make a playa out of you. How's that for service?"

Jimmy's frustration dissipated. "You're right, I don't take enough chances. I guess in my line of work, I'm always on the verge of failure. Just promise me you'll be a gentleman. I really care for Ella. I want her to get the best version of me."

"That's what I'm trying to do—make a better world for a better Jimmy. Now then, what shall we do tonight?"

"I usually watch TV," Jimmy said. "I'm a big fan of those unsolved crime shows."

"Ah yes," James said, nodding his head. "There's nothing more relaxing than watching the equivalent of murder porn." He and Jimmy shared a laugh over the remark and settled together on the sofa.

A couple hours later, tiredness beckoned them to bed.

Jimmy hadn't been asleep for long when he heard splashing water. "A little late for a bath," he remarked to himself. The splashing became increasingly louder, eventually resembling a chaotic thrashing. Jimmy got up and jogged to the bathroom.

"James! Are you okay in there?" Jimmy attempted to turn the doorknob, but it was locked. He pounded on the door. "James, open the door! James!" The door groaned as it slowly opened. The bathroom nightlight had given up its faint, golden hue to a sinister red. From where Jimmy stood, no one was in the bathtub. Terror gripped him. "James?" he whispered.

A slimy blue arm flopped over the side of the tub with a moist thump.

Jimmy didn't want to go any closer, but his body took on a mind of its own, dragging his feet forward. With each terrifying step, his blood chilled within his shivering soul. He came to the tub and peered into it.

A dark, human-like form was lying beneath the pale blue water. Its open, luminescent eyes were like a cat's caught in the beam of light. Air bubbles drifted from its slitted nostrils to the surface.

Jimmy leaned over the tub, his fear-laden lungs firing heavy breaths through his trembling lips. "J-J-James?"

The blue, mottled creature sprang up and grabbed Jimmy, yanking him into the slimy water. Jimmy screamed, then—

He woke from the blood-freezing nightmare and clawed his way from under the covers. Jimmy stumbled through the shadows of his dimly lit bedroom, the cold floor frosting his bare feet. The pounding of his hammering heart echoed in his ears as the remnants of the horrid nightmare clung to his fevered mind. *Where the hell did that come from?* he thought. After a few minutes, his breathing slowed and his body untensed. His dry throat begged for water. He got up and went to his bedroom door, easing it open so as not to wake James.

Jimmy sneaked his way to the kitchen and filled a glass with tap water, finishing it in three large gulps. He muffled a burp into his clenched hand and placed the empty glass in the sink.

As he navigated the shadow-soaked living room, he felt compelled to check on James, if only to show himself that his twin hadn't turned into an alien terror. The numbing nightmare had left a residue of anxiety on his psyche—a pale blue stain, to be exact.

Jimmy slid his feet lightly over the carpet until he reached the edge of the sofa where James lay sleeping. As he stared at James, he remembered the vivid nightmare and James' troubling reaction from earlier, as if he had caught him planning something sinister. "*What are you up to, James?*" he thought.

James startled Jimmy when he suddenly rolled over on his side, exposing his back. There was enough light for Jimmy to notice a bold blue line behind each ear. They were about a half inch in width and followed the curve of the ear. *What are those?* he wondered. *Guess we're not so identical after all.*

When he'd seen enough, Jimmy returned to his bed and lay on top of the sweat-soaked covers. Despite his efforts, the terrible images from earlier clung to him like oil, robbing him of his sleep—his peace. *Should I be afraid of you, James?* Paranoia burrowed into his mind like a hungry worm, leaving him uncertain and on edge. Then, as if to confirm his darkest suspicions, the words of Stephen King came to him: "Perfect paranoia is perfect awareness." *That it is, Stephen,* Jimmy thought. *That it is.*

# 7

As the blackness of the night gave way to the golden tinge of dawn, Jimmy finally fell asleep.

A short time later, the sound of James milling about the apartment woke Jimmy from his all too brief slumber. Wearily, he crawled out of bed, stretching broadly, and rubbing his scratchy eyes.

James was whirring about the apartment like a frantic fly looking for a way out of a window.

"Where are you, ya stupid key card?" he mumbled, as he looked under the sofa cushions and beneath the coffee table.

Jimmy slipped past him unnoticed and went to the kitchen. He took a bowl from the cabinet, filled it with Honey Nut Cheerios, and doused it with the milk he pulled from the fridge. Then he took a spoon from the silverware drawer and plopped onto a kitchen chair. He had fed the first bite of cereal into his mouth when James popped in.

"Found it," James said, holding up the plastic key card that allowed him access to the elevator in the parking deck of the building that housed Tannen Windows. "Hey, listen. I'll need to borrow the keys to the Kia. I can't get to the restaurant tonight in a rickshaw, can I?"

"Oh, right," Jimmy said, slumping over his breakfast. "I almost forgot about the date with Ella. Do you have everything under control?"

"No problems there," James assured him. "I'm going to leave work a bit early, get a haircut, and do a power workout. I'll shower and change at the gym. That'll give me time to get to the restaurant early so I can get the lay of the land. Also, I want her to think that I arrived early because I couldn't wait to see her. That should put us on her radar," he said slyly.

"Please be gentlemanly and don't lay it on too thick," Jimmy said. "If she agrees to see me again, I don't want her expectations to be too high. Which clothes did you pick out? You're not going to dress like a slob, are you?"

"Would you dress like a slob?" James asked.

"No."

"Then neither will I—I have your taste in clothes, remember? Hey, you're going to look great tonight, so no worries. You aren't nervous, are you?"

"Nervous? Try terrified. Tell me again that you're not going to blow it tonight with Ella."

"Geez, Jimbo. I'm not going to blow it tonight with Ella. She was quite open to the idea of meeting you for dinner and drinks. Just relax and think good thoughts."

*I have thoughts, my friend, but they ain't good,* Jimmy mused.

James noticed The Thoughtful Jimmy Look. "Don't fret, Jimbo. Remember: I'm going to be the new and improved Jimmy."

"Yeah, yeah, I remember."

James smiled with satisfaction, like a salesman who'd made the tough sale. "Now you're talking," he said. He grabbed his garment bag, snagged the keys from the counter, and left Jimmy to his breakfast.

Jimmy finished eating, then rinsed out his bowl, leaving it in the sink. He showered and dressed, then took a long walk to clear his head. He still worried that Ella might be scared away by James and his annoying overzealousness. He hoped he was wrong.

# 8

Jimmy had been strolling through a small business area near his apartment for the last few hours. The quaint and eclectic collection of stores included a thrift store, a vintage guitar shop, a used bookstore, and several other private purveyors of all things cheap and interesting.

Before Jimmy knew it, it was late afternoon, and he was famished. He wanted something high in protein, so he stopped in a deli situated along the shady, calm stretch of sidewalk.

Despite it being past most people's lunch hour, the store was buzzing with activity. He looked with sympathy at the two employees who were running the counter, ringing up sales, and filling the food orders by themselves. The dozen or so people who wanted their order five minutes ago outmatched them. There was yelling and tension. *God, how do those poor employees stand this?* Jimmy thought. Then, despite the deafening din of chaos, Jimmy noticed something peculiar, yet impressive: While everyone else was agitated and impatient, the two employees maintained serenity and focus. It was as if they were only dealing with a couple of people in line. The ruder the customers were, the more the two smiled—warm, genuine smiles. In meeting the loud demands, they were efficient, not rushed. When they thanked each customer, they seemed to mean it. Nothing disturbed them. They were simply... happy.

When Jimmy got to the counter, there were only a few customers left behind him. He got the same cordial greeting that the previous customers had received.

"Thank you for choosing Goldman's Deli, sir. What would you like today? And please, take your time. There's no rush," the young man said.

The next customer stepped to the counter next to him and received the same polite greeting from the female employee.

"Um, let's see," Jimmy pondered. "I'll take a Turkey and Swiss sub on wheat bread, along with lettuce, tomatoes, onions, and mustard. Oh, and a bottle of water, please."

The employee inputted the transaction into the cash register. "That'll be $7.40, sir." After taking Jimmy's money, he said, "Make yourself comfortable. I'll let you know as soon as your sandwich is ready. I'm Ricky. If you need anything else, just say the word, and I'll get it taken care of right away."

Jimmy decided that if anyone deserved a proper, heartfelt attaboy, it was Ricky. "I appreciate that, Ricky," he said. "You know, I'm very impressed with you and your coworker. No matter how crazy things got, you two were calm, polite, and professional. I don't know what you're getting paid, but both of you deserve a r aise."

Ricky's face brightened even further. "That is very, very kind of you to say, sir. I absolutely adore working at the deli, especially when it's busy. Isn't that right, Marchelle?"

Marchelle was smiling ear to ear. "I wouldn't want to work anywhere else. In fact, I agreed to work extra hours this weekend to cover for Tyler. He never seems to want to work."

"Oh my gosh, what a coincidence," Ricky said. "I'm coming in early that morning cos Terrence is gonna be running late again. What can I say? I'm a company man through and through."

"Wow, you two sure are team players, all right," Jimmy said.

"Yes siree," beamed Ricky. "I'm always happy to serve. Speaking of which..." He turned and went to a metal prep counter stocked with various ingredients and breads. Marchelle soon joined him there.

Jimmy stepped aside for the next customer but stayed near the counter while his sub was being prepared. He watched as Ricky and Marchelle expertly pieced together each sandwich, all the while whistling. Jimmy grinned, as he continued to be amazed at the young employees' positive attitudes and talent. But he stopped grinning when he noticed the bold blue line on the backs of their ears.

# 9

**12:08 a.m.**

Throughout the evening, Jimmy remained distracted. He'd tried watching TV and reading, but his concerns wouldn't give him the respite he was seeking. Was there a connection between the markings on the deli employees and the ones on James? More worrisome, he was wondering what was happening with Ella. *I'd have had her home by now,* he thought. He lay in bed, jittery and troubled. He nearly leaped from his skin when he heard the key turning in the front door lock. He held his breath, listening. He got up and went to the door, pulling it open far enough to see into the living room.

James took off his shoes to minimize the noise and crept into the living room like a thief. He stripped naked, then folded his clothes and laid them on the coffee table.

Jimmy was about to go out and ask him how things had gone, but stopped when he got a closer look at James' body. He gasped at the dry and withered skin that was hanging off in opaque patches. It was as if James had been trapped in the desert. He reminded Jimmy of a petrified mummy. Jimmy closed his door as James walked past.

James entered the bathroom and turned on the tub's faucet. He held his fingers under the water flow until the temperature felt right, then climbed in and relaxed.

On the other side of the bathroom wall, Jimmy sat anxiously on his bed, trying to make sense of the strange goings on. Troubling questions plagued his mind. *Why is his skin flaking off like scales? What's wrong with him? Is that why he needs to soak his body every night?*

After about twenty minutes, the whishing of the water stopped, followed by the sound of it swirling down the drain. Jimmy heard James leave the bathroom and enter the living room. He waited for a moment, then cracked his door and peeked through the sliver. He saw that James' skin had returned to normal, like a wilting flower saved by the rain.

James sighed with contentment as he stretched out on the sofa and pulled the blanket to his chin.

Jimmy wondered how the date with Ella had gone, though worried was more like it. Caution told him to wait till morning to find out, so he crawled into bed and fell asleep. The sound of gentle crying haunted his dreams.

# 10

Something crashing to the floor startled Jimmy awake. He got out of bed and went to investigate.

He entered the kitchen and saw James leaning against the counter, staring at a shattered coffee mug on the floor. The twin looked mournful and worried.

"Glad that isn't my favorite mug," Jimmy quipped.

James didn't respond, didn't move.

"Did something go wrong last night?" Jimmy asked.

James continued staring down at the broken mug. "Sorry, Jimbo," he muttered. "Turns out she's not that into you after all."

Jimmy's stomach flipped at the news. "What happened? Did you say anything to offend her? I told you not to push too hard."

James sprang at Jimmy. He glowered at him as he stood toe to toe, his eyes smoldering with anger.

Jimmy refused to look into those eyes—eyes of rage, eyes of malice. He felt James' hot breath huffing on his face, mingling with the icy sweat that was there, making him shiver.

"You know, Jimbo," James growled through gritted teeth, "sometimes there is no perfect you. It's like trying to make chicken salad out of chicken crap."

Jimmy backed away. "I'm sorry, James. I'm just really disappointed. You're right; I set you up for failure. I shouldn't have expected so much from you."

James relaxed, as the tension drained from his body. "You know what, Jimbo? I think I'm going to take the day off—do some thinking."

Jimmy was hesitant to ask the question trapped in his throat. "Think about... what?"

James turned and went into the living room, dropping onto the sofa littered with his crumpled pillow and wrinkled blanket.

Jimmy followed him, repeating his prior question. "Think about what, James?"

James was pensive. "I think it's time for a new adventure. I've experienced enough of your life to know that you're holding yourself back." He leaped from the sofa, his face gleaming with excitement, then grabbed Jimmy by his shoulders. "Think of it, Jimbo: We can just pack up whatever we can cram in that godawful car of yours and drive until we find a place to start all over—a new life with a new you. What do you think?"

Jimmy's emotions wavered between suspicion and apprehension. What was happening? Had he allowed James to wield too much power? Something was different; something was wrong. He felt it in his bones. He wanted some time to think things through, to find answers. He needed to stall. "That's a lot to think about, James," he said, trying to minimize the nervous quaver in his voice. "Why don't you clean up the mess in the kitchen and make yourself another cup of coffee? I'm going to hit the head."

James looked skeptical, saying nothing. Each second of silence felt eternal, like an endless flow of time. Then: "Yeah, I'll do that. Would you like a cup?"

Jimmy felt like he could breathe again. "Yeah, that'd be great. Give me extra—" He saw the look of exasperation on James' face. "Right—you know how I take my coffee."

"Jimbo, when are you going to learn that I know what makes you tick?"

His words frosted Jimmy. "Of course you do. Well, duty calls." He left James and went into the bathroom, closing, then locking the door.

As Jimmy was urinating, he glanced at the inside of the bathtub. Despite rinsing out the tub after his soak, James had missed some moist flakes of skin collected around the drain. Jimmy finished urinating and rolled off a foot's length of toilet paper, which he used to remove the scales. He held them close to his eyes, examining them, wondering what he was seeing. *What are you, James?* He thought of confronting the imposter, but remembered the dark, intimidating side of him he'd shown earlier in the kitchen. Still, he needed answers—answers that James might not be willing to provide. To find out what James had been doing, he decided to go to the office. *And just how are you going to pull that off, Houdini?* he asked himself. His nerves felt taut, like piano wires. He jumped when the voice bellowed from the kitchen.

"Hey, Jimbo! Did you fall in? Coffee's getting cold!"

Jimmy had seconds to decide what was going to happen next. *We don't know anything yet,* he thought. *Act naturally until you decide what to do.* He wadded the sample up and tossed it in the wastebasket. Then he flushed, washed his hands, and took a deep, soothing breath before joining James in the kitchen.

"Here you go, brother," James chirped, passing the hot mug of coffee to Jimmy.

*Play it cool,* Jimmy told himself. "Thanks, I can sure use this. I've got a busy day ahead."

"Really?" James asked between sips. "What do you have planned?"

The question caught Jimmy off guard. He panicked as his imagination shifted into overdrive. He was relieved by the quickness of a plausible reply. "I was thinking that, since you're taking the day off, I might drive to Ipswich. Maybe I'll visit Guthrie Center or do some window shopping. I'll decide when I get there."

James squinted at him, his eyes teeming with doubt. "Since when do we like visiting out-of-town stores and museums?"

Jimmy paused. He took a long sip of coffee to buy himself some time before answering. "I've decided to take a page from your playbook. I'm trying new things."

James grinned. "Now that's what I want to hear. I'm telling you, Jimbo, there's a big old world of possibilities out there for us. I'm going to make a new man out of you yet."

"I wish you the best on that one," Jimmy said with faux pleasantness. "I think I'll get dressed and head on out—let you enjoy some downtime. You've been running yourself ragged. You look exhausted."

James considered the idea. "Yeah, I could use some rest. I didn't sleep well last night. Like you said, I'm exhausted."

"Good," Jimmy said, retreating to his bedroom. He got dressed in casual business attire while James called the office. When he came out, fifteen minutes later, he found James passed out on the sofa. *Thank God—an easy escape,* he thought.

Tip toeing past the sofa, Jimmy stealthily collected his keys and opened the front door. He was about to step out when a voice came from the living room like a phantom wind.

"Hold on a minute there, Jimbo. I'm thinking it might be fun to tag along. What do you think?"

Jimmy's body twitched as if a hot electrical current had passed through it. He gulped thick spittle, as his brain rushed through believable excuses for not taking James along on the imaginary trek. Fortunately, his imagination whizzed to the rescue again. "Shouldn't you be planning our next great adventure? I'm dying to hear all about it tonight."

"Ooh, yeah. That's a terrific idea you have there. I like the way you think. Have a great day, Jimbo."

"Thanks," Jimmy said. He closed, then locked the door. He took a moment to let his overwrought nerves settle before heading downstairs to his car. He needed to stay on top of things. He had an office visit to make.

# 11

Jimmy nearly forgot about how difficult it was to find a place to park on the large parking deck. Fortunately, he found one close to the building's elevator. He turned off the engine and collected his thoughts. He realized the need to pick up where James had left off without missing too many beats; otherwise, he might draw attention. *I hope I don't blow my cover,* he worried.

Jimmy climbed from the car and was about to slam the door shut when he noticed something in the backseat. It looked like a piece of cloth to Jimmy, but he wasn't certain. He opened the rear door, leaned inside, and grabbed it. It was a six inch long, thin strip of fabric with a yellow floral pattern. Upon further inspection, he found a dark smudge, but the dim garage made it difficult to tell what it was. He eased out of the car and straightened up, holding the cloth strip closer to his face. The stain was crimson. He gasped and dropped it, watching in horror as it performed a feather float to the smooth concrete. "Oh my God," Jimmy muttered to himself. "What did you do, James? What did you do to Ella?"

Jimmy bolted to the elevator that would deposit him in the lobby of Tannen Windows on the third floor. Inside, he kept jabbing the third-floor button as if doing so would make the elevator go faster.

When the elevator doors swished open, Jimmy walked briskly to Ella's cubicle. Along the way, his co-workers stared at him. There was no 'hello'—no 'how are you?' Jimmy saw one of his work buddies, Taron, heading his way. *Finally, a friendly face,* he thought.

"Morning, Taron," Jimmy said casually, trying to conceal his distress.

Taron ignored Jimmy, as if Jimmy were invisible. Taron shoulder-bumped him as he passed by, throwing Jimmy off balance, then kept going, leaving Jimmy mortified. "Hey, Taron, what the hell?"

Without stopping or looking back, Taron gave Jimmy an over-the-shoulder bird.

*This can't be good,* Jimmy thought. As he speed-walked to Ella's space, he passed by another office neighbor, Anya, who was typing on her keyboard. "Somebody's working hard," he quipped. He paused when he heard her whisper, "Butthole." He opened his mouth to say something in response, but let the matter go. He had business that was more important—the business of Ella.

Jimmy jittered as he hovered outside Ella's cubicle, working up the nerve to enter and talk to her. When he finally peeked inside, the space was empty. His knees tottered, and he thought he might throw up. *God, please let her be okay,* he begged.

Hoping to find answers, he headed toward his own cubicle. Perhaps James had unknowingly left some clues behind.

Jimmy traveled around the corner and into his space, where he sat down at his small desk. It was far more neat and organized than he remembered. *James: ever the eager beaver,* he thought. He noticed the blinking yellow light on his desk phone, showing he had messages. He picked up the receiver, placed it to his ear, and poked the flashing button.

"You have twenty-one missed messages," the female voice informed him. "First message..."

"Hey, jackass," the gruff voice said. "You promised me that the first shipment of windows would arrive this past Thursday. Where are they? If I were you, I'd quit ducking my calls and make this problem go away. I play golf with your company's vice president. I'm sure *he'd* take my calls."

Jimmy trudged through ten more messages that followed the same path. James had been over promising and under delivering. *No wonder his sales are going through the roof,* Jimmy thought. He hung up the phone and went to see David Munch, a solid salesman and sometimes confidant.

Along the way, he kept his eyes forward; the hateful stares were tough to tolerate. He felt like a serial pedophile doing a perp walk.

He was relieved to find David in his cubicle working. "Knock, knock. You have a minute?" Jimmy asked.

David looked up from his desk. His face fell in disgust. "What the hell do you want, brown-noser? Running out of people to screw over?"

His harsh words stung Jimmy. Their working relationship had always been pleasant. Clearly, that had changed. "David, what are you talking about? Why's everyone giving me the skunk eye?"

"Why do you think, Jimmy? You steal all the good sales leads, promise clients the sun and the moon, then screw them over as well. And now you're angling for that sales executive opening. You know how much that job means to me. What's happened to you, Jimmy? We used to be friends."

Jimmy felt betrayed himself. But what was he going to say—*Sorry, but my magical twin has bent all of us over our desks.* "David, I'm so sorry about everything," Jimmy said. "I've been struggling lately, not that that's an excuse. Look, I'll contact those angry clients and tell them I messed up. I'll ask every one of them to allow you to handle their accounts; that should drive up your sales. As for that promotion, I don't deserve it; you do. I'll do everything in my power to help the suits see that you're the only person in sales who can do the job right. How am I doing so far?"

David looked unmoved by Jimmy's change of heart. Then his skeptical scowl softened. "I guess everyone deserves a second chance. But good luck making things right with everyone else. You can't treat your co-workers like trash and expect them to like you again." He sighed. "But then again, they're good people, and good people know how to forgive, even if it's a moron like you."

Jimmy felt a glimmer of hope that things had not passed the point of no return. Suddenly, Ella and the bloody sliver of fabric returned to his mind like a bolt of horror. "Say, David, is Ella around?"

"I don't know. I haven't seen her yet. Try her cubicle."

"Are you guys talking about Ella?" This was Patti Wright from next door.

"Yeah. Is she here? I really need to talk to her," Jimmy said.

"I heard Barry telling someone that she called in sick this morning."

Barry was the floor supervisor.

"Don't know what's up with that," Patti added. "That girl's a workaholic."

Queasy and wobbling, Jimmy leaned against a partition. "I really need to tell her something. It's important. If you happen to have her phone number, I'd like to give her a call. I can find out how she's feeling while I'm at it."

"Give me a sec," Patti said. She scrolled through her contacts for the number.

"What happened last night?" David whispered. "Word is you two had a secret date planned."

Jimmy didn't answer—couldn't answer.

"Here you go," Patti said, handing Jimmy a pink post-it with Ella's phone number scribbled on it.

"Thanks, Patti," Jimmy said while taking the post-it.

"Tell her we miss her and hope she feels better soon," Patti said.

"Will do. Thanks again," Jimmy said.

When Patti disappeared back into her cave, Jimmy returned to David. "Thanks to you, too, for leveling with me. My particular brand of bull crap is over and done."

"I'm glad to hear that, Jimmy. Up until now, Ella was your only friend left. Tell her I said hi."

"You got it, bud," Jimmy said before returning to his cubicle. He sat down, dialed the number on the post-it, and listened for the ring. His heart leaped when someone picked up.

"Hello?" asked the lifeless murmur on the other end of the line.

*Thank God, she's still alive,* Jimmy thought. He wasn't sure where to begin. "Hi, Ella. It's Jimmy. I heard you called in sick. You sound a little rough. Are you okay?"

There was a quiet pause, followed by a pathetic whimper. "I told you last night, I'm not going to make any trouble for you. I didn't go to the hospital or the police. I just need some time to heal up. Please, you got what you wanted. Just leave me alone, so I can try to get enough of my self-respect back to return to the world. Why can't you just... just..." Ella's painful sobbing sounded like that of a hysterical trauma victim, which, of course, she was.

Jimmy's heart flooded with despair; he shook with guilt and rage. What had James done to her? *The animal raped her. That's what he did to her,* he thought. Tears pooled in his eyes. He could barely speak, but knew he had to. "Ella—oh my God, Ella. I am so, so sorry for what happened to you. I'm gonna set things right. He's gonna pay for this."

"Who? Who's gonna pay for this?" Ella yelled. "Someone is already paying for this: *meeee*! That was the deal, right? I keep my mouth shut and you don't cut my throat. At least that's what you said when you held it to my throat. I'm begging you, leave me in peace."

"Ella, I—"

Ella ended the call.

Jimmy stared at the phone in his hand. He closed his eyes and gritted his teeth in anger. He slammed the phone against its base so hard it cracked. "You're going to die, you bastard," he growled. "And then I'm going to have a word with Madam Ona."

He rushed from his cubicle, almost pancaking Barry.

"Whoa there, son," Barry said. "I thought you weren't coming in today. What with Ella out, I thought some bug might be going around."

Exasperation filled Jimmy's voice as he spoke. "Yeah, I thought I'd picked up something, but it turned out to be a bad choice of food," he blurted. "Look, Barry, my stomach is a raging mess, so I think I'll take a sick day after all. I'm sure whatever I have will pass."

"I hope it does, Jimmy. In fact, I was coming to see you about something concerning. I've been getting complaints from your coworkers and a couple of prospective clients. We really need to talk about this. When will you be back?"

Jimmy was shaking and perspiring. He was standing in front of Barry, but in his mind's eye, his body was in his car, racing toward James with violent intentions. "I don't know, Barry. Soon, very soon. Now, if you'll excuse me..." Jimmy pushed past Barry and jogged to the elevator.

On the way down to the parking deck, he went through a few scenarios for killing James. But first, he had to overcome a major hurdle: James might already be sensing the danger. Jimmy thought of the iconic religious acronym WWJD, then asked himself, "What would James do?"

# 12

By the time Jimmy made it upstairs to the apartment, his fury had turned to fear—fear of what James was capable of. He hated himself for his cowardice. He stood in front of the apartment door, fidgeting with the keys in his hand. He willed his dancing nerves to still. *There's always the chance he may not know what you know. Just be cool. There's no need to rush this*, he thought. When he felt ready, he unlocked the door and entered the apartment.

James was lying on the sofa, watching TV. Without looking up, he said, "How were things in Ipswich?"

Jimmy's anger returned. He pushed it down into his guts, where it churned like bubbling lava. The innocuous question reminded him he might have the advantage of James' ignorance, something that could buy him enough time to devise a clever plan. "Lovely as ever," Jimmy said nonchalantly. "I wish you'd have come along after all."

James rose from the sofa, then stretched and yawned. "What'd you do first?"

Jimmy felt as if he were taking a pop quiz. "Um, let me think. Oh, I was famished by the time I got there, so I had some lunch."

James's face became slack, his eyes unreadable, unsettling. "What did you have?" he asked with a hint of suspicion.

Jimmy hesitated too long. "A cheeseburger... with sweet potato fries. Oh, and an iced tea. They have the best iced tea."

James crossed his arms over his chest. "Who has the best iced tea? You didn't say."

*He's on to me,* Jimmy thought. He feigned offense. "Why all the questions? I'm starting to think you don't believe me."

James' accusing eyes locked with Jimmy's. "Your jaw muscles are tense; you're also tapping your leg. I believe that's always been our tell in tense situations. Are you sure there's nothing troubling you? Why do I feel like you're keeping something from me? If you have something you'd like to get off your chest, just say it."

Tingles of terror began at the bottom of Jimmy's feet and slid like icy vines up his legs and to his groin. *Calm... calm... calm...* he reminded himself. With effort, he maintained eye contact with James, hoping that he wouldn't see the fear in his eyes, the mirrors of his soul. Using humor as a gambit, he joked, "Okay, you caught me. I can't live with the guilt another second. I ate an entire Snickers bar on the way up so I wouldn't have to share. But God help me, guilt never tasted so good. I'm afraid of what I might do next."

Though it was only a few seconds, it seemed like hours before James responded. "You should be afraid," he said menacingly. Then he grinned and chuckled good-naturedly. "I've been using your toothbrush to clean around my toenails."

Jimmy was relieved the ruse had worked. "That's okay. I farted on the TV remote," he said, chortling along with James.

James stopped laughing and began scratching his arms and neck as if he had fleas. "You know, Jimbo, I believe I'm going to have myself a long, hot bath. My skin's been feeling dry and itchy lately."

*I'll bet it has, you freak,* Jimmy thought. Then he said, "Have at 'er. I think I'm gonna crack a cold beer."

"Sounds good; save one for me," James said. He turned and walked to the bathroom. When he got there, he stopped. "Jimmy, Jimmy," he muttered. "How come I still can't be sure if you're lying to me?"

Jimmy was mute.

James burst out laughing. "Gotcha! You really need that beer, huh? Relax already."

Then he entered the bathroom, closed the door, and ran some water for his healing bath.

The possibility that James might be on to him petrified Jimmy. *He likely suspects me,* he thought. *If I'm gonna act, it has to be now while he's sitting in the bathtub; otherwise he could put up a fight I won't be able to win. I'll figure out what to do with his body later.*

Jimmy searched the living room, then the kitchen, looking for a weapon. He had no idea what he'd need to do the job. Stabbing would be messy; bludgeoning would be worse; strangulation would require too much effort. He found inspiration sitting on the kitchen counter: a toaster.

Jimmy unplugged the appliance from the socket and saw to his chagrin that the cord was only two feet long, making it too short to toss into the tub from the bathroom outlet. Then it occurred to him he needed a bigger element of surprise, such as bursting into the bathroom with weapon already in hand. It required plugging the toaster into a wall socket located outside the bathroom, adding more distance. He remembered he had a few extension cords in the catchall drawer near the sink. He yanked the drawer open and plundered through the disparate items until he found the cords.

Linking them to the toaster, he went to a small lamp table a couple of feet to the right of the bathroom. He plugged the cord into an open socket and took stock of the length—it was long enough.

*Make it quick, or this could go the other way in a second,* Jimmy warned himself. He heard splashing in the bathtub, then silence. He pictured James reclining in the water, relaxed and unsuspecting. He loosely held the toaster in his left hand while gradually turning the doorknob with his right. He gave himself a mental countdown. *Here we go. One... two... three!*

Jimmy charged into the bathroom and tossed the toaster into the tub, where it flashed brilliant sparks before plunging the room into darkness. He was relieved when he didn't hear any movement in the water. Still, he wanted to make sure James was dead. He pulled out his cellphone and shook it until its flashlight came on. Then, with mild trepidation, aimed it where he knew a gruesome sight waited. As soon as the beam displayed the empty tub, he felt someone shove him from behind, making him land face first in the water.

James leaned over Jimmy, forcing his head under. "You're so sly, but so am I, Jimbo," he snarled.

Jimmy pushed against the bottom of the tub with his palms, struggling to get free from James' murderous grip.

James grunted from the effort that it took to hold Jimmy down. The drops of hot sweat on his ghoulish face cascaded down his throat and onto his chest like salty rain.

Jimmy swept his hands around the tub, feeling for the toaster. He felt a surge of adrenaline when he located it. Using all his strength, he swung the toaster behind his shoulder, connecting with James' skull, causing him to loosen his grip.

"*AAAAGH!*" James bellowed, touching the side of his head. He felt a knot forming as blood trickled to his ear. Bright pinpricks of light blinked before his eyes.

Jimmy threw himself backwards, landing on the hard tile, and coughing up warm water.

Seeing Jimmy prone, James lunged at him. "I knew you were up to something!"

Jimmy swung the toaster at James' head again, but this time, James was ready. He grabbed the toaster and twisted it from Jimmy's hand. "What's good for the goose is good for the gander," he chuckled, as though he were more amused than angry.

Just as the weapon was about to strike him, Jimmy rolled to his right, and the metal box smashed against the floor with a resounding crack, shattering the tile, and crushing the toaster. He scooted backwards until he felt the wall pressing against his back, then braced his feet against the broken tile, pushing himself up the wall to a standing position. However, he wasn't fast enough to ward off James, who grabbed him by his hair and slammed his head into the glass door of the medicine cabinet. Broken glass clattered into the sink. As if reading the other's mind, each of them reached into the sink and armed himself with a large shard of glass. They raised their sharp weapons in the air, preparing to deliver a death stroke. But, like in any duel, only the quick and dead remain. After the murder, it was the quickest of them who growled, "I've got something for you, Madam Ona."

# 13

The bell over the door of Madam Ona's shop tinkled melodiously.

Like an actress taking her cue, Madam Ona appeared from the back room and went to greet her customer. "Well, well, Mr. Louder. How nice to see you again."

"Please, it's Jimmy."

"Of course. Have you returned to pay your bill? I must say, you look more relaxed since your last visit."

"If by relaxed, you mean relieved that I came out of this adventure alive, then yes, I am relaxed. I nearly died because of you and that body double. Still, I have to admit, I'm a better man for it. Now then, I remember telling you I always keep my word." He took out his wallet, opened it, removed five one hundred-dollar bills, and slammed them down on the counter. "Now, if you'll excuse me, I have a mess to clean up. You won't be seeing me again."

Madam Ona picked the bills off the counter and straightened them before placing them in the cash register. She turned and watched her former customer hastily leaving her store for the last time. It was then she noticed the long blue line behind each of his ears.

# DOUBLE SHIFT

I'm very passionate about the exciting work I get to be a part of each day here at the cloning lab. Everything about it always seems new to me. Mans' seemingly god-like ability to create life from little more than a strand of DNA and a few tiny cells has intrigued me for a very long time. This job gives me a front-row seat to the whole miraculous process.

I'm fortunate to be working with a small group of brilliant, visionary experts in the field of human duplication. The only drawback is that I'm considered the bottom face on the totem pole as the newest and youngest addition to the team. That means I'm assigned most of the mundane tasks, such as writing up reports, analyzing data, and so on.

The only time I'm allowed to visit the part of the lab where the fully formed specimens are stored is near the end of my shift. My job is to check vitals and to make sure that all the equipment is working correctly.

The scientists keep the clones in tall, Plexiglas tubes attached to individual control panels. The cylinders contain a thick, transparent liquid that keeps the bodies suspended. Seeing them up close creeps me out a bit. Sometimes, one of them will twitch, and I half expect it to become conscious and start clawing its way out.

Still, I can't help but marvel at these incredible new beings. For example, there are two things that I find particularly remarkable about them. The first is how rapidly they grow. The second is the exact likeness each one bears to its donor.

It's time for me to begin my nightly tasks. I'm gradually working my way down the rows of encasements, noting any changes, and making necessary adjustments.

Ah, finally, the last one. Oh, no, this can't be real. Is that me floating in there? I have to get out of here! Hey, who's holding me? Ow! Is that a needle going into my neck? Oh God, I think I'm going to faint. I... feel like I'm... fading... awaaay...

I'm very passionate about the exciting work I get to be a part of each day here at the cloning lab. Everything about it always seems new to me.

# THE DARK DEAL OF BILLY TWANG

*The following article by staff writer, Sherbert Spooner, appeared in the June 11th, 2021 issue of Rag, a music magazine devoted to fans of rock, blues, and Norwegian Zydeco.*

# Day 1

As I drive down this seemingly unending road, I notice it is lined by oaks as ancient as Keith Richards. Their gray Spanish mosses sag like testicular tinsel from the crotch of a mighty Christmas tree. The black beast of pity is slowly swallowing my excitement about meeting the man himself: Mr. Billy Twang. I ponder the unfairness of visiting this legendary artist, not backstage at a packed arena, but in the dreariest of settings: an old folks' home. He has a dark, yet fascinating story to tell—one of hardship, riches, fame, and demonic deals.

I nearly drive past the entrance before the sign jerks me away from my lugubrious thoughts. Closer to Heaven Retirement Home is a modest brick facility nestled inside the bosom of a lush and gentle forest. I am serenaded by the sweet, lulling songs of the birds who share this bucolic setting with their elderly neighbors.

It's almost as if they are saying to the residents, "Why don't *you* get the hell off *our* lawn?"

I walk up the steps and onto a dusty, narrow porch decorated with spider webs and dirt daubers nests. Plain wooden rocking chairs rest side by side, as if they are in military formation, making the front of the building look like a Cracker Barrel in Fallujah. I press the button on a small, pollen-covered intercom at eye level beside a secure entrance. There's no reply. I press the button again, this time holding it down for several seconds. I hear its shrill wailing through the door. I continue to wait, but still no one arrives. With my finger hovering over the button, I see a plump, black woman making her way towards me along a brief hallway. Judging by her attire, I presume she's part of the staff.

When she arrives, she pushes through a single glass door and into a small vestibule where another glass door separates us. Her lips curl when she looks at me, as though I disgust her. "May I help you?" she asks.

"I'm Sherbert Spooner from *Rag* magazine," I inform her. "I have an appointment to interview Mr. Twang."

"Mr. Wang dead. That Chinaman went to meet whatever god them people worship over a month ago."

"No, no, no. I'm here to interview Billy *Twang...* T-W-A-N-G."

"He ain't Chinese, then?"

"No, ma'am. I'm certain he is a proud American."

"Aw right," she lazily replies. "Just turn and face the camera so I can get a good look atcha."

I'm confused by her odd request. "But you can clearly see me through the glass. We can't be more than two feet apart."

She scowls. "We have security protocols in place here, Mr. Cracka Ass Interviewer from

Ragu magazine. Now step in front of the damn camera!"

"Fine," I say, before turning to face the camera

"Now turn to your left," she orders me.

"I will not turn to my—"

"I said turn to your damn left, Mr. Ragamuffin Writer Man!"

"It's *Rag* magazine, you stupid..." I mumble, before complying.

"Now turn to your right."

I blindly follow, hoping to gain entry at some point.

"Then turn yourself around."

I begrudgingly follow this directive, as well. "What now?" I ask.

"*Ya do the Hokey Pokey, cos that's what it's all about,*" she sings, before breaking into hysterical laughter.

"ENOUGH!" I yell. "I want to see your supervisor!"

"Oh, chill the hell out," she says through a jagged smile that houses more gold than a Vegas pawn shop. "I don't get paid crap for this gig. The only fun I can afford to have is at other people's expense."

Madea's stunt double pushes the button that unlocks the main door. At last, I'm allowed inside. I'm wondering how to convince her to show me to Billy's room without jumping through any more hoops of humiliation. "Where can I find Mr. Twang's room?" I ask.

She gestures towards a long corridor. "You go halfway down this hall till you get to Room 128," she sneers.

"And that's where I'll find Mr. Twang?"

"Naw, that's Ms. Handy's room. She pees the bed a lot, so it'll prepare you for the smell.

What cha wanna do is keep on-a-truckin' till you get to the end of the hall. From there, you'll hang a left and keep goin' till you reach the end of that one. Then you'll turn around and come back cos you done went the wrong way. So now, you gonna go down to the other end of the hall and stop at the last door on your left."

"Is that where he is?"

"No. Now you're totally screwed, cos you don't know where in hell you are. Just yell for me."

"What's your name?"

"My actual name's Odessa, but I want you to call me Shuga B. Sweet. That there was my stage name back in the day when I stripped. Once you done hollarin', and makin' a big ole jackass outta yourself, I'll waddle down there in my own sweet time and take you to Mr. Twang's room. Can you handle all that, or should I shift to a slower gear?"

I weigh the prison sentence that I would receive for her brutal murder against the sublime satisfaction of completing a rare interview with a veritable rock and roll icon. In a voice devoid of all pride and self-respect, I murmur, "Got it."

She tilts her head and glowers, waiting for something more to be added from me.

Understanding her meaning, I say, "I've got it... Shuga B. Sweet."

"Hallelujah, let's go," she says, slapping her beefy hands together. "Sooner I get you to that old fart's room, sooner I can visit the commode and break up this log jam. Damn cheese—it's the snack food of the devil!"

Holding down my bile, I follow the inspiration for Nurse Ratched in *One Flew Over the Cuckoo's Nest* down a hall lined with residential rooms. A sad symphony of despair seeps from the dank rooms of the old and forgotten. A plea for comfort enters my ears, along with a discussion with imaginary people. Further down, I hear a rousing rendition of "Party in the USA" being sung in an ancient warble that is raw from age. It sounds like Karaoke Night in Pompeii just before the lid blew off Mount Vesuvius.

From there, we take a shadowy stairwell up to the second floor and down a dingy corridor to Room 209. Giddy, childlike excitement soon replaces my frustration. I am seconds away from an experience I will relive as I lay on my deathbed. I am breathless when I enter.

There he is—the one and only William Andrew Twang, otherwise known as Billy Twang. He is the famous founder of one of early rock's biggest and most influential acts, Billy Twang and the Next Big Thang.

Billy was once a vendor of celebrity phlegm at flea markets throughout the Southwest before fate plucked him from obscurity. Despite his lack of notable charisma or movie star good looks, destiny placed him on a stage that was a million dreams away from the small Texas town of Shitzley, where he was born and raised. For one glorious moment, he held court before millions of adoring fans with a wiggle in his walk and a giggle in his talk. Gone now are the sinister black jeans, red velour jacket, and his infamous Chihuahua skin boots. The only reminder of Billy's rebel look is his famous blue ponytail.

The former globetrotting entertainer is leaning forward, his elbows resting on his knees, as he watches the TV screen a few feet away. He sits enraptured by a show on Discovery Channel titled, *The History of Yarn.*

"Sum bitch," he mumbles to no one in particular. "I always thought they got yarn from matin' an afghan sweater with a wooly worm. Who da damn thunk?"

I clear my throat to get his attention, but I get no response. After a few awkward seconds, I clear my throat a second time, only louder.

"Sorry, but I don't collect celebrity phlegm no more," he informs me.

I introduce myself. "I don't sell phlegm, Billy. My name is Sherbert Spooner, and I'm a journalist with *Rag* magazine. Our office contacted you about doing an interview with me. Do you remember that? Do you remember agreeing to an interview, Billy?"

"'Course I remember," he says without taking his eyes from the television. "I can remember everything, includin' what I had for dinner a week ago. Oh Lord, wait—we had peanut butter and shrimp casserole," he says with tangible sorrow and regret. Then he becomes agitated and terrified, as if he's falling down a pitch black hole, barreling toward some sort of hellish nightmare. "Why the hell did you make me remember that horror?" he pitifully asks. "I just wanted to die; I mean *really* die. I had the screamin' squirts for nigh on three days. Maintenance had to come by and paint the bathroom."

I attempt to console him. "Billy, it's all right. Why don't we focus on the here and now? Turn off the TV and let's go find a nice, pleasant place to chat. What do you say?"

Billy calms down a tad. "Well... I guess we might as well. It don't look like they're ever gonna show some graphic footage of a wooly worm matin' with a sweater. I was hopin' there'd be some saucy action, to look at—you know, like when they show them half-nekkid jungle women with their knockers hangin' out. Ya ever notice how droopy them things are? It's like they been breast feedin' one of them big ole African elephants. Poor things. They probably get chaffed knees, what with their jelly jugs rubbin' up against 'em like that. The clumsy ones probably trip over 'em."

His abhorrent remarks stun and disappoint me. "Wow, Billy. I have to tell you that I find your observations disgusting and offensive."

"Is that so?" he responds heatedly. "Have yourself a gullet full of that damn, nasty crap casserole from last week, and then talk to me about disgusting and offensive!" He takes a moment to settle down before continuing. "Speakin' of crap," he says in a milder tone, "let's go shoot some!"

And with that, we begin our slow, purposeful trek down another long, dreary hall that reeks of industrial strength disinfectant and remnants of life-threatening casseroles. With each smashed cigarette butt and cockroach we navigate around, we draw closer to our destination, where a life and career-altering discussion is about to begin.

**W**e're nestled in some well-worn chairs in a sun-drenched common room, surrounded by tall windows. There is a stillness and peacefulness about this space. It's the perfect setting to begin the conversation that I have traveled all this way to have.

"Now, Billy, it's the stuff of lore that you rarely give interviews, and on the infrequent occasions that you do, you are often taciturn and guarded. I appreciate how difficult it is for you to talk about your upbringing, as well as the complicated journey of your band. I want you to know that I, along with your fans, and both of my readers, will be grateful for whatever tidbits you choose to share with us. My only hope is that perhaps—just perhaps—you'll share as much of your odyssey with us as possible, despite your strong desire for privacy."

"All right, I'll tell ya anything you wanna know."

His words catch me off guard. "I… don't understand. When my office contacted you for this interview, you said you didn't like speaking to columnists."

"Oh. I thought they asked if I'd mind speaking to communists. You don't strike me as a commie."

"I'm not."

"Well, in that case, I'll tell ya whatever you wanna know.

"Okay, let's start with your earliest days."

"Well, that's kind of interesting," he says, as he stares through one of the many windows that offer a soothing view of the surrounding woods and a nearby methadone clinic. "We'll start when I was about five or so. My mama was a sweet and simple woman. Her mama was a Cherokee Injun and her daddy a recovering Irishman. She figured that was why she grew up to be an angry drunk who made bad real estate decisions.

"Now then, my pappy was tougher than a Piggly Wiggly pork-chop—a manly man's man, you could say. He woke up every mornin' at two o'clock, downed three pots of scaldin' black coffee, raised a barn, and endured at least two pit bull attacks before ever leavin' home. Then he walked twelve miles down a mine-laden dirt road to get to his job at the iron mill. It was there he worked in the sweltering Texas heat, forging anvils with his bare hands. With a pinch of chaw between his cheek and gum, he'd scratch his butt while recitin' the stoic philosophical musings of Marcus Aurelius and the enchanting poetry of Browning and Yeats. I remember he worked odd hours; his shifts were at five, seven, nine, and eleven. He was a remarkably large man whom the townsfolk looked to as a source of order, strength, and, occasionally, shade.

"I had a big brother named Delmar who went into the entertainment business before I did. He brought joy to thousands of children, despite having Irritable Bowel Syndrome. Maybe you've heard of him—Squirts the Clown? He died during an unfortunate incident involving a butt plug and an ornery bull. We don't need to go there, though."

"Thank goodness," I say before steering Billy to another topic. "It's been said that many artists have a story to tell about the moment they heard the clarion call to perform. Was there a moment in your young life that inspired you?"

"Sure was. I remember it like it was yesterday. I was sixteen at the time. I'd worked up the nerve to ask this pretty little thing named Delilah to the prom. I nearly fainted when she said yes.

"When we got to the prom, I noticed a few of my buddies standin' near the punch bowl, laughin'. I asked Delilah to excuse me while I said a quick hello to 'em. Turns out, they were spikin' the punch with cheap grain alcohol. Well now, bein' one of the guys, I had a smidge. I was wantin' to take another snort, so I looked around to see if Delilah was watchin'. She was very religious, so I knew she'd disapprove. When I saw her yackin' it up with some girls on the other side of the gym, I took the opportunity to throw back some more hooch. Before long, I was staggerin' drunk. Well, wouldn't ya know it, Delilah saw me and came stompin' over; I knew I was done for. When she got there, she could tell right away that I'd been imbibing. Bein' the good girl that she was, she insisted that I take her home immediately. I tried talkin' her out of it, but she had made up her mind. I was too drunk to drive, and I knew it, but she kept on demandin' that we leave.

"Anyhow, we had driven a couple of miles when we came to a dangerous piece of backwoods road nicknamed 'Don't Take This Curve Cos It'll Kill Ya.' I know I should've been more careful, but Delilah wouldn't stop cryin' and yellin', so I sped up. She was still hollarin' at me when she met her end."

I'm touched by Billy's openness and vulnerability. "I can understand how that tragic car crash changed your life, Billy."

"Car crash? Naw, there weren't no car crash. I got tired of Delilah's constant complaining, so I pulled over, yanked her out of the car, and chucked her whiny butt off a cliff. That's when I realized that girls were too much of a distraction from what I really wanted to do: play guitar."

"When did you pick up your first guitar?"

"It was Christmas of '59 when I asked Santy for a new guitar. I was so happy on Christmas mornin' when I found this one big present under the tree with a tag that read, 'To that peculiar one with the dopey face.' Brother man, I couldn't wait to unwrap my first-ever guitar."

"Why were you so certain it was a guitar?

"They used cellophane for wrappin' paper."

"What happened next?"

"Before I knew it, I had that guitar in my hands, playin' some wicked, avant-garde types of chords until Delmar pointed out that I was playin' the wrong end of the guitar. So, I flipped it around and started blarin' such hits as, 'Blue Suede Shoes,' 'Rock Around the Clock,' and 'I am a Pretty Little Dutch Girl.'

"On that last one, Mama turned to Pappy and said, 'You just had to have another kid, didn't ya?' while Pappy mumbled, 'Why us, Lord? Why now?'

"I ignored their hurtful remarks and went outside to put on a concert for the dog. Now that's a curious story right there. Pappy named our dog, Private First Class Myron Feldstein, after a fella he'd served with in WW Two. He said he felt a sense of obligation after shooting the private, whom he'd mistaken for the composer of 'I am a Pretty Little Dutch Girl.'

"Now Private Feldstein (the pooch, not the soldier) was a very unusual dog. He'd converted from Judaism to Islam six weeks earlier and assumed such practices as not eating any dog food that contained pork byproducts, and takin' his dumps in the direction of Mecca. I know this all might sound a little weird, but honestly, you should have seen his prayer rug—*very* stylish. At least he wasn't as loony as our neighbor's dog, who was a Boston Terrier. He had this annoying New England bark. Every time a stranger came on their property, he'd go, 'Bak! Bak! Bak!'

"Anyhow, I listened to records and figured out chords that I never knew existed. After a while, I met up with a fella who I'd spend the next several years performin' with: Swanky Diggs. But that's gonna have to be a tale for another day."

Billy appears to be getting tired, so I suggest we work on the interview some more tomorrow.

I roll him back through the breezeway toward the nearest entrance. Due to security concerns, the single glass door is locked, so I press the buzzer on the adjacent wall to request re-entry. The single glass door is locked, so I press the buzzer on the adjacent wall to request re-entry. I am met by Shuga B. Sweet, who asks us to identify ourselves. I sob.

# Day 2

Billy and I have made our way out to the courtyard today. The warm sunshine, colorful azalea bushes, and the musty stench from an overflowing cigarette butt receptacle heighten his alertness. I can tell something is bothering him. I ask him if anything has happened since our last conversation.

"Lost a good friend last night," Billy groans. "I only knew him for a few months, but still we'd gotten close. It was all so sudden, but not altogether unexpected."

"Heart Attack? Cancer?" I delicately ask.

"Naw, it was suicide over the Peanut Butter and Shrimp Casserole that's on the menu for next Thursday. We all figured he just couldn't face another day of knowin' that gut bomber was comin' 'round the mountain again."

"Billy, I was hoping we could pick up where we left off yesterday. We were just about to discuss your relationship with your bandmate of many years, Swanky Diggs. Do you feel up to talking about him?"

"Sure, why not? I first met Swanky when we were fifteen. He was a quirky little squirt, even back then. His parents were part of an early hippie sect called the People's Asparagus Movement. Folks were always laughin' about the peculiar way they dressed and how funny their pee smelled. Swanky's folks were so engulfed in this movement that they went so far as to have their names legally changed. His old man's name became Peggy, and his old lady started goin' by Stool Softener. Guess she never had none of that Peanut Butter and Shrimp Casserole!"

Billy throws back his head and laughs at his own joke. Unfortunately, his head goes far enough back to hit the center of the butt receptacle, catching his blue pony tail on fire. After I beat it out with an azalea branch, Billy catches his breath and returns to his story.

"Despite bein' their only child, Swanky's folks never coddled him. Even as a little tike, they expected him to sweep the porch, feed the chickens, and manage their investment portfolio. They were artisans, so they taught him how to make crafts from everyday items. He was a quick study, and by the age of twelve, he had mastered the art of makin' bongs outta Christmas ornaments. I still got one with the three wise Rastafarians he made for me."

"I see. Tell me how you two first met."

"We met in Mrs. Petermeir's tenth grade class. Besides providing us with a proper education, she taught us valuable lessons from her experiences, like surviving a dust storm, livin' through a depression, and being cautious of whom she called, 'Kooky Krauts.' She said she developed her distrust of the Germans from a romantic relationship she'd had with a German soldier at the height of World War One. As she told it, she'd been servin' as a nurse at a frontline M.A.S.H. unit when the Military Police brought the soldier in as a prisoner. The doctors put her in charge of treatin' him for an aggressive form of gooch rot. Over the course of the treatment, the two star-crossed nymphos formed a strong bond and eventually fell hopelessly in love. Unfortunately, it wasn't meant to be. I recall how she'd become somber and teary-eyed when recounting the events that had led up to the dissolution of their all-too-brief romance. She told us he'd made plans for the two of 'em after the war, but she just couldn't make peace with his expectations. Although she admired his appreciation of lagers and fine automotives, she felt she had to draw the line at invadin' Poland."

"Billy, let's get back to your relationship with Swanky."

"Sorry 'bout that. Looks like I hung a left at the wrong corner again, huh? Now, where was I? Oh yeah! We hit it off pretty good, Swanky and me. One day, I invited him over to my house after school. He had to get the okey-doke from Peggy and Stool Softener, but once that was settled, he came on over.

"The first thing I showed him was my guitar. 'Let's hear what you got,' he said, so I lit into some heavy, experimental rock fusion. I was wailin' away with some complicated chords until Swanky pointed out that I was playin' the wrong end of the guitar. I turned it the right way and started crankin' out some of the classic artists of the day: Jimi Hendrix, The Who, The Archies.

On that last one, Mama and Pappy came into the room. Pappy told me I wasn't his son while Mama tried to pull her head off.

"Swanky snatched the guitar out of my hands and said, 'Let me show ya the real deal!'

"I sat there in astonishment, as Swanky tore through a right many rock and blues tunes. He flew up and down the neck of that guitar like a boy possessed. When he finished, he put the guitar down and said, 'What d'ya think?'

"I turned to ask my parents the same question, but they had quietly snuck out during Swanky's tour de force. I learned later that they had called Peggy and Stool Softener to see if they'd be up for makin' a trade."

"That must've been pretty tough on you at that impressionable age," I say. "Did you feel any bitterness, particularly against your father?"

"A little at first," he answers. "But I'd pretty much gotten over it by the time he went to Glory."

"So he died shortly after that?"

"Oh, he didn't die right then. Naw, he ran off with this bug-eyed, fatty waitress named Glory. I recall that one of her boobies was bigger than the other one. The disproportionate weight made her list to one side, so she was always walkin' in circles."

"But your father did die at a relatively young age, I understand. How did he pass?"

"Now that's kind of a peculiar story," Billy says.

"Yes, Billy. That seems to be the pattern regarding some of your anecdotes. Please, continue."

"You betcha! Pappy and Glory, along with Delmar and me, were watchin' reruns of *Hee Haw* on the TV. Pappy was kicked back in his recliner, sippin' iced tea out of his favorite Bama Jelly jar. Glory was sittin' on the couch clippin' her toenails. Glory's toenails were real thick, see, so she cut 'em with one of them big Ginsu steak knives. Well sir, when she sawed off a big ole grungy chunk, it flew through the air like a cannonball, and did a belly flop right into Pappy's tea jar. We reckoned he never heard the splash, cos he didn't hesitate to throw back a hearty swig. Well, the next thing that happened was his eyes started buggin' out of his head, as he tried to yack up Glory's big yella toenail. Sensing the danger, Delmar sprang into action and threw Pappy on the floor. Then he jumped up and down on his big beer belly hopin' to dislodge the nasty thing. When that didn't work, Glory took off like she'd lit too big a fart and ran to get the vacuum cleaner to suck it out. Before she could get back, Pappy breathed his last."

"Did he manage any last words?"

"Yep. He said, 'Tell Glory I love her. Then go and tell my mistress I love her more.'"

"Oh my goodness, Billy. That was horrible. I can't imagine the shock your family felt dealing with such a bizarre and unexpected death. I would think that the way your father died left you shaken and confused."

"Oh yeah, I was confused all right, what with him swallowin' one of Glory's toenails. He usually just chewed on 'em."

Pushing away my disgust, I say, "Billy, I *desperately* want to get back to your early work with Swanky."

"Sure thing," he says. "Swanky and me got to be pretty tight—like brothers even—except his parents never had sex with mine (although sometimes they'd go on nude picnics together). We'd jam, hang out, paint the dog, and occasionally write songs together. The first one we worked on was a tender love ballad written by Swanky right after a romantic breakup. It was called, "I Pooted On Your Sandwich." That one really moved me cos it emanated from Swanky's broken heart, as well as from his digestive tract. It also taught me some good rules when it came to love: Be grateful for the experience, love till the very end, and never leave a PBJ unattended if Swanky is mad at cha.

"Shortly after we graduated from high school, Swanky and I put together some interesting bands.

"We named the first one, The Run-Overs. That one broke up when our lead singer lived up to our name while crossin' a busy highway.

"The next band had a name that appealed to folks who liked to throw back a few cold ones. We called ourselves The Empties. That one fell apart after we realized that The Empties too often described the parking lots of the bars we were playin' at.

"Now the rock 'n roll pie had a lot of fingers in it by then, so we turned to a new genre that was hot at the moment: Christian rock. After the success of *Jesus Christ Superstar*, and *Godspell*, we figured we'd be a hit. We dubbed ourselves The Beatitudes and performed Beatles songs with altered lyrics. We jammed on such titles as 'Hey Judas,' 'Got to Get You Into my Eternal Life,' 'The Long and Winding Road to Damascus,' 'Six Days a Week,' 'Evolution No. 9,' and my personal favorite, 'While David's Harp Gently Weeps.' The critics at the time must've also been in a biblical frame of mind, cos, brother, they crucified us. Their cruel assessments disheartened us so much that that group fell by the wayside as well.

"After all that, Swanky and I decided to take a break from the band format and resigned ourselves to performing as an acoustic duo."

"Really? You guys were an acoustic duo?"

"Oh yeah. We played some Crosby, Stills and Nash before they brought that southern man hatin' jackass, Neil Young, onboard. Neil Young is a whiny, nasally commie whose voice sounds like his nose is packed with snot. That boy doesn't need a band—he needs a decongestant. We also performed some early Eagles and Allman Brothers. And every once in a while, I'd play solo on some of the old Archies songs. On those particular nights, I'd see Mama come in, weep into a hanky, then saunter away. And if I listened carefully, I could hear Pappy wretchin' in the parkin' lot."

"How long did you guys go on as an acoustic act?" I ask.

"Longer than we wanted to, that's for dang sure," Billy says. "We were mighty thankful when the Lord sent us a couple of gifts in the form of a red-hot bass player named Sven the Mexican and his drummer buddy, Cable Man."

"Tell me how their arrivals came about."

"That's gonna have to wait for another time. Nude Bingo starts in less than an hour, so I have to get ready."

"It takes you that long to get naked?"

"Heck no! It takes me that long to hide, so they don't drag me down there to look at all them nut-draggers and boob-saggers."

I thank Billy for his time and tell him I'll return in a few days to hear the rest of his story. He bids me a gracious adieu, pops a wheelie in his wheelchair, and steers his butt chariot away to a broom closet near the end of the hall.

# Day 3

It's a rainy, somber day—the kind of day that is tailor-made for old movies on TV, moments of quiet reflection, or colonoscopy preps. Billy's mood reflects the inclement weather. He sits near the rain-spattered window in a state of deep gloom. He hardly notices me, as I place a chair next to him and sit down.

"Billy?" I ask. "Are you up for a talk today? I can come back when you're feeling better."

Without raising his head, he mumbles, "I want to get it out. I want to get it all out now."

"Okay, then, Billy. Just say whatever you feel compelled to share."

He looks confused. Irritated. "No, no!" he exclaims. "I'm talkin' about the broccoli jello they fed me this mornin'. I want it out of me right now!"

I ask Billy if he needs a moment to regurgitate in the bathroom. He thinks I say "refrigerate" and shares that he keeps his mini fridge in his bathroom because it makes the storage of his stool samples convenient.

It is now that *I* wish to regurgitate, but not in Billy's bathroom—definitely not in Billy's bathroom. I push down the gorge that's rising through my throat like molten sickness. Once the urge to vomit has passed, I prod Billy to continue his story. I am happy when he does so.

"Billy, in our previous conversation, you were about to tell me about Sven the Mexican's and Cable Man's journey to becoming members of the band."

Billy smiles at the recollection. "Oh yeah, ole Sven and Cable Man. Me and Swanky had put up ads all over town: record stores, telephone poles, community bulletin boards. It had been almost a month, and we hadn't had a single hit. One Saturday afternoon, Swanky and I had just come back from lunch at Pizza Slut."

"I think you mean Pizza Hut."

"No, it was like Pizza Hut, but with hookers for waitresses. Boy, howdy, you should've checked out their Meat Lovers Special."

"Billy, you've strayed again."

"Right. So Swanky and I were over at our rundown apartment pickin' through some tunes when the telephone rang. Now today, you young fellas snuggle your phones up against your willy. But back then, they hung on walls or sat on tables in your living room and bedroom. I only mention this because it was the phone on the kitchen wall that rang. Swanky ran to get it, you know, just in case it was somebody respondin' to our ad. Anyhow, he tripped over the coffee table and stumbled toward the window. His arms were pinwheeling, and his eyes were as big as the steerin' wheel on a Greyhound bus. He couldn't stop himself from crashin' through the window and landin' on top of a man below who was walkin' his weenie dog.

"Well sir, that little sausage dog got loose and ended up right in front of a city bus that ran over its tail. I heard the dog's name used to be Precious, but after the accident, the owner changed it to Beaver."

"Billy, let's stay focused. The phone rang and..."

"Oh right. Sorry. Okay, so I answered the phone and said, 'Hello, who's this?'

"The fella said, 'Ola, my name's Sven the Mexican.'

"At least I think that's what he said. He was kind of hard to understand with that thick Swedish accent. He went on to say he was calling in response to our ad.

"Accordin' to him, he was a seasoned musician with some club experience. Well, needless to say, I was tickled pink. I told him we were lookin' to add some people to our lineup and asked him if he'd meet us for an audition. He said, 'Si, señor,' in that same Swedish accent, then started talkin' about a drummer he knew who might fit the bill. I told him the more the merrier.

"We agreed on when and where, and that was that."

"My understanding is that you guys met in an old, abandoned factory. Walk me through the audition."

"Swanky and I often passed by a former factory that had man-ufactured heat-seekin' lawn darts. It had been shuttered for years, so we picked that for the site of our first jam session with the other fellas. I recall it was on a cold Tuesday afternoon when Sven the Mexican and Cable Man, the drummer, showed up."

"I've always wondered," I say. "How did he end up with the name Cable Man?"

"His mama named him after his daddy," Billy explains.

"So, his father was a cable man?"

"No, his daddy was a plumber. You're a big boy, you do the math."

I nod, indicating that I understand his implication. I press on. "I know that Sven's last name was Rodriguez, but I don't recall ever learning Cable Man's last name. Did he keep it secret on purpose?"

"Everybody has a last name. It's just that Cable Man couldn't remember his. When he was a young'un, a propeller from a small airplane, that just happened to be flyin' overhead, broke off and lodged in his noggin. The doctors were afraid to remove it. They didn't know what kind of damage it might do, so they left it in.

Poor Cable Man had a hard time gettin' through doorways and narrow halls. He quit school early cos he was tired of knockin' his classmates unconscious every time he looked around to see who was callin' his name. To keep him out of trouble and elevators, his folks bought him a cheap drum set, which he played religiously. Later on, he and Sven crossed paths and started workin' together as a rhythm section. Once they were tight, they signed on with some popular local yokel acts. The cash started trickling in, and soon Cable Man had enough to pay a back-alley doctor to yank the prop out of his skull. Then one day, fate stepped in, and Sven saw our ad. Shall I continue?"

"Yes, please," I eagerly say.

"Cable Man and Sven the Mexican showed up that day with their gear, and we got down to the business of makin' music. I don't know how to explain it, other than to say it was like a lightning bolt hittin' a hamster: explosive, but without all the guts and cedar shavings. From the first go 'round, we clicked on every cover song: 'Fortunate Son' by CCR, 'Jumpin' Jack Flash' by the Stones, and 'I Think I Love You' by The Partridge Family. I remember that last one because Pappy appeared out of nowhere, puked on the floor, and stumbled off mumblin', 'All it would've cost me was a dime at the drugstore.'

Billy takes a dramatic pause in his story. "Now listen up, sonny," he says, leaning closer to me for emphasis. "This here is the important part—the moment when we became Billy Twang and the Next Big Thang.

"Ole Swanky says to us, 'I got an original piece that I want to show you guys. It's four chords and the truth—nothin' more, nothin' less. Dig it.'

"Well, let me tell ya, Swanky lit into some honky tonk power chords that filled my soul with rock 'n roll. It was like Stevie Ray Vaughn had enticed Chuck Berry into meetin' him in a cheap motel and takin' part in a crazy, stinky, monkey sex, three-way with Pat Benatar, producing a two-headed, one ball, sasquatch named

Roarin' Rock 'n Blues. When he was done, I slapped some greasy lyrics on it, and it became our first big hit, 'You're in the Wrong Hole.'"

I'm beyond excited. I have learned the origin of the song that brought about the Billy Twang and the Next Big Thang era. Now the questions are coming to me with the speed of Budweiser distancing themselves from Dylan Mulvaney. "So," I ask, "Was that early record the catalyst for your first album, *Sniff my Finger*?"

"Oh yeah!" Billy exclaims. "We spent the next few months perfectin' our sound. The songs fell out of the sky like Lizzo with a parachute malfunction. We were brothers after that, except, unlike Hunter Biden, nobody planned on bangin' the other guys' widows."

"Walk me through the first round of success," I say.

Billy takes his time. "This is the hardest part—the dark part," he fearfully mutters. "You gotta understand: We were four young men who had waited all their lives for one bite of the apple. The problem was that the record company wanted us to take three more bites. And if those bites didn't leave a mark, then the label would do the equivalent of what's called a Turkey Drop. That's when you dump a fat, ugly girlfriend before your buddies find out you're datin' her. Yep, it was all comin' unglued. The ideas dried up faster than Whoopi Goldberg's ovaries. And like Madonna yankin' her drawers down for skin mags back in the late 1800s, we were young and needed the money. We were, in a word, very desperate."

"Billy, that's two words," I inform him.

"Oh finger me, grandpa—you wanna hear the story or not?" he irritably asks.

"Of course, Billy. Please, continue."

"Okay, then. That's when Sven the Mexican offered up a solution. Ya see, he'd been dabblin' in the dark arts. I'm talkin' evil stuff that can take over your mind and soul, like Satanism,

Demonology, or FanDuel. He told us that if we'd swear an allegiance to the demon, Oompa Loompa, the creature would bestow on us the gift of never-ending hits. What wasn't to like?

"The ceremony required us to slice our palms with a sacred dagger, then recite an ancient chant. The closest thing we had to a sacred dagger was a steak knife that Swanky had filched from a Waffle House. We used it to cut ourselves, then rubbed our bloody palms together, while chanting, 'Inna-gadda-da-vida.'

"Sittin' here now, with the benefit of hindsight, I'm ashamed I went through with the ceremony. I took some comfort from the fact that 80s punk rocker, Billy Idol, performed a similar ceremony by chanting, 'Here she comes right now, mony-mony.'

"Anyway, that's when we came up with new hits like, 'I'm Only Usin' the Tip,' followed by 'Don't Be Paranoid—There's No Camera in the Teddy Bear,' and the chart topper, 'I Swear to You: This Has Never Happened to Me Before.'"

"Ooh, ooh!" I shout. "I know those! They're classics!"

"Classics, but at a cost," Billy somberly says.

I ask him to explain.

Billy lowers his head like a drawbridge. "Every contract has a stipulation. For us, it was our eternal souls. That was somethin' I found to be a little silly, cos I've never heard of a temporary soul. It makes it sound like a dang Hertz rental. Anyhow, we had our hits, sold out big venues, and got celebrity tables near the meat display at Outback Steakhouse. But like Travis Kelce, we knew we now belonged to an entity darker than the night, and that there would be no escape. We didn't want the demon writin' mean songs about a messy breakup, so we sauntered along meekly. Helplessly. Eventually, the time came when we had to pay our dues. And unlike Planet Fitness, it was a heckuva lot more than ten dollars a month."

I swallow hard. Do I really want to hear the truth behind the unusual and premature deaths of the members of The Next Big Thang? I realize and accept that this interview must end as it began: with the truth. I deftly guide Billy toward the interview's inevitable conclusion. "Tell me, Billy, how did you feel about the passing of your brothers—your bandmates?"

"Have you ever seen the movies, *The Omen* or *Final Destination*? he asks in a barely perceptible whisper.

"Yes, Billy, I have. Both films feature a series of horrifically violent and preordained deaths."

"That's right," he says. "I always knew that Sven would be the first to go. After all, he was the one who first signed on the dotted line. Many folks were perplexed over how a man could die in such a sequential way. But I knew—it was time for him to pay his tab."

I speak softly, carefully. "If you're up for it, Billy, please walk me through his last day as you understand it."

"It all started simple enough," Billy begins. "Apparently, Sven was battling a raging case of athlete's foot. Within weeks after the initial diagnosis, the disease had spread up his leg to his knees. His podiatrist solemnly advised him to consider getting his affairs in order. When Sven told him he didn't think the condition was terminal, the doctor became embarrassed and said, 'By golly, you're right. Never mind.' Then he directed Sven to a nearby Walgreens for a medicated foot spray.

"The story goes that when Sven got home, his wife, Mona, was hosting a Mary Kay party in the livin' room. Sven said a quick que pasa to the attendees and headed upstairs to the bathroom to spray his fungus. What he didn't realize was that he had the nozzle pointed the wrong way, so instead of sprayin' his foot, he took a heavy blast of fast-actin' Tinactin straight to his peepers.

"Sven's eyes were ablaze in fiery agony, as he bolted from the bathroom screamin' like a bobcat. In his panic, he tripped on the hallway rug and went tumblin' butt over elbows down a flight of stairs. Then he spilled out into the hallway outside the livin' room where Mona's party was raging in its raucous, all-pink glory.

"The best way to describe the ensuing melee is to think of Sven as a stick of dynamite and the party as a cozy campfire.

"At the sound of their screaming, Sven sprang up and attempt-ed to run away. In his frenzy, he ran straight into a wall that pro-pelled him backward into a table full of Mary Kay products, then into his brand new 47-inch color television. The TV crashed to the floor, causing an electrical fire that quickly spread to the flammable Mary Kay products. There was a loud *WHOOSH* followed by a curtain of famished flames that ate their way through the livin' room like Michael Moore at an All You Can Eat Buffet.

"Mona and her guests stampeded like terrified buffaloes out the front door and into the yard. Poor ole Sven followed right behind 'em, still blind and screamin'. That's when one guest yelled, 'Get away from me, you wailin' whack job,' and started strikin' Sven upside his head with her heavy purse.

"To flee the assault, Sven ran across the yard and out into the street, where a large collection truck from Industries for the Blind struck him. The impact of bein' hit by well over 5,000 pounds of irony sent him flyin' through the air, over a neighbor's chain-link fence, and into his yard, where six Rottweilers were housed. It turned out the neighbor had gone fishin' for the weekend and had forgotten to feed his large-breed eatin' machines. Well, you can guess the rest.

"Mona, a former exotic dancer who had once shared the stage with a rotund stripper named Shuga B. Sweet, was the first to in-form me of the tragic news. In her usual buck-toothed babble, she explained that the doctors had treated Sven for a range of injuries, including seared retinas, carpet burns, smoke inhalation, a head contusion, fractured ribs, dog bites, and the pièce de résistance, rabies. Apparently, the stupid neighbor had never bothered havin' any of his dogs vaccinated. The whole ordeal caused so much trau-ma and shock that Sven ended up dyin'.

"As for Cable Man, he had the most cringeworthy demise. It was winter in Aspen, see, and Cable Man loved to go up and ride the slopes. He also liked to ride the snow bunnies, but that's a letter to Penthouse sort of tale. Anyhow, it was late morning, and he was jonesin' for a drink. It's like he used to say, 'It's ten o'clock in the mornin' somewhere.' After a couple hours of drinking, he'd gotten good and snookered. This left him open to suggestions from the other drunks in the resort's clubhouse. How the heck anyone could talk a man into strippin' nekkid and ridin' a mountain chair lift in the dead of winter is still a mystery to me.

"Witnesses said that when his car reached the highest point, it snagged on a pulley. Then the chair's safety bar inexplicably opened, and he fell off. But it got worse—Cable Man's grape pouch had frozen to the seat. They said after he fell, he bounced up and down like he was hooked to a bungee cord. He dangled from his grotesquely extended sac for hours before someone got close enough to pour some warm water on it to free him. By then, he'd been dead for hours from the bitter cold. In my nightmares, I can see him there, swingin' wildly in the high winter winds from a yard-long, fleshy tentacle. It chills me to this day.

"Turns out, there was a silver linin', though. Before his funeral, his kin couldn't find a tie to go with the suit they were buryin' him in, so they painted tasteful red stripes on his stretched out strip of balls, and tied it around his neck. I gotta say, ole Cable Man looked pretty dapper in his testicle tie.

"When Swanky went, I knew my end was near. I loved Swanky. He'd been with me from the beginning. He inspired me, taught me, and promised me in bed that it had never happened to him before."

"I have to believe that his passing was likely the hardest for you to process," I say with deep compassion.

"Yep, it was," Billy groans. "But I take comfort in knowin' that he went out like a warrior.

"Years after the ritual, Swanky tried gettin' out from under the demon's thumb by becomin' a Christian, and joinin' a church called Our Lady of the Barcalounger.

"One day, some of the church brethren decided they wanted to join the local church softball league, so that's what they did. This is where Swanky's story drew to its awful conclusion.

"Originally, the church invited Swanky to join their praise band, but it was the up-and—coming softball team that drew him in. All they asked for was a mascot, so there was no need for him to endure lengthy training sessions.

"After a lunchtime pow-wow at The Sizzler, Swanky and the brethren sealed the deal. Immediately, the team began thinking of a cool and tough-lookin' character for a mascot to represent 'em. Then an idea hit 'em.

"The team piled into the church van and drove to this place called Crazy Cal's Discount Costumes. Once they got there, they started lookin' for somethin' fierce and menacing, like a shark, a pirate, a tiger, or a bear. Unfortunately, they only had about fifty bucks between 'em. Crazy Cal had one costume that he would part with at that price: a sweaty and slightly used lobster suit that someone had recently worn at the grand opening of a local Red Lobster. Although it seemed like a lame mascot, the brethren begrudgingly agreed that the giant claws did look a little intimidating. They weren't happy about namin' the team The Pit-Stained Lobsters, but Quentin Tarantino's lawyers were just as unhappy about their original choice: The Inglorious Baptists. Anyhow, they bought the stupid thing and left.

"A few days before their first game, the brethren, sans Swanky, began to think that it wouldn't make for a flamboyant entrance to simply have a big lobster waddlin' onto the diamond to lead 'em out, so they got an idea to spice things up. One of 'em found a used circus cannon on E-bay. They bought it with the notion of firin' Swanky the Lobster out over the diamond and into a safety net about fifty yards away. Lookin' back, it may have saved them all a lot of heartbreak and expense had they gotten Swanky's input first.

"When game day rolled around, a frightened and significantly better-informed Swanky changed his mind. Said somethin' about how they'd never mentioned anything about a cannon, and he wanted out. But since Swanky was a little guy, and it's hard to fight back in a lobster suit, they were able to overpower him and stuff him into the cannon.

"Now the first thing you need to know about firin' a cannon is not to use too much gunpowder. This became apparent to the brethren after they messed up calculating the bodyweight to airspeed ratio and loaded the cannon with way too much of it.

"Decidin' to leave the details to the devil, they picked a child to come down out of the stands to light the fuse. Soon, there was a loud BOOM! High-pitched screamin' echoed through the bright blue summer sky, as a flamin' lobster streaked speedily toward the horizon. Swanky's velocity was so great, and his trajectory so high, that a low flyin' Cessna snagged him with its tail fin and whisked him away to parts unknown.

"The church, upon hearin' the news, located the pilot, who had traveled to Cancun for a Drag Queens for Trump rally. He informed them that he didn't find anyone hangin' from the plane, so Swanky could've fallen off anywhere along the Texas/Mexico border.

"There was a brief search, but despite the effort, they couldn't find him. From what I heard, they still don't know where Swanky is.

"Well, just like Lia Thomas' parents, the brethren were guilt-ridden and disappointed. After some prayer and a couple of forced lobotomies, they decided to quit church softball. There was talk of a Hatchet Throwin' Club, but after hearing about the plan, the church excommunicated the brethren on the grounds of bein' idiots.

"As for the fate of Swanky, a story is told down Mexico way of a giant, scorched lobster stumblin' around aimlessly through the dusty streets of Santa Rosa, muttering over and over again, 'Play ball. Play ball.'

"But that's only a legend. I, alone, know the truth: Swanky landed in the arms of the demons who eagerly awaited him. And now, there's only..."

"You," I finish for him. We sit in silence, as if deciding who should end the interview. The quiet is all encompassing and absolute, like Bank of America Stadium during a Carolina Panthers game. After what feels like an endless moment, I ask the final question. "Was it worth it, Billy?"

He smiles, but only slightly. It's the kind of smile that says, "I have accepted my fate and am at peace with it," or "I just crapped my pants, and now you have to smell it and pretend that you don't." Eventually, he looks at me, then speaks the last words I shall ever hear from him.

"Some folks live their whole lives dreaming, but never touch those dreams," he murmurs. "Some folks trade their gifts for a safe, normal life. But some folks throw themselves at their destiny like we did. As for me, I have found my dream, met it on its own terms, and lived to tell my story—my story to you. I'm glad we talked—set the record straight. I guess that's all I have to say."

Billy and I sit for a while longer. The air is fragrant with the smell of daffodils, roses, and the sweet stink of the cheap cigar that Shuga B. Sweet left smoldering in a nearby ashtray. As our time together ends, I stand and gaze lovingly, respectfully, at the man, the legend, Billy Twang. In that last moment together, I find myself wondering, *Should I tell him he crapped his pants or pretend that I don't smell it?*

---

It's a few days after my last visit with Billy that I learn of his death. Perhaps it was the dark demon collecting his final payment that ripped Billy from this world and dropped him into an eternal realm of darkness. Or maybe it was the eye-watering butt funk from Shuga B. Sweet that had nauseated me over those few days. Most likely, it was the ghoulish menu of Closer to Heaven that eventually took its toll. I suppose I may never know. One thing that I do know is that for one brief, shining moment, I stood before greatness. Billy

Twang has now passed into history, and with him, the Next Big Thang. We'll never see the likes of them again. However, with plates such as Shrimp and Peanut Butter Casserole, it's probably for the best.

—Sherbert Spooner
June 11, 2021

# THE SCENE OF THE CRIME

It all went down on Highway 52 in Winston-Salem, NC. Alex Carrington, a twenty-two-year-old police rookie, pulled over a reckless driver by the name of Michael Joseph Watts. It turned out Mr. Watts was a violent felon on parole. For him, a simple traffic citation was a ticket back to prison. The blunt in his hand, along with the unregistered 9mm tucked under his seat, would seal the dea l.

Officer Carrington didn't know that he was about to cause a fierce competition between Watts and the police in and around Winston-Salem. The culprit's gun was the starting pistol—the contest began once the bullet hit Carrington.

This was music to Owen's ears.

Owen, now in his thirties, was sitting on an overburdened swivel chair in his bedroom, devouring a jumbo-sized bag of Nacho Doritos, and washing them down with two liters of marshmallow crème soda. Like other social castoffs, he walked alone: no pals, no girlfriend, a crappy job, overweight, and living in a house that had once belonged to his parents—his dead parents. It was his house no w.

It saddened and haunted Owen that the house where he'd celebrated many wonderful Christmases and birthdays had not so long ago been a murder scene. His guilt over not rescuing his parents still overwhelmed him. *Where was I when they were being killed?* he'd asked himself countless times. *What was so important that I couldn't be here?* He was grateful that his recollection of the event was hazy. The only thing he remembered was that they'd died violently in their kitchen. *Maybe it's better that some things go unremembered,* he thought.

Owen led a sedentary life and was often bored. Enjoying an occasional walk on the wild side kept him occupied. To do this, he stayed up late, using a police scanner that he'd bought at a police auction.

A scratchy voice pierced the silence, breaking his boredom. "All units, we have a code 10-1, a code 10-1 on Highway 52 southbound near the Clemmonsville Road exit.

"We're on it," another voice responded.

Owen picked up his laminated sheet of police codes. The catalog said that code 10-1 meant someone had shot an officer. And if the incident had happened on Highway 52, it must've been a traffic stop gone south.

"Whoa, now we're cookin'," Owen said, rubbing his chubby palms together.

Most of the radio calls that Owen listened to were mundane: loud music, neighbor disputes, fender benders. Then there were calls like this one that made his heart race. It was like what emergency dispatchers and first responders normally say about their jobs: long periods of dullness interrupted by short periods of excitement fueled by adrenaline.

Owen stayed glued to the radio like a basketball fan listening to the Final Four. After several minutes, a police officer broke in to confirm that there was a uniform down and unresponsive. He told the dispatcher to order the paramedics to hurry, though he didn't do so in a G-rated manner.

A short time later, the dispatcher interrupted again with a critical update. "All units in the area of South Clemmonsville Road: We've got a 10-32. Please proceed with caution. The suspect exited his vehicle on Konnoak Drive and is armed and running. We've got a chopper in the air, surveying the surrounding area. Witnesses reported a white male about 5'10" and 190 lbs. He has short black hair and is wearing jeans and a white t-shirt with the sleeves cut off."

"Roger that," several officers answered.

"Ooh, the plot thickens," Owen said with twisted glee. He rocked back and forth as he listened for the next transmission.

Soon, the dispatcher rewarded his patience. She alerted the officers who were pursuing the perp that the police chopper had spotted him running through backyards in the 3200 block of Renon Road, a lower middle-class neighborhood close to Owen's.

"Oh my God, this could get crazy," Owen chuckled. Soon, he could hear a helicopter and police sirens. At first, he was excited, but his enthusiasm soon morphed into deep concern as the noises drew closer. "Uh-oh, what's happening?" he gasped. By the time everything was on top of him, Owen had become distraught.

The pilot got on the radio. "Guys, he's a hundred yards west of you!"

The neighborhood dogs were barking their heads off, further adding to Owen's distress. Panicked, he wondered if he should go hide in a closet, the bathroom, or the basement. The chase lost all of its entertainment value; it was hitting too close to home.

Owen heard someone collide with the garbage cans in the alley behind his house. "Oh crap,"

he said breathlessly, his pulse pounding like a 1980s techno beat.

"Stop! Drop your weapon and lay face down on the ground! I said, stop!" The voice was coming from overhead.

*That's the chopper!* Owen thought. He heard his kitchen door exploding inward, followed by soprano screams.

"Shut up! The cops'll hear you," a voice barked.

"Please, don't hurt us," said a man.

"Just take what you want and leave," added a woman.

*Oh my God! Is that Mom and Dad?* Owen asked himself in terror. The memories of the horrible night that had happened the year before sent a chill of fear and disbelief through him.

"No, no, no," he mumbled, unaware that he had even spoken. "This isn't happening."

The chopper pilot alerted the officers underneath. "This is Big Bird! We've got a 10-23! He just entered the white house, third from the south corner!"

Owen glanced down at the code sheet. It corroborated the obvious: He had a cop-killer in his kitchen. But who was with him, the ghosts of his parents? "Please, don't let this be real," he begged. "It's not possible. There's no way that..."

*BANG! BANG! BANG!*

The booming gunshots brought shrill ringing to Owen's ears. Stomping feet rushed through the house like a stampede of horses.

Owen clung to his chair, his breath coming in sharp gasps, his eyes round with fear.

CRASH!

*There goes my front door*, Owen thought, as an icy bolt of electric terror blasted through him.

"Drop it! Now!" someone yelled from the living room.

The warning preceded a flurry of gunshots that sounded like fireworks. Something heavy hit the floor so hard Owen could feel the vibration through his feet. Then the lights shut off and every-thing was quiet.

A chill rolled through Owen; he remained motionless. His breathing was quick and strained. The Doritos and marshmal-low crème soda were backing up on him. He waited for some-one—hopefully, a police officer—to make his presence known. Only silence met him. The radio that moments ago had been alive with the sounds of utter mayhem had gone lifeless.

When Owen's overburdened heart couldn't handle the sus-pense any longer, he pushed himself out of the swivel chair and tip-toed to his bedroom door. He pressed his ear against the thin wood and listened; no sound came from the other side. He eased the door open and peered into the pitch-black hallway. His throat was dry, and his body racked with acute apprehension. "H-h-hello? Is anybody th-th-there?" he croaked. Nothing.

Pushing through his frigid fright, Owen left the safety of his bedroom and slipped out into the hall, but remained close by, in case he had to high-tail it back there. He stood rigid, hoping to hear or see something, but nothingness greeted him.

Owen went to the living room first to assess the damage. The room was dark, save for the weak illumination from the streetlight that stood just beyond the house's scraggly front lawn.

Broken lamps and vases littered the dim room. Someone had overturned one of the wingback chairs. The ugly couch, with its outdated fabric, was askew.

*CRUNCH!*

Owen stopped. He'd stepped on something light-colored and crinkly—a tape outline of a person. The sight of the tape left him shaken and repulsed. A stiff crimson stain coated the carpet within and just beyond the dry tape. Owen stepped over the gruesome discovery and headed towards the mangled opening of the door. When he got there, he barely managed to stop himself from walking through the yellow police tape blocking his doorway, like a plastic cobweb. "What the..."

The loud crackling of the police scanner startled Owen, as it revived itself.

"We've neutralized the gunman," the voice said.

"You've taken the gunman down?" the dispatcher asked.

"Affirmative. We're checking the house now for residents."

Owen's chest heaved in time with his racing heartbeat. *What just happened?* he
wondered.

The mysterious calmness of the house left Owen frightened and confused. So did the bloodstain, but not from its presence—it was the lack of the body it had leaked from. *Where the heck did everybody disappear to?* he wondered. Silent seconds passed. "What's going on?" he shouted to the empty house.

Owen needed to get the lights on; the breakers were in the basement. Unfortunately, the door to the basement was in the kitchen, the place where his parents had suffered execution for the crime of being at home.

Owen's dark imagination seized his frantic mind, as he pictured his parents' corpses sprawled on the floor, punctured by bullet holes, a look of horror and surprise etched on their faces. He choked back a sob. "Oh, Mom... Dad." His melancholy became fearfulness, as he wondered what he might find there: rotting bodies? Shifting shadows that resembled those of his deceased parents? Despite his trepidation, he felt compelled to visit the room of distant ghosts to make sense of the night's supernatural events.

Entering the kitchen, he came across two faded body outlines on the dingy linoleum floor.

The pond of dried blood that surrounded them made it difficult to tell whose was whose. He swooned. "I think I'm going to be sick."

From the bedroom, the scanner shattered the eerie quiet again, causing Owen to jump.

"Dispatch, we have a 187 here."

"Got that—a 187," the dispatcher repeated, before handling the request. "We need a coroner and CSI unit at 1106 Waters Street.

"Copy that. We're en route."

Owen had memorized several codes. The lowest ones signified mundane incidents, such as drunken disturbances or abandoned vehicles. The authorities assigned the higher codes to critical events, such as homicides, robberies, or assaults. Owen didn't have to remember what a murder victim was.

Tears burned his eyes. "God, why are you making me relive this?" Owen asked the quiet heavens. "I can't lose them a second time. Please, whatever this is, make it stop!"

"Unit 11, do you have a name yet on those 187s?"

"Give me a second to check for some ID."

Grief paralyzed Owen. *I can save you some time, officer,* he thought. *They're my parents.*

A short time passed before the officer reported. "Let's see. According to some mail on the kitchen counter, we've got Joe and Angie Mellish."

A distant voice bled through. "Hey, Frank! We have one in the back bedroom."

"Check for ID!" Frank answered.

*One more?* Owen thought. *Who else was...* His stomach fluttered.

"Got it Frank!" the officer hollered. "His name was Owen Mellish!"

# FEEL MY PAIN

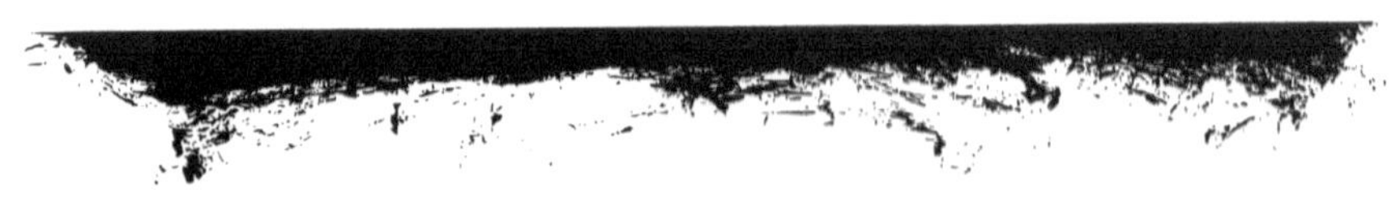

CRRRAAACK... BOOM!

Jagged streaks of ice-white lightning crisscrossed the black October sky, heralding a deep thunder that made the earth tremble in its wake. Swollen clouds wept rain over an infinite line of evening rush hour commuters as they crept along the water-choked interstate. The storm intensified the eeriness of the witching season, the time of year when the thinnest of curtains separates the world of light and darkness. For some, this is when the evil aura of demons, witches, and monsters supplants the benign aspects of everyday life. The noise emanating from the closet door no longer resembled that of a rusty hinge; rather, it resembled a demonic entity desperate to escape. The flow of air through a vent transformed into the eerie sound of a hungry corpse, slowly making its way through the ductwork that leads to their bedroom. For most, October 31st was a night for children to dress up and go trick-or-treating, while adults would attend parties with more potent treats.

Chad was eager to get to such a party, but the storm was calling the shots, slowing all movement to an eternal crawl. Despite upping the car's defroster, he struggled to see beyond the blurry taillights of the vehicle stalled in front of him. He watched the melting colors running down the clear canvas of the wet driver-side window, the city's glowing skyline painting it in soft hues. Torrents of loud rain rushed downhill from the roof of his slate-gray Mercedes AMG, rolling off its polished back like watery fingers unable to take hold. The custom-designed interior held the sweet scent of genuine hand-stitched leather, expensive cologne, and top-shelf whiskey. The car had cost north of $130k, but Chad Swinton, corporate attorney extraordinaire, made four times that amount. He was twenty-nine years old and already he was holding the tiger of success by its tail with one hand while tickling its testicles with the other. However, I-40 couldn't care less about his accomplishments on this hellish Halloween night when rain fell hard and bad things happened.

Chad was benefiting from the wait. He was drunk, and he knew it; courtesy of the fifth of Johnny Walker Scotch that he kept tucked away in the top drawer of his $15,000 custom desk. But how many times had he driven drunk? He couldn't say for sure—kind of like not being able to remember how many drinks he typically downed at one sitting. An alcoholic's math is always fuzzy. He was feeling the effects of his overindulgence: disjointed thoughts, thick tongue, bleary eyes.

Chad switched on the car's state-of-the-art head unit. A talk show he enjoyed was hitting a station break for local news. The lead report was about an altercation at a convenience store at Stratford Road. The police had taken down two allegedly armed gang-bangers named Tyrese Jackson and Michael Taylor. It turned out they were neither armed nor gang-bangers.

"Sniff, sniff, sob, sob," Chad said indifferently, mockingly. "My parents made it out of the hood and became successful. You could have, too." Chad's empathy withered under the glare of his blessed ignorance of what it means to struggle for hope, dignity, and purpose. Unlike his parents, he had never known poverty, only privilege, something he took for granted. He could scarcely imagine that his parents, now prosperous business owners, had grown up attending public schools, working summer jobs, and wearing second-hand clothes. Chad was their overindulged offspring, who enjoyed the benefits of a classical education, a sports car at sixteen, and $200 sneakers, a reward for excellent grades. With a law degree from Yale, and some influential allies, he'd landed a prime position at the largest and most prestigious law firm on the eastern seaboard. His life was one of prominence, power, and conspicuous consumption.

But that life changed the moment a sickly, yellow light brightened the interior of the Mercedes.

Chad flopped forward to get a better look, his body straining against the seatbelt. Several yards ahead, an LED road sign loomed in the furthest right-hand lane.

*POLICE ROADBLOCK AHEAD*
*PREPARE TO SHOW I.D.*

A greasy lump formed in his gut, as an unpleasant scenario played out in his dark imagination. He pictured a cop, annoyed about having to spend his evening working in the incessant rain, looking for drunks. The next scene picked up with the same cop observing the expertly styled, affluent metrosexual sitting in a car that exceeded the value of his own house. Chad envisioned the look of glee on the cop's face as he yanked him from the car after failing a breathalyzer test. The conclusion featured him standing handcuffed in the downpour, looking like a drowned rodent, as he watched his career, future, and the accouterments that come with a cultured life wash away.

Chad's nervous fingers played drum rolls on the steering wheel as the distance closed. He felt like a condemned man being dragged to a prison's death chamber. Frustrated and afraid, he threw his head back and hollered, "Dammit, Chadwick!"

As if in answer to an unspoken prayer, he saw an exit a short distance before the checkpoint. He smiled at the opportunity fate was affording him. "Chadwick, m'boy, therein lies your salvation," he said, much relieved.

Chad anxiously waited, the exit seeming a hundred miles away. "Come on, come ooon," he urged the halting traffic. His impatience grew as he neared his escape route in painful increments. "Almost there," he reassured himself. Finally, he accessed the exit and followed it to MLK Jr. Boulevard.

Not realizing that he'd been holding his breath, Chad exhaled, emptying his lungs and filling the car with the rank scent of stale whiskey. Although he'd narrowly escaped a sure trip to the drunk tank, he realized that the danger wasn't over; he was still wobbly from the alcohol. *Let's hit some back streets and see where they take us,* he thought.

A few blocks later, he saw a street he recognized. Fifth Street ran from the center of downtown for several miles before connecting with Highway 66 South. From there, he had the option of taking the rural two-lane highway through a few small towns before returning to the interstate. Then he would take the second exit, putting him within a few miles of his house.

Chad turned right onto Fifth Street and drove cautiously, working to keep the Mercedes between the lines. As a lawyer, he'd heard about this area of town. But until tonight, he'd never had a reason, or a desire, to pass through it. Rundown rental properties, brothels, liquor stores, and crumbling schools populated this section of the city. The low-income residents shared the poverty, violence, and hopelessness that permeated their community.

A few blocks in, Chad slowed down to ogle some hookers standing on the porch of one of the slum houses. He noted their cheap, ratty wigs, and the tight Daisy-Duke Shorts that outlined their sex. Undersized halter-tops strained against their fleshy cargo. Brightly colored eyeshadow accentuated unnaturally thick eyelashes that resembled tarantulas.

A small group of men lined up on the porch appeared to be waiting for some action. Most of them wore tank tops or sports jerseys, with baggy pants that hung down to their upper thighs, exposing their underwear. As Chad passed by, one of the johns nudged another and pointed out the Mercedes. Chad realized he was sticking out like a sore thumb in his luxurious sports coupe with its vanity plate that read *Up R Class.*

Along the way, a menacing pit bull chained to a shoddy, hand-made doghouse barked his displeasure at him as if to say, "Move along, rich boy. Ain't nothin' to see here."

As Chad ventured deeper into the world beyond his life experience, he became more paranoid.

Ahead, a green stoplight hung over an intersection. Four or five men—Chad couldn't be sure, his vision as foggy as the wind-shield—were taking shelter under a Plexiglas bus stop on the corner. As he neared the intersection, the light turned red. He dreaded the thought of stopping, but he'd already drawn too much un-wanted attention; speeding through the signal would be a bad idea.

When Chad stopped at the corner, he avoided looking at the group. In the tail of his eye, he saw one of the men approaching the passenger side of his car. *Oh hell,* he thought. *Just stay calm, and let's get out of here as soon as that light changes.*

*Thunk—thunk—thunk*

"Hey, bruh!" the stranger shouted, tapping the window. "You get lost, or you lookin' to buy?"

When Chad didn't acknowledge him, the man pounded the window with the side of his fist. "Who the hell you think I'm talkin' to, bitch? You bet-tuh look at me when I'm speakin' to yo uppity, black ass!"

At that moment, a teamster couldn't have driven a straight pin up Chad's tight sphincter with a sledgehammer.

The angry man stepped back, looked the car over, and ad-dressed his companions. "Yo! Y'all come check out diss ride!"

One man pulled the hood of his jacket over his head, ambled around to the driver's side of the Mercedes, and began yanking the door handle.

Chad's adrenaline flooded his quaking body like jet fuel, quickening his heartbeat, and turning his bowels into Jello. He needed to flee—now! But rather than ripping through the stop-light, he turned right and barreled down a side street.

Unlike the major stretch, this road was narrower and had fewer streetlights. Chad drove erratically, twice hitting the curb. *These people are crazy!* he thought. *How do they live in all this filth? What a bunch of useless, sorry—*

**THUD!**

He felt the car lurch as something large hit its front and rolled over the roof. Immediately, he stomped the brake pedal, causing the car to hydroplane a short distance before screeching to a stop on the rain-slick street.

"Crap! What kind of junk did I just hit?" he growled. "These people better not have screwed up this car. It costs more than every dump in this project!"

Chad climbed out of the car, keeping a watchful eye out for anyone who might pose a threat. The coast was clear. Soon, annoyance returned to him like a searing heat. *Great! I'm soaking wet. Now my upholstery's gonna get stained*, he worried.

Chad walked to the front of the car to survey the damage. The object had smashed the grill and dented the hood. Then he went to inspect the rear of the car. He felt pleased upon discovering that the trunk remained undamaged. He figured whatever he'd hit must've flown clear.

"Aaaah... Aaaah..."

Chad faced the sound. A dark shape was moving in the middle of the road. *Tell me I didn't run over one of these street gangsta's watchdogs. Now, who'll guard the meth lab?* he thought, snickering. As he approached the groaning mass, he made a mental note not to try moving it. *On top of everything else, I don't need rabies.*

When he was within a few yards of the obstacle, his stomach forced itself up to his throat.

He'd hit a person... and they were still alive.

Chad knelt beside the victim, getting a better look. The child couldn't have been more than ten or eleven. Chad turned to his side and vomited at the gruesome state of the young boy's ruined body. His upper torso was facing up—the lower half in the opposite direction.

"Oh, God," the child moaned. "Somebody help me!" Blood gurgled in his mouth, preventing him from saying more. Thin rivulets of crimson and gray leaked from his ears. The rain washed it away, seemingly intent on purifying him. The rough asphalt had shredded what looked like a Grim Reaper costume. In his clenched hand was a plastic Halloween treat bag. The impact of the car had knocked his sneakers off: one was lying on the sidewalk, the other hiding somewhere in the shadows. He looked into Chad's terrified face, his eyes frightened and pleading. "Please, call somebody. Oh, Lord, I'm scared to die."

Chad squeaked when the child grabbed his forearm. Then the injured boy coughed out some words—ones that Chad would want to forget.

"Please, sir. Don't let me die here. I don't want my momma to see me in the street."

Chad felt conflicted. The child was only a 911 call away from getting urgent medical assistance. But at what cost to himself? The authorities would know immediately that he'd been driving drunk. Chad trembled at the realization that he would lose everything he'd worked for. The bad press would destroy the firm. His sense of self-preservation overrode his compassion as he made his decision.

"Shhhhh, be quiet," he told the struggling child. Looking around and not seeing any witnesses, Chad felt the same comfort of relief as when the God of Lucky Breaks had bestowed the exit upon him.

He wrestled his arm free of the boy's grip, then leaned in close enough to be heard over the unforgiving rain. "Sorry, mah man. I know you're hurting and all, but if you think about it, I've done you a favor." Chad waved his arm in a sweeping gesture, displaying the impoverished neighborhood. "I mean, daaamn, son. Is this all you have to look forward to? Nah, it's best if you stay here and die like a good boy. Unlike you and your peeps, I've got a life to live."

Chad rose, then stood over the moribund child. His face was a cruel, expressionless mask as he watched the dying boy reach his hand up to him as if begging for mercy. He couldn't be sure if it was tears or raindrops rolling from the boy's eyes. He didn't care, and he didn't stick around to find out.

As Chad zigzagged his way back to his car, he realized that he might not yet be in the clear.

His legal skills were useful when he recalled a case involving a hit-and-run driver caught through wreckage evidence. Chad thanked his benevolent gods again and walked around the car, picking up several chunks of his front grill. Confident that he had gathered them all, he nonchalantly tossed them into the car and sped away. He never looked back.

Sticking to his original plan, Chad followed the quiet back roads to the interstate. From there, he drove until he came upon the exit that would get him back home, hopefully without further incident.

Chad was relieved when he reached the ornate iron gates of Kellington, a private, upscale community. He punched in his code and waited as the two large gates grudgingly opened.

Careening through a world he better knew, Chad felt safer by the moment. The contrast between the derelict neighborhood he had managed to escape and the opulent enclave he was now traversing did not escape his notice. He'd taken for granted the magnificent community that was home to top-tier surgeons, bankers, and upscale attorneys such as him. Never before had he marveled at the towering oaks on either side of the road; their rich, green canopies shielding residents from the sunlight like gentle green hands. The grounds of the stately homes were resplendent with beautiful and meticulously landscaped lawns. This universe belonged to Chad and he to it.

Chad directed the Mercedes along his house's circular drive-way, taking care not to hit the stone fountain at its center. He pressed the blue tooth button on the steering wheel, opening the massive garage door of his Georgian colonial-style house.

He pulled in, parked alongside his expensive Vyrus 987 motorcycle, and killed the sports car's rumbling engine. Closing the garage door, he quickly entered the house and went directly to the bar in his study.

After pouring himself a double-bourbon, Chad walked over and collapsed in the plush, brown leather sofa, wallowing in his predicament. He placed his forearm over his eyes and tried to relax. Almost immediately, the mangled boy appeared in his mind's eye, causing him to jolt forward in terror as he teetered on the edge of a scream. "Get it together, Chadwick. You've got this," he mumbled to himself.

After sucking down the liquor in two big gulps, Chad stood and began pacing the room. Throughout his life and career, he'd always evaded trouble and its inconvenient consequences. This skill had also helped his corporate clients, who sought to exploit the legal system for their benefit.

Chad continued pacing, repeating his brain fuel mantra: *For every problem, there's a solution... for every problem, there's a solution...*

After a bit, it occurred to Chad to check the news. His hand was shaking so badly that he almost dropped his cellphone. He went to a local news app and searched for any word on the child. His heart clenched when he came to a story about the accident.

*Local police are investigating what appears to be a fatal hit and run in the Northeast part of the city. The incident occurred in the two hundred block of Samuel Street between the hours, 8-10 PM. Now that authorities have notified the victim's relatives, we can identify the deceased as ten-year-old Cameron Miller. It is thought that he was heading home after going trick-or-treating. Detectives interviewed several residents and learned that no one recalled witnessing or hearing anything unusual. Investigators have found no evidence at the scene, making it difficult for the make or model of the vehicle to be determined. Police are asking anyone with information to contact the Anonymous Hotline at 1-800-TIP-LINE.*

*—Reported by Emily Newsome*

As Chad remembered the fragments in the car, his pulse began returning to normal. "Thank God. Can't believe I had the presence of mind to collect all those pieces. Who da maaan?!" he crowed.

Drenched in rainwater and sour perspiration, he threw back another tumbler of Jim Beam, then went upstairs to shower.

Once there, Chad used the shower's voice activator to turn itself on. Then he accessed the water temperature panel on the bathroom wall screen, bumping it up to a soothing ninety-eight degrees. He peeled off his soaked clothes and dumped them in the hamper. Then he entered the oversized shower and allowed the balmy waters to wash away his stress.

As he reflected on the incident, he felt a twinge of guilt. Then he remembered what he had said to the boy: *I know you're hurting and all, but if you think about it, I've done you a favor.* He convinced himself that this was so. *Yeah, he's better off,* Chad continued telling himself. *I only did what I needed to do. I certainly contribute more to society than a homeboy ever would've. Just saying.*

Finishing what he considered a cathartic cleansing, Chad instructed the shower to turn itself off. Rubbing his damp scalp and body with an Egyptian cotton towel, he walked over to the bathroom vanity. "Now I feel almost human again—at least as much as a lawyer can." He giggled at the remark but stopped when he looked at what someone had drawn on the steamed mirror.

**I don't feel better off**

Chad leaped backward. "What the hell?" he puffed. He wrapped the towel around his middle, then cautiously entered the bedroom. He tiptoed to the nightstand by his bed, opened its top drawer, and removed a Sig Sauer 9mm. He searched the room's walk-in closet, as well as under his bed, but found no one.

All at once, a series of crashes erupted from the downstairs study, startling Chad.

He removed a pair of sweatpants from his dresser and pulled them on. Then he left the bedroom and jogged to the staircase, stopping at its top. "I hope your gun is as big as the one I'm holding!" he warned. The only response came from the pounding storm and its angry thunder.

Chad made his way downstairs to the entrance of the study. Craning his neck, he glanced inside before defensively jerking his head back. He had seen no one, so he reasoned the person was hiding or had moved to another room.

Upon entering the study, he saw that someone had smashed every bottle from his bar against the walls. His face flushed with indignation. "Are you kidding me?! Do you know how much that stuff costs?!"

"Momma saw me!" the angry voice boomed from the dining room.

Chad froze. "What's that supposed to mean? Who the hell are—

"You're right," said the voice. "I am better off... better off than you."

Chad was unnerved, but he also felt taunted by the stranger. Anxiety turned to outrage. "You arrogant mother—" He charged toward the voice, his gun raised.

He rushed into the formal dining room, skidding to a halt. He looked under the long cypress table. Nothing.

Curious as to whom the intruder might be, Chad began thinking through plausible possibilities. Finally, he hit on what he thought was the right answer. Someone had seen the accident, saw he was a man of means, and then followed him home. He wondered if the visit was about revenge or extortion. It didn't matter, he figured. All he needed to do was to lure the person out, then shoot him. The claim of self-defense would be a no-brainer.

"I'm sure you don't know who I am, but I can make a lot of bad things happen with a single phone call," Chad said. "Or you can come out and talk with me, face to face. I'm sure we can come to some kind of reasonable agreement."

Several small objects flew into the room and scattered on top of the polished table. Air whooshed from Chad's body as the sticky sweat returned. His eyes broadened when he recognized the fragments of the Mercedes' grill. "What do you *waaant*?!" he yelled.

He walked beside the table and stopped at the entrance to the adjoining kitchen. Written in mud on the floor were the words...

**For every problem, there's a solution**

For one of the few times in his life, Chad didn't feel cocky or in control. He felt powerless, and it was a feeling he didn't care for.

He crept into the kitchen, taking care to lay each foot on the floor as gently as possible. Suddenly, the lights went out. "Oh, crap. What now?" he muttered. Nervously, he felt his way through the dark to the granite island in the middle of the room. He opened a drawer and retrieved a flashlight, turning it on.

Chad took a hesitant step. A sudden yelp escaped his lips when he almost slipped on something slick. He shone the flashlight on the floor. The treat bag the boy had been holding glowed in the bright beam. He shuddered.

The sound of something moving around in the nearby garage startled Chad, causing him to recoil.

Clutching the Sig Sauer in his right hand and the flashlight in his left, he eased across the floor, stopping at the door that led to the garage. Tucking the flashlight under his arm, he turned the knob and eased open the door.

Leaning in, his shaky hand bounced the flashlight's beam over the large, shady area. "Okay, you've gotten my attention. Come on out and we'll talk," Chad said. Garnering no movement or response, he added, "Look, I'm gonna lay the gun down. That way you're safe to come out and make your pitch. Fair?"

"Put it down and come see me. I want you to see *meeee*..." the phantom voice hissed.

Pimples of terror carpeted Chad's skin. "Okay, b-but remember, you can't c-collect from a dead man," he stammered.

"I don't agree with that," the voice rumbled. Then: "I'm way-tiiing..."

Chad's knees threatened to give way. His throat was dry, his form frigid with fright. "All right, I'm coming down. I-I trust you to have enough good sense to work this out with me. I can m-make it worth your while."

He put down the gun, then descended the four wooden steps to floor level, the concrete cold against his bare feet. He guided the ray around the dim garage. "Hello?" he squeaked.

Chad gasped when the flashlight went out, his heart pummeling against its bony cage. "Dammit," he murmured. He beat the flashlight against the ball of his palm to revive it, without result. He stopped when he heard something that sounded like the snapping of dry sticks.

*Skoosh... Skoosh...*

A soft shuffling was coming in his direction. Chad's insides tingled. After a moment, he detected something directly in front of him... gurgling... panting. Panicked, he hammered the flashlight with greater speed and force. Finally, it returned to life.

The broken boy stood in front of him, still wearing the tattered, blood-soaked Grim Reaper costume. His upper half was facing away from Chad; his lower half toward him. Gradually, his upper body made sickening pops, as it turned around until it realigned with the rest. The thing gave an evil sneer, its cracked teeth dangling from bleeding gums. The neck, crooked and swollen, looked as though it might burst from a buildup of gore and shattered bone. "Remember me?" Cameron hissed.

"Oh no. N-n-noooo," Chad huffed. Tied to his terror, he was afraid to move, unable to flee.

The living corpse glared at Chad, its blood-tinged eyes bulging to where they looked ready to pop free of their sockets. With a crack, the neck of the ravaged thing gave way, causing its head to sway from side to side. Dead Cameron lifted his loose head in his hands, stretched the neck, and pushed his ashen face so close that Chad could smell the rot inside him. "Feel... my... pain."

Breaking free of his trance, Chad ran to a side door. He turned its deadbolt, yanked it open, and bolted from the garage.

He barreled down the long driveway and into the flooding street. In an act of defiance, he turned and lifted his middle finger. "Haunt *this* you useless piece of—

**THUMP!**

Chad rolled end-over-end along the roof of the braking Jaguar XF, before crashing to the ground in a cracking heap. His bouncing body felt like a rock skipping across a pond filled with razor blades. Nerve endings screamed as he scraped over the unmerciful blacktop, deep strips of skin ripping away. After what seemed like an eternity of unrelenting agony, he finally skidded to a stop.

The car's driver jumped out, then raced through the downpour toward the writhing figure, desperately praying that the person was still alive. Kneeling beside the man, he immediately recognized his neighbor: the *vindictive*, wildly successful, *vindictive* attorney. "Oh, dear," the man said as he considered the depth of his dilemma.

Chad, though barely conscious, worked up enough breath to speak. "Thank God. It's you, Bill. Please help... me."

Bill didn't respond. His frantic mind was busy deciding whether he should be compassionate or practical. *I want to do the right thing,* he thought, *but this guy could ruin everything for me, Rebecca, and the kids.* He looked into Chad's eyes and winced at the awful solution.

"Bill, p-please. Get help," Chad begged.

Bill continued staring at him.

Chad felt a fear that went beyond his grievous and possibly fatal injuries. He recognized the cold-blooded look in Bill's eyes... knew it well. "Bill, for the l-love of God."

Bill made his decision. He scanned the surrounding houses anxiously for any lights or movement. Because each home sat on generous acreage, they were far apart. He figured this played to his advantage, as if he were destined to escape. He rose and ran to the Jaguar, then sped away, never looking back.

"Oh, God! Oh, God!" Chad whimpered. "Please don't let me die in the street. I have too much left to do. This isn't fair!" Tears mixed with pelting rain cascaded down his raw face.

Then Chad noticed people gathering around him. Looking up, he saw five African-Americans looming over him, their faces scowling, piercing eyes full of hatred. They wore the fashion of the backstreets, with thick rain plastering it against their pallid skin. Four of the group were young men in their early twenties. Two of them resembled crack-ravaged skeletons, while the other two bore multiple bullet holes. One female, a teenager, appeared pregnant. Her broken, battered body looked like Conor McGregor had pummeled it into a powder. The last revenant, an elderly woman, had leathery skin that suggested decades of abusing alcohol and cigarettes.

Chad's body seized up. He thought perhaps that shock was playing tricks on his eyes, causing his meager conscience to fill his head with guilt about the avoidable death he'd caused. He opened his mouth, pushing the rain out so it wouldn't choke him. "What are you people d-d-doing here? How'd you get into this... neighborhood?"

The quartet parted as if to make room for another person. Chad's throat refused to give up a scream when the corpse of the child he'd left to die joined them.

As Cameron spoke, a thick goop dripped from his mouth and onto Chad's face. "Sorry, mah man. I know you're hurtin' and all, but look around you."

Chad looked at the other ghostly figures. "Please, don't do this. I'm... I'm sorry."

The Cameron-thing's face was expressionless, cruel. "Shhhhh. It's best if you stay here and die like a good boy."

As Chad's vision dimmed, the last things he saw were the grinning corpses reaching down to take him. This time, he screamed.

Hours later, the shattered body of Chad Swinton lay on a cold metal drawer inside one of the morgue's refrigerated units.

The ding from the rear entrance's motion detector alerted Steve, the sleeping morgue attendant, that someone was there to either drop off or claim a body. He rose from his chair, stretched, and gazed at the monitor that displayed the loading area. Two young black men dressed in cheap but tidy suits were waiting at the backdoor with an empty gurney. On top laid a long, black, plastic bag.

Steve pressed the intercom button. "You guys here for a pickup?"

One man looked up at the camera and flashed an OK sign.

"I'll buzz you in," Steve said.

The two men entered and made their way to the autopsy room, the gurney's wheels squeaking over the scuffed floor of the otherwise silent hallway.

Steve shuffled papers on his squat metal desk, working to make it appear as though he'd been wide awake, and engaged in some important activity before the drivers arrived.

The unsmiling men entered the open room, stopping to stare at Steve.

"So, who ya here for?" Steve asked.

One of them reached into an inner pocket of his jacket and retrieved a form, handing it toSteve.

Steve gave the paper a cursory glance. "Okay, you're wantin' Swinton, Chadwick. He's right over here: drawer #9."

The two men waited as Steve opened the small, sealed door.

After sliding the drawer out and yanking back the cover on the body, Steve stood back and sang, "Ta-da!" He expected a laugh, but none was forthcoming.

The men wheeled the gurney beside the stainless steel drawer, unzipped the body bag, and spread it open to receive the freezing corpse. Once they had secured Chad's ragged remains, they steered the gurney to the loading area, Steve following them.

As they put Chad's body into the back of the hearse, Steve cocked his head in concentration. He had a strong feeling he'd seen the two men before. As they were getting into the vehicle, Steve called out to them. "Hey, guys! Don't I know you two from somewhere?"

The driver looked at Steve; his face was blank, his eyes dead. "We were here a short while back," he said flatly. "My name's Tyrese. He's Michael. See ya 'round."

As the hearse pulled away from the loading area, Steve noticed the name of the funeral home on the back window: Cameron Miller Mortuary.

# DON'T BE LATE

## I

B ryan Blanch sped from his luxury New York apartment as though his life depended on it. *I've got about ten seconds to make it to the elevator if I'm gonna hit the lobby by seven-fifteen. It's that or I'm gonna be late*, he scolded himself.

Arriving at the elevator, Bryan pressed the down-button at least twenty times in rapid succession. When it got around to reaching his floor, he wasted no time getting into it.

Once he boarded, Bryan became irritated when the sliding doors didn't close as fast as he wanted. *Why aren't they as quick as the ones in science fiction shows?* he wondered. Bryan kept jabbing the first floor button with violent intent. The journey down was slow and agonizing. The cruel metal box became a trampoline as he jumped up and down on its floor. After what felt to him like an eternity, the doors opened at a speed he found downright sadistic. The entire experience reminded him of how much he despised the lazy lift. Its timing was one of the few things he couldn't manipulate or control.

Bryan erupted onto the sidewalk, filled with the daily parade of the white-collared undead. Threading himself through the horde, he began power-walking at the pace of an outright jog. He preferred to walk to the office. Buses were too slow, and hailing cabs in lower Manhattan was a hit-or-miss proposition.

One of the first things he had done, after moving into his posh Manhattan apartment, was to plan the quickest and most direct route to the Miser Building where he worked. It was where the prestigious Fortune 500 Company of Tyler, Milford, and Drake made their top executives prosperous by keeping a select group of clients fat, dumb, and happy. The big boys hailed Bryan as one of the most gifted efficiency experts on the East Coast.

One of Bryan's most noteworthy talents was the ability to recall every number, person, place with exact detail. For example, he remembered that Walter Shimmel, the Director of Human Resources, had hired him at 3:08 p.m. on April 11, 2015. Bryan's mental files were accurate, useful, and weaponized. Without notes or mercy, he could offer cold numbers, overly complicated charts and graphs, and empirical data to executives who needed to trim the human fat from their corporate bottom line. Because of his peerless expertise, he'd ascended the corporate ladder to a staggering height, much like his corner office on the coveted twenty-ninth floor. There, he would come face-to-face with the man who would change his destiny.

Bryan was going over his notes for his afternoon presentation to the muckety-mucks when his phone buzzed.

"Mr. Blanch?" asked Marta, his executive secretary.

Bryan huffed with annoyance at the intrusion. "Yes, Marta. What's this about?"

"There's a gentleman here who says he has important business to discuss with you."

"Does he have an appointment?"

"No, sir, but he's very insistent that you give him a moment of your time."

Bryan's mouth slumped as he mulled over his decision to accommodate the uninvited visitor. *Guess I could use a break to refresh,* he reasoned.

"Okay, Marta. Send him in. But it'd better be quick."

"Yes sir, Mr. Blanch."

The stranger entered Bryan's considerable corporate sanctum, or as he called it, "The Butcher Shop."

Being very detail-oriented, Bryan took immediate notice of the tall, lean man. He was wearing a pressed blue suit with creases so sharp, you could use them to slice meat; at its base were black Italian shoes polished to perfection. He sported a simple but tasteful necktie that was nestled into the crisp collar of a brilliant white shirt. His dark sculpted hair crowned a handsome face that exuded intelligence, sophistication and confidence. His gaze was intense, but not threatening.

After cordially introducing himself to the stranger, Bryan offered him a chair, but the man declined.

"Let us see what happens next before I take a seat," he said, with an elegant German accent.

"As you wish," Bryan said, before taking a seat himself behind his expansive desk. "I rarely take meetings with people who don't have an appointment. That you're meeting with me tells me that my receptionist found you charming and persuasive—you sound a lot like me."

To Bryan's chagrin, the witty remark drew no reaction from the man. Dropping his smarmy grin, Bryan cleared his throat and took it from the top. "Look, whoever you are, I'm a very busy man; I must insist that you get to the point. Tick Tock, Tick Tock," he said, tapping the face of his Omega wristwatch."

A mischievous smile grew across the face of the curious visitor. "Oh, believe me, Mr. Blanch, this will not be a waste of your time. In fact, I think you're going to enjoy the proposal I'd like to pitch to you today."

"That so?" Bryan asked with a dash of smugness. "Talk to me, but like I said, make it quick."

"Yes, Mr. Blanch—Tick Tock, Tick Tock. My name is Gunther Schmidt. I represent a prominent multinational corporation with vast experience dealing with clients from all backgrounds over the years. In that time, our proud company has expanded to such a degree that it requires a good bit of creative and efficient reorganization."

"And the name of that company?" Bryan asked.

"I'll get to that later," answered Schmidt. "For now, let's just say that it's an organization I'm sure you're familiar with. Think Amazon, Walmart, and Berkshire Hathaway, only bigger."

The man did not yet impress Bryan. "Am I supposed to play Twenty Questions? Look, state your business or get out."

"I fully understand your impatience, Mr. Blanch; I'm a busy man myself. I'm also a very particular sort of man. You see, I'm not here to impress *you*. I'm here to find out if you can impress *me*."

Bryan narrowed his eyes at Schmidt. "If I didn't already impress you, why'd you come here?"

Schmidt sniffled with laughter. "There it is, right there. You are very sharp, my friend, very sharp. I've come to you because of your well-earned reputation for meticulous planning and dispassionate decision-making. But it's your penchant for achieving results with precision and well-reasoned forethought that impresses me the most."

Bryan leaned forward, his interest now piqued. "Continue," he said.

"I'd like to offer you a challenge. If you prove to me you can deliver a special item at an exact time and location of my choosing, I can assure you we will do business together for a very long time. It will be most lucrative. However, if you are incapable of completing the task, there are no worries. You will still receive a handsome cash reward for your time and effort. It's a win-win, wouldn't you say?"

Schmidt's glowing compliments pushed Bryan's super-inflated ego to the point of a near explosion. However, that he was also entertaining the possibility of failure on Bryan's part was humbling. Although he was a tad uneasy by the man's reluctance to share any more details about his business, it excited him to put his skills and reputation on the line to humble Schmidt. "Let's hear the challenge," Bryan said with eagerness.

"The rules are quite easy to understand," said Schmidt. "However, it's the finish line that will be nearly impossible to cross."

"Oh, I think my skill set might surprise if not astonish you."

"All right, then. Are you familiar with the rest of the Lower East Side of Manhattan?"

"Know it like the lines on my face," bragged Bryan. "Keep it coming."

"Ooh," cooed Schmidt. "Now I'm even more impressed with you. Some might view your statement as arrogant or reckless, but I call it moxie.

Schmidt inspected the two leather chairs in front of Bryan's dark mahogany desk. He selected his favorite and sat down. "I told you I'm particular," he said, winking at Bryan. He gracefully crossed his legs, then straightened the left cuff of his trousers until it was just so. Reaching into his inner jacket, he extracted a small, cream-colored envelope about the size of an invitation.

"Is that invite for me?" joked Bryan.

"Yes, I suppose it is," Schmidt said with a slight laugh. "If you can meet my expectations, that is."

"I'm listening," Bryan responded.

"Very good." Schmidt allowed a moment to pass before speaking again, as though he wanted to form the most cogent and succinct way of explaining his directions. "I want you to deliver this envelope to me at a building at 104 Beaumont Street at 11:09 a.m. on Tuesday, May 11 of this year—that's two weeks from today. Because you are reputedly a stickler for planning and punctuality, I expect effort on your part—no cheating. You may not use any form of transportation other than your own two feet. No clever tricks such as standing nearby, watching the time click past—I expect constant movement. You need to plan your route so that you arrive at the time given. If you are not standing in front of that building with this delivery at exactly that moment, you will have failed this assignment."

"Who says I'll even take you on? You seem flaky, not to put too fine a point on it."

"Then I'll have to move on to a more talented and ambitious individual. And you will always wonder when or if you'll have this opportunity again."

Bryan tried to keep his face from showing the momentary doubt that had broken off a small crumb of his bravado. Forcing a casual tone, he said, "As they say on the award shows," 'The envelope, please.'"

Demonstrating some theatrical flair, Murphy lowered his arm like a drawbridge and presented the envelope.

With an equal amount of dramatic panache, Brian pulled the card from Schmidt's outstretched hand, as though he were plucking a delicate rose. Holding it up to the overhead light, Bryan looked at the envelope with an obvious air of suspicion. "So, what's inside?"

"Your final directive. You are to open it after you arrive, and not before. Follow it to the letter."

"How do I know you're on the up and up?"

"If you decline the offer, I will be on my way. Tick Tock, Mr. Blanch. Tick Tock."

Bryan could think of fifty reasons to throw Schmidt out of his office, but only two to play the game: his ego and reputation. "Okay, I'll bite. I'll see you in a couple of weeks," he said.

"Yes. I've faith that you will. Now then, do you fully understand the terms that I've just presented to you?"

"Be in front of the building at 104 Beaumont Street on Tuesday, May 11 of this year at 11:09 a.m. with this delivery. Not earlier.

Not later. Got it. In the vault," Bryan beamed, pointing to his brain.

"Outstanding. Oh, one more thing—and this is, of course, your decision. You may want to keep this little test of your acumen to yourself, rather than bragging to your colleagues. Consider what they, your stockholders, and your employers will make of your inadequacy should you crash and burn? Food for thought, food for thought."

Schmidt smiled, then stood and headed for the two large, hand-carved wooden doors of

Bryan's spacious office. He reached for the doorknob, then stopped. "Oh, and just for the record, I'm hoping you pull this off. I so want to be impressed. It would be amazing to have a man with your abilities aboard. Good day, Mr. Blanch... and good luck."

# 2

When he returned from his presentation, Bryan began mapping out his necessary departure time, as well as the most efficient and barrier-free route. He questioned the wisdom of playing a game with a man he'd only just met. However, he felt more enthusiastic and exhilarated about his job than he had for a long time. For him, it was the challenge of it all. The task allowed him to showcase all he had learned from childhood through college and his years as a practiced and accomplished professional. The mantra his father taught him as a child stuck with him: "Early is on time, on time is late, and late is don't bother showing up." Except for this time, that old advice wouldn't be helpful. He couldn't be early, and he couldn't be late. He had to arrive on time, down to the absolute nanosecond. *What was it, 11:09 a.m.? Not 11:08 or 11:10,* he reminded himself.

The game was officially afoot.

# 3

After work, Bryan made the journey to 104 Beaumont Street. The building was still a work in progress. Twelve stories of iron scaffolding pushed toward the city sky. A large wooden sign posted outside the protective chain wire fencing displayed the finished apartment building, as well as information regarding the construction company and the bank that was financing the project.

Bryan stared at the building's great steel skeleton and sneered. "I own you, you quirky German."

Each morning leading up to the delivery, Bryan got up at 5:00 a.m. With a stopwatch in hand, he stood in front of his office building and walked the ten-block route, timing it. He repeated the ritual three times before heading to work each day. He was a tad doubtful at first. It took him over two dozen tries before he figured out the exact speed that he had to walk in order to arrive at the agreed-upon time.

When the day arrived, Bryan took some time to relax with some light yoga before heading to work. He didn't want his anxiety and adrenaline forcing him to lose focus or to rush.

Bryan struggled to concentrate throughout the morning. He kept nervously checking the time. *Get downstairs at ten-nineteen—SHARP!* he ordered himself. By nine-thirty, he had nearly worn a path through the carpet, pacing relentlessly, and squeezing a rubber stress ball.

By ten o'clock, he couldn't take the tension any longer, so he left for the lobby early. He got strange looks from the people coming and going as he fidgeted on a seat, tapping his legs, and mumbling to himself. He garnered more stares when his watch clicked to ten-nineteen. "It's about damn time!" he shouted.

*Ready, set, go!* thought Bryan, as he leaped off the lowest step of the building where Tyler, Milford, and Drake loomed over the city. He walked to the prescribed place he'd embedded in his brain to the point of muscle memory. Down sidewalks and alleyways, he followed his route with commitment, determination, and focus.

There were only two blocks left. *Keep at this pace,* Bryan's mental coach reminded him. *From this point, it should take you forty-seven steps before you reach the flower shop doorway.*

It's been said that men plan, and God laughs. Such was Bryan's misfortune when, just before reaching the flower shop, a couple walked out. Bryan couldn't avoid the collision. The man was pushed back by the impact, but the woman fell down. The man started yelling at him, but the only voice filling his mind was his own . *"Crap! Why'd this happen now?"*

"You idiot!" screamed the man.

*How long has it been since I hit them?* wondered Bryan.

"... sue you for everything..."

*Relax and check your stopwatch.*

"Where do you think you're going?"

Bryan had to do some quick recalculations. *I know I should step onto the corner curb at 14th Street at eleven o'six. I'll just jog slowly until my stopwatch hits that time.*

Once Bryan was back on schedule, he relaxed. However, the calm dissipated when it occurred to him that he couldn't remember if he'd put the envelope in his jacket pocket before he left for the office. *You moron!* his racing mind screamed. He needed to keep passing the landmarks on his route on time, so stopping to check for it would only complicate things. As he walked, he tapped his pockets, hoping to find the irksome envelope. He was relieved when he felt it tucked inside the pocket of his inner jacket.

Bryan could hear his heartbeat in his ears; his breathing was heavy and quick. Owing to his nerves, he hadn't eaten breakfast, and now he was feeling a tad queasy and light-headed. His mind became both friend and foe. Finally, he spotted the building about fifty yards ahead.

...thirty yards

*What if I don't make it?*
...ten yards
*What if I do?*
...five yards
*Look at the watch*
...four feet
...*three, two, one*
...curb
...*eleven o'nine*
"I maaade iiit!" Bryan yelled.

He threw open his jacket, removed the envelope, and ripped it open. "So," Bryan said through a cocky smile, "what's next, you pompous jerk?"

Inside the envelope was a thick card containing the final directive:

LOOK UP ^

As Bryan peered upward, his smile became a wide-open mouth of stupid confusion, as a half-ton girder dropped on top of him.

Traffic screeched to a stop. People screamed and gawked at the pulverized sidewalk in front of 104 Beaumont, where a man of impeccable timing and execution had just stood in triumphant.

Across the street, Bryan felt confounded and afraid as he appeared beside the handsome man in the elegant blue suit.

Schmidt grinned as he continued to stare at the mad and grisly scene across the street. "Wow, I am impressed," he commented. "You were right on the mark. You know, some people disparage the tardy by saying they'll be late for their own funerals. But you weren't, my friend. No, sir—you are as advertised! I'm so glad to have you on board with the company. As I told you: We're growing larger every day. But with you there to help with our ongoing expansion, I'm confident we'll be able to service the many for a very long time."

Schmidt's face beamed with satisfaction as he placed his arm around Bryan's slumped and trembling shoulders. And then they were gone.

# THE DRAINING ROOM

## I

Kyle rapped on the rear service door of the funeral home, hoping someone would soon come and open it. It was frigid this time of year in the Kentucky hills, particularly at this late hour. The biting winter wind cut through his frame despite his heavy coat. Each time his bare knuckles smacked the dented metal door, an icy shock pulsed up his arm, reminding him he was within minutes of hypothermia. The wind roared, blocking out all sound beyond the door, including footsteps. It had been a good ten minutes of pounding at this point. He'd give it one more before giving up. He balled his fist, preparing to deliver a heavy hammering. Suddenly, there was a light metal clanking emanating from within the door. *It's about time,* Lyle thought.

A tall, spindly man with patches of wiry brown hair on his otherwise bald head stood in the doorway. His cheeks were sallow and his skin loose on his skeletal form. The blue lab coat he wore was wrinkled and stained—with what Lyle did not want to know.

"Mr. Crayton? I'm Lyle. I hope I came to the right door."

"You needn't have beat the door so hard," Crayton sneered. "We don't move fast around here. It's not as if our clientele have anywhere to be." He pushed the door further out, stepped to one side, and with a dramatic flip of his hand, beckoned Lyle inside.

"Thank you," Lyle said, stomping snow from his frozen shoes before entering. "I was beginning to think I might freeze to death out there."

"Well, if you had, you'd have been in the right place," the morose man said with no hint of humor. As he spoke, Lyle couldn't help but look at his teeth, or rather, what remained of them.

They were small and cracked with black splotches near the top from lack of care. His breath stank of stale coffee and gum disease.

Crayton allowed the heavy door to slam shut, causing Lyle to jerk. "You might want to toughen up, boy. Otherwise, you'll be afraid of everything else in here."

The interior hallway felt like a furnace compared to the outside chill. Lyle unbuttoned his coat and slung it over his shoulder.

Seeing Lyle making himself comfortable, Crayton said, "That door gets opened a lot during the day and sometimes at night, so I like to keep the hallway warm. It'll be cooler in the prep room. Now, who did you say you were?"

"I'm Lyle Blaylock. We spoke on the phone a few nights ago. I answered your ad. You hired me as an apprentice."

"Oh, right... right," Crayton said, nodding his head at the recollection. "I recall you sounded very earnest." He walked past Lyle, waving his hand in a come-along motion. The blue shoe booties the curmudgeonly corpse handler wore slid smoothly and silently down the wide hall, creating the illusion he was floating rather than walking.

Lyle nervously followed him. The place was already putting his nerves on end, his neck hairs as well. A harsh odor—something like formaldehyde—made him queasy. The hallway was eerily silent. The only sound was the slap of his damp shoes on the pale green linoleum floor. It looked older than dirt—probably the only flooring the depressing old building had ever known. He noticed some pale parallel tracks leading to a pair of swinging double doors ahead. He presumed they were from the gurneys that taxied the dead around before their journey to the earthen hole where they'd be planted like holly bushes and forgotten.

Crayton continued. "You said that you haven't got any experience in this field, but were eager to learn. I like initiative. Besides, it's not as though we have a lot of qualified applicants way out here in the sticks. The ones who have come through have been few and far between—the job's not for everyone."

"I plan to stick around as long as you'll have me, Mr. Crayton. The funeral homes back where I'm from require a one-year college certificate just to begin an apprenticeship."

Stopping at the thick plastic doors, Crayton turned to Lyle and grinned. Lyle didn't like that grin. It was better suited for a jack-o'-lantern than a man. And inside a creepy funeral home, in the shadowy portion of a one-light town, it was undeniably sinister.

"You hear that?" Crayton whispered.

Lyle swallowed hard. "Hear what, sir?"

"Exactly," Crayton said. "Not a single complaint about your lack of training. But we'll take care of that right and proper. Let's start with getting you suited up. Wouldn't do to get fluids all over that nice, clean shirt and those fancy pants, would it?"

"No sir. I'd like to avoid that at all costs."

"That's what I figured. Come with me."

Upon entering the room beyond the doors, Crayton handed Lyle an oversized pair of surgical scrubs and pointed him to a small, grungy bathroom to change.

When he finished dressing, Lyle placed his street clothes on the bathroom counter and joined Crayton, who was leaning over the naked body of a paunchy, middle-aged man, inspecting his mouth.

Crayton glanced up, noticing Lyle's return, then gestured towards a wall shelf. "Grab that face guard and a rubber apron, then come over here. I want to show you something."

Lyle put on the protective gear and stood opposite Crayton at the stainless steel table. Trying to calm himself, he held his breath, as he had never seen a dead body up close before. He didn't want to appear overwhelmed. But despite his efforts, his vision swam, and he dizzied.

Crayton snickered at Lyle's reaction. He went to a noisy refrigerator, retrieved a bottle of Gatorade, and brought it to Lyle. "Here, take this. It'll restore some electrolytes. That is, unless you'd rather puke and pass out."

Lyle gratefully took the bottle and drank half of it in one long pull; he quickly felt better.

Once his embarrassment subsided, he thanked Crayton and refocused. Hoping to avoid humiliation once more, he kept his gaze low, anticipating the start of what he hoped would be the first in a series of lessons.

"Now listen, boy," Crayton said. "When the bodies arrive, we first have to prep them. That means we remove their clothes and personal effects—those go to the family. Then we place the deceased on this table for inspection. We have to check out all the orifices, and yes, it's as unpleasant as you think. I like to start at the top and work my way down. I check the mouth for dentures, the nose for snot, and the anal canal for waste. Once I'm finished with that, I use this hose to rinse down the table. Last, I wash the body with a mild disinfectant—hair too. Can you tell me what you think comes next?"

"We... have to drain the blood and clean them out for the embalming process?"

Crayton's macabre smile returned. "That's right, that's right. Now then, look around, and tell me what you see and what you don't see, as far as equipment is concerned."

Lyle scanned the room. He'd read a lot about body prepping, so he had a good idea of what he was looking for. But this facility was so old and cheaply maintained that it lacked any of the equipment found in modern funeral homes.

The only machine he saw was what appeared to be an outdated embalming pump. Its tall glass canister sat on top of a squat console that had a dial and two meters on its front. The apparatus made Lyle think of a blender. A long tube with a thick needle at its end was attached to the bottom of the console.

Lyle surveyed the rest of the room, but saw no additional equipment. What was missing? Then it hit him. "I see the pump for the embalming fluid."

"Very good. Continue," Crayton urged.

"What I don't see is the vacuum for removing the blood and organs. Don't you have one?"

"Used to. The thing gave out some years back. I haven't replaced it."

"May I ask why?"

Crayton sighed. "In case you haven't noticed, Lyle, this is a very small operation in a very small town. There's not a lot of money to be made. Folks around here are mainly out of work miners, store clerks, or food servers. They don't have a lot of disposable income. And like most people, mainly the young, they expect to live forever. Also, funeral expenses aren't the first things that come to mind when you're trying to keep the groceries coming or your truck from being repoed. That's one reason I've had to do things the old-fashioned way. That leads us to the next room. Follow me."

Lyle grabbed the half bottle of Gatorade for safety purposes and followed Crayton into an adjacent room. Ceramic tiles covered the walls, their grout stained black with gunk and neglect. The concrete floor slanted toward a drain in the center. A couple of feet underneath the ceiling, a thick steel rod ran wall to wall. From its middle hung a thick chain attached to a pulley system; a meat hook dangled at the end. Along a wall was a swath of pegboard covered with various types of knives, clamps, and other tools of butchery, including a bone saw. A washtub lay on the floor underneath a shelf lined with used two-liter soda bottles.

Crayton strutted around the brightly lit room, as if he was proud of the display.

Lyle felt frozen. He surmised the horror that took place in the room. He couldn't bring himself to speak. Crayton spoke instead.

"This is the draining room where we empty the corpses. I know it may seem shocking to you—barbaric even. But it serves two essential functions. By keeping the costs down, folks can afford to bury their kin with dignity and respect. That's good for them and helps me to keep my business open. But it's the second function of this room that gives them so much more: life.

Crayton shuffled to Lyle, placing his bony arm around his slumped shoulders. "I need you to pay attention to what I'm going to tell you. You may find it unsettling. Frightening. And maybe it's best if you do. You see, out of all the equipment that I've owned, the most important are those soda bottles and that washtub."

Crayton could feel Lyle's body quaking, could hear his staccato breaths trying to escape his lungs.

"I... I... don't understand, Mr. Crayton."

"Then I'll explain it to you. Like lots of other scary stories, this one began one bitterly cold night—just like this one..."

# 2

*Knock Knock Knock*

Crayton was mopping up when he heard rapping on the back door. He thought it odd—he wasn't expecting any body drop-offs, and the showroom had been closed for hours. Wanting to be sure of what he'd heard, he took a moment to listen. Silence. "Hmmm," he muttered, then went back to mopping.

*KNOCK! KNOCK! KNOCK!*

Crayton felt startled. Someone was certainly at the door. He put the mop down and entered the hallway. He hesitated. "Who's there?" he hollered.

Whoever was at the door didn't answer. Crayton waited, uneasy.

**KNOCK! KNOCK! KNOCK!**

His apprehension gave way to annoyance. "All right! All right! I'm coming!" He stomped down the hall, ready to tell off the impatient visitor.

When he opened the door, no one was there. He called out, but no one answered. He chalked it up to high winds, being tired, or both. After closing and latching the door, he went back to finish cleaning.

Crayton stopped in his tracks when he saw the man... the creature... the whatever it was... standing in the prep room, leering at him. It was at least seven feet tall, with a ghoulish, elongated face. Its withered skin was pale gray, the color of a granite headstone. Gnarled hands with filthy, cracked claws dangled from grotesquely long arms that hung to its knees. It wore rags that reeked of dirt and rot. Its dead, black eyes bore an icy hole through Crayton's soul.

Working on bodies in varying degrees of trauma and decomposition had made Crayton immune to the horrid images of death. But the frightening being was different. It barely looked human, much less alive. It stared at Crayton as if it was sizing him up for a meal.

"You're the proprietor of this establishment?" the creature growled.

"Th-th-that's right. How did you get in here?"

"You'd be surprised what we can do."

"What do you want from me?"

"I don't want anything from *you*. I want something from your dead."

Crayton shivered. "What could you possibly want from them?"

"Their insides and their blood."

"Why would you want that?"

The terrifying creature walked to within two feet of Crayton and looked down at him.

Crayton was too scared to meet the thing's haunting eyes. When it spoke, its low, hissing voice felt like broken glass under his skin.

"My kind has lived quietly in these woods for many years, sustaining ourselves by feeding on animals. You've probably stumbled upon their eviscerated remains."

"Folks figured that bears or wolves did that. Why are you after them?"

"We need the nutrients contained in their blood and organs—a type similar to that of humans, but not as powerful. Consuming all of you would better fit our needs, but we don't think it wise. It would draw unwanted attention to us, which might well mean our extinction. Therefore, we take whatever the woods offer us. Until now, we've bothered no one, and no one has bothered us. We'd like to keep it that way, but our bodies demand a change."

Crayton was panting from fear. "What kind of change?"

"The animals have been little more than a weak substitute. Our hunger and needs have increased. What we now require must be human. It gives us our life, our vitality."

Crayton saw where this was going. "And you think that these people, though dead, can meet your needs?"

The thing nodded. "Their harvest is weaker than that of the living, but it will sustain us better than the animals do."

"So, if I provide you with a steady food source, you'll leave us be?"

"Yes, but we'll need to be fed regularly."

"How much blood and organs do you need?"

"One body every ten days will suffice."

Crayton mentally crunched the numbers. He worried. "You have to understand. I'm a small town undertaker. There may be times when I'll come up short. I can't go around killing my neighbors. I wouldn't even if I could. Besides, in a town this size, questions would be raised."

The creature's malformed face hardened with thought. Then it gave Crayton a solution.

# 3

"So, you're telling me you're providing them with human remains?" Lyle asked, sickened by the idea.

"It's for all our sakes," Crayton said. "It's up to me to try to preserve our way of life, pitiful though it is. The bodies are going to be emptied anyway, so why not use them to save my neighbors? At least, that's how I square it."

Lyle shook again. "And that man who's laid out in the prep room?"

"We'll bring him in here and string him up by his feet. Then we'll field dress him just as you would an elk or a deer. Blood goes in the bottles, guts go in the tub. What's left we give to the earth. We leave the creatures' items at the edge of the woods and collect the empties the next day."

Lyle felt weak and nauseous. "I don't know if I can do this, Mr. Crayton. I understand your reasons, but there's something about using people for monster food that doesn't seem ethical... holy."

Crayton used a softer tone. "Look, son. This is how it's got to be. Trust me, you'll get used to it; my other apprentices did. Like you, they couldn't afford the price of a certification course, so they came here to learn the craft and hone their skills. But they also found out what it means to serve a greater purpose."

Lyle's heart overrode his mind's concerns. "All right, Mr. Crayton. I'll help you."

Crayton cocked his head, eyeing Lyle warily. "I need to be able to count on your discretion, Lyle. You'll get a good education from me, but you can't tell a soul what we do here. It'll cost me my business and perhaps some innocent people their lives. Understand?"

Lyle searched himself for the answer. "I came here to learn an important skill, and that's what I mean to do. I suppose that if it helps your neighbors, I can live with it. You have a deal, Mr. Crayton."

Crayton slapped his hands together, rubbing his palms. "Well then, young man, let's make a mortician out of you!"

A few weeks passed as Crayton carefully and patiently educated Lyle.

Lyle was sickened at first by the visceral procedure involving the removal of innards and blood. But like the apprentices before him, he learned to treat the bodies as what they were: vacant vessels.

Crayton accompanied Lyle on his first few trips to deliver the food to the creatures. Soon, Lyle thought of it as little more than delivering groceries. Per Crayton's instructions, he always returned the next day, collected the empty bottles and washtub, then took them back to the mortuary for cleaning and storage. On one such day, he found Crayton prepping a new arrival. Normally, the mortician went about his work dispassionately. But today was different. The man looked scared—worried.

"I'm back with the items, Mr. Crayton. I can start with the cleaning, then help you with the body whenever you're ready."

Without looking up, Crayton said, "You're probably a bit worn out from the trip. Why don't you help yourself to a Gatorade?"

"Sure thing, sir. I don't want to lose too many electrolytes," Lyle snickered.

Crayton smiled at the remark, though it appeared disingenuous. "No, Lyle. We don't want that."

Lyle fetched a Gatorade from the refrigerator and joined Crayton at the prepping table. He took an ample swig and tried not to burp—it seemed disrespectful. "Business has slowed down quite a bit, hasn't it, Mr. Crayton? Do you think you'll have enough bodies to keep those things sated?" As he drank more of the Gatorade, he felt a slow guilt building in his heart, as he considered the callousness of the question.

"Unfortunately, I don't have any more customers booked anytime soon," Crayton said somberly. "Mr. Tiller, here is the last meal I can offer for at least a few more weeks."

"That's not good. What do you typically do in a tight situation like this?"

Lyle grew groggy. His body felt rubbery, his head light. The Gatorade dropped from his hand, clattering to the floor.

"Same as I always do," Crayton said sadly. "Hire a new apprentice."

# ABOUT THE AUTHOR

P.D. Williams is an author, composer, and multi-instrumentalist. Several popular horror anthologies and e-zines, as well as many national and international horror podcasts, have featured his short horror fiction. He resides with his amazing family in North Carolina. For more info on the author, visit his website at **pdwilliamsauthor.com** or at **P.D. Williams Horror Writer** on Facebook.

Please, feel free to post a review of this collection on Amazon.

# MORE CHILLS FROM VELOX BOOKS

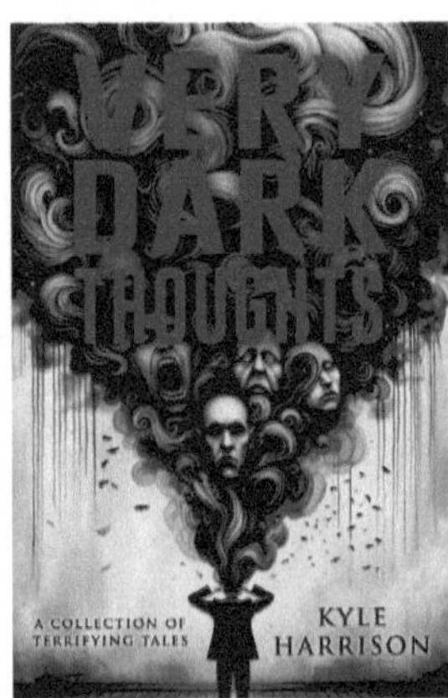

# MORE CHILLS FROM VELOX BOOKS

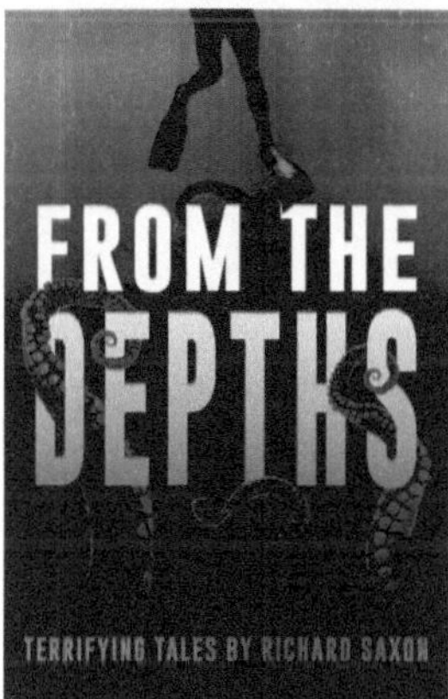

www.ingramcontent.com/pod-product-compliance
Lightning Source LLC
Chambersburg PA
CBHW031034310726
48969CB00007B/1980